ONE FOR THE ROAD

ONE FOR THE ROAD

Mary Ellis

SEVERN
HOUSE

This first world edition published 2020
in Great Britain and 2021 in the USA by
SEVERN HOUSE PUBLISHERS LTD of
Eardley House, 4 Uxbridge Street, London W8 7SY.
Trade paperback edition first published
in Great Britain and the USA 2021 by
Severn House, an imprint of Canongate Books Ltd,
14 High Street, Edinburgh EH1 1TE.

British Library Cataloguing in Publication Data
A CIP catalogue record for this title is available from the British Library.

ISBN-13: 978-0-7278-8998-0 (cased)
ISBN-13: 978-1-78029-727-9 (trade paper)
ISBN-13: 978-1-4483-0448-6 (e-book)

Typeset by Palimpsest Book Production Ltd.,
Falkirk, Stirlingshire, Scotland.

To Donna, Linda, and Donna – my three Kentucky gal-pals

ACKNOWLEDGEMENTS

I would like to thank the wonderful tour guides at Jim Beam Distillery in Clermont, along with those at Angels Envy Distillery, Evan Williams Distillery, and the Jim Beam Urban Stillhouse, all in or near Louisville. Plus I'd like to thank Barrel House Distillery in Lexington, Kentucky for a thorough explanation of making small-batch bourbon, with a special thank you to Betsy Bright, tour guide extraordinaire, and Bobby Downing, lead (master) distiller. Thanks also go to my husband, Ken, who makes research fun, and Pete and Donna Taylor, who willingly provide my Kentucky home away-from-home. Where would I be without friends and family?

AUTHOR'S NOTE

Although the Black Creek and the Founder's Reserve Distilleries in my story are fictional, the Kentucky Bourbon Tours and the small craft tours are very real and loads of fun!

ONE

'There it is!' Jill exclaimed as they passed a bright blue road sign. '"Welcome to Kentucky – the Blue Grass State". I'm so excited I could spit.'

Michael Erikson, her videographer sidekick, took his eyes off the road long enough to scowl. 'Don't you dare! I just had this car washed and detailed. What's so exciting about the countryside of Kentucky? We're talkin' grandma rocking on every porch and pickup trucks driving like an Indy race.'

'Sounds like the perfect spot for a travel piece.' Jill rubbed her stomach with a circular motion. 'I can almost taste the flapjacks, corn pone and deep-fried everything now.'

'You don't even know what corn pone is.' Michael slugged his cold coffee with a grimace.

'No, but I aim to find out. This could be my big chance to advance beyond travel features and blogging to the news service. We have ten expense-paid days to discover why thousands of tourists flock to bourbon country every year.'

'You don't even like whiskey. You drink grocery store wine out of a cardboard box.' Michael held his gut while he laughed.

'This will be bourbon, not whiskey.' Jill pulled down the vanity mirror to check her teeth for remnants of lunch.

He shook his head. 'Bourbon is a type of whiskey. If we're doing this, partner, start doing your homework.'

'I intend to, tonight. I would've already if the boss hadn't handed us this at the last minute. Besides, my wine comes in bottles with real corks.' Jill lifted her chin with indignation.

'Yeah, right. I stopped at your apartment last Christmas, remember?'

'Of course I do. What woman could forget a pair of lime-green, six-toed socks?'

'What can I say – they were on sale. We're on the outskirts of Louisville. Better program the GPS with the hotel's address.'

'We're not staying at some boring chain hotel.' Jill produced a cat-in-the-cream grin.

'I get the feeling I'm not going to like this.' Michael rubbed the back of his neck.

'Why on earth would we stay in Louisville when the charming town of Roseville is close to two distilleries? If you recall, bourbon distilleries are why we're here.'

'This motel in Roseville . . . is it one of those turquoise mom-and-pop's with a soda machine permanently out of order?'

'Absolutely not. We're staying at Sweet Dreams Bed and Breakfast. The online pictures looked gorgeous, truly elegant and historical.'

'In other words flowery wallpaper, lace doilies, and threadbare rugs.'

'Have you ever even been to a B and B?'

'Yup, remember my ex-fiancée, Cindy? She took me to one in the Alleghany Mountains. Each night I expected Jack Nicholson to axe his way through the door. I didn't sleep a wink.'

'If anyone was going to take an axe to your head, it would have been Cindy.' As usual, her insult had zero effect on him. Jill shook her head. 'This place serves a gourmet breakfast each morning, plus either tea with scones or cocktails and canapés in the evening. Sweet Dreams is not only in the heart of bourbon country, but the proprietor might be a long-lost relative of mine, which for now we'll keep quiet about. And her husband owns a craft distillery outside of town.' She braced herself for Michael's next parlay – which never came.

'Now that might come in handy,' he said. 'Having a bourbon master at our disposal could produce some great footage. Plus I can start my Christmas shopping.'

Jill chuckled at his unexpected reaction. Like her, Michael had been born and raised in Chicago's suburbs. 'We're not going to become nuisances, are we?' she asked. 'The boss wants a positive spin on this travel story.'

'I won't become a nuisance, but you'd better not drink any hundred-proof bourbon or you'll start singing "A Hundred Bottles of Beer on the Wall".'

'I don't even know the words. Can you get us a cash advance from accounting? Most likely not everyone takes American Express along the backroads.'

The ace videographer winked. 'I'm way ahead of you. This assignment will be as easy as sippin' lemonade on a hot summer day.'

Jill punched the address into his GPS and settled back to relax. Maybe two weeks of low-pressure interviews and personal interest vignettes – not to mention product sampling – would be fun. It would be nice to escape the office gossips for a while, who were always wondering if she and Michael were dating. They never had and never would. For one thing, editing audio and video segments to make people stop what they were doing and book a trip was hard work. Plus office romances never turned out well. And a third reason? Jill didn't want anyone standing in the way of her advancement. She couldn't tread water in Chicago forever, growing more bored each day. It was time to go after what she wanted in life, even if it meant moving across the country or halfway around the globe.

'We're here, Sleeping Beauty,' Michael whispered in her ear.

'For cryin' out loud,' Jill snapped. 'A simple nudge would've worked.'

'Welcome to Roseville. How could anyone fall asleep on roads that twisty?'

'Old-fashioned streetlights, people milling around the town square, even a gazebo with bandstand? Looks like we just stepped into a Norman Rockwell painting.'

'You're not kidding. Roseville has more going for it than I expected. I've counted six bars that sell craft beer and local wines, besides the bread-and-butter of the county. A few places even have live music on Saturday.'

'Heck with the nightlife.' Jill craned her neck out the window. 'They have art galleries, dress shops, a jewelry store, and even a wholefoods grocery. I want to move here. Towns this quaint are only on greeting cards.'

'You'd do anything to get out of Chicago. Just remember, jobs for journalists in places like this don't pay squat.'

'Money isn't everything. Let's stop for a minute and check out that bakery.' Jill pointed at a tiny store with a bright red awning.

Michael ignored her and turned at the next corner. 'No, we'll check in first and get something to eat later.'

'Fine, but I'll pick the spot. I'm dying for a piece of pizza.'

They had no trouble finding the three-story, white colonial on a tree-lined street a few blocks from downtown. And they would have no trouble finding the distilleries tomorrow. Plenty of signs pointed to Founder's Reserve north of town and the Black Creek Distillery twenty miles to the south.

Michael parked at the curb and grabbed their bags from the trunk. 'I hope you reserved two rooms instead of twin beds in the attic.'

'Don't be ridiculous. I even asked for rooms in separate wings.' Jill took her suitcase from his hand and marched up the front steps. Just as she was about to knock, the door swung open.

'Welcome to Sweet Dreams,' said a seventyish, silver-haired woman. 'I'm Mrs Clark. You must be Miss Curtis and Mr Erikson. Please come in.'

'Hi, I'm Jill and that's Michael.' Jill stepped across the threshold into the foyer. 'Wow, your home and your town are adorable.'

'A newborn baby is adorable,' she said with a laugh. 'I would describe my house as colonial Williamsburg-on-a-budget.'

'Well, I think it's gorgeous.' Jill had been expecting overdone Victorian with tons of knick-knacks, but her décor was almost austere.

'Any house rules we should know about, ma'am?' asked Michael, pragmatic to a fault.

'Let's see . . . Your rooms have deadbolt locks, but the back door is always open in case you go out later. Breakfast is at eight thirty in the dining room or later by request. Tea and scones are available in the library at four and then at six o'clock I provide wine, beer or bourbon with a light snack.' Mrs Clark pulled two skeleton keys from her pocket.

'What about the rule "you break it, you bought it"?' Michael asked.

'Good grief, young man, accidents happen. Where are you folks from?'

'I'm from Chicago. He's from the moon.' Jill took the key from her. 'Thanks, Mrs Clark. I would love tea this afternoon.' Jill started up the stairs, then turned back to Michael. 'I'll be in my room. See you later.' As much as she liked her partner, she needed some space after several hours in the car.

'Thank you, ma'am.' Michael took the other key from Mrs Clark. 'While you research, I'll catch a few winks,' he called.

His words drifted up the steps as Jill opened her door on a four-poster bed, leaded windows, and a working fireplace. 'I'm never leaving.' She flopped across the embroidered coverlet.

Since tomorrow she'd be interviewing bourbon aficionados, Jill buckled down to several hours of online research and found plenty of information on the tours, as well as restaurants along the circuit. Fourteen major distilleries offered tours in the top half of the state, but Jill wanted some small-batch producers too. After printing out her research in the B&B's office, she found Michael checking his emails in the library.

'I'm ready for anything.' She plopped into a chair by the fire. 'Did you know how many types of whiskey there are? Besides Kentucky bourbon and Tennessee sour mash, I read about Scotch, Canadian, and American blends.' Jill ticked each off on her fingers. 'Each one supposedly tastes different.'

Michael closed his laptop. 'I could've told you that much on the drive down. What else did you find out?'

'Plenty. Considering how many people home-brew beer these days, distilling your own spirits could be the next wave of the future.' Jill smiled smugly.

Michael rolled his eyes. 'It's been done. They're called moonshiners and it's against the law. Let's hope we don't come within ten miles of anyone's illegal still. Don't you watch anything other than the cooking channel on TV?'

Jill ignored the question. 'I also learned that making bourbon is more complex than I thought. Competition between distilleries can get downright cut-throat.' She pulled a sheet from her printouts. 'Listen to this news story about a brawl at a county exhibition. "Police called to break up a fight at a small-batch competition. Ten people were arrested for malicious destruction of property and two for carrying concealed weapons".'

'What's the big deal?' Michael asked.

She arched an eyebrow. 'You don't think twelve people getting thrown in jail is a big deal?'

'Jill, Jill. They were just good 'ole boys blowing off steam on a Saturday night. The "malicious destruction" was probably a busted table and a few chairs. And the concealed weapons? Some guys probably forgot they were carrying. The article didn't say firearms had been discharged, right?'

She stared at her mild-mannered videographer. '*Who are you? This is so not like you.*'

'Look, we live in Chicago where law and order are mandatory for society. These people grew up with a different mindset, but deep down their moral and ethical codes are the same as ours.'

Jill wrinkled her nose. 'So a few broken chairs and split lips are OK as long as there's no gunplay?'

'Exactly. Did you know one of the major bourbon producers can trace his family tree back to Frank and Jesse James?'

'I did not.'

'We'll have fun getting this story. And we'll get to see how America looked a hundred and fifty years ago. That will make great video footage.' He held up two thumbs.

'As colorful as that sounds, let's book only tours with high AAA and AARP ratings, instead of Joe Bob taking folks up the mountain to Uncle Jethro's still. And no local contests unless you hire armed bodyguards on your own dime. We don't want to explain *that* on our expense report.' She handed him the printouts.

'Trust me, I'll work out an itinerary that'll snag us an Emmy. Plus, don't forget I've been working out for three years. You'll be perfectly safe with me.' Michael pulled up a sleeve and flexed his bicep.

Jill started to heckle, but stopped when they heard loud voices in the next room.

'What in the world are you serving our guests?' thundered a male voice.

'Miss Curtis asked for tea and scones, so I baked these fresh.'

Recognizing the second voice as Mrs Clark's, Jill and Michael sat very still.

'People don't come to Roseville to drink tea with their pinky fingers sticking out. This ain't London, England,' grumbled the male, presumed to be Mr Clark.

'I'm merely fulfilling a guest's request.' Mrs Clark wasn't backing down.

'At least put a bottle of my bourbon on the tray with some smoked sausages. That gal ain't travelling with her mother. There's a man with her.'

Jill rose from her chair, but Michael clamped a hand around her wrist. 'Don't interfere,' he whispered. 'We're guests in their home.'

Jill knew Michael was right, but she hated hearing a woman being bullied. Unfortunately, their marital squabble wasn't over.

'Where are you going, Roger?' Mrs Clark asked.

'Back to the plant, where else?'

'You just got home and haven't had supper yet.'

'What are you, my mother? Keep the supper warm till I get back.' He punctuated his demand with a loud thud.

Jill sat very still, afraid to move, while Michael ran a finger inside his shirt collar.

Suddenly the door swung wide and a burly man stomped into the room. A small brown beagle followed close at his heels. When the dog spotted Jill he ran straight to her and rose up on his hind legs to be petted. The man, however, stopped dead in his tracks when he noticed his guests. 'Didn't know you two were down here. Sorry, you shouldn't have heard that.'

Except that he didn't sound very sorry.

'Every couple fights,' said Michael.

Having nothing nice to say, Jill remained silent.

'I'm Roger Clark. That's my mutt, Jack. Just push him down if you don't like dogs.' He set down a tray with a bottle, two snifters, and a bag of Smokies. 'Try a sample of the best bourbon in the county.'

'Thanks, we sure will.' Michael stood to shake their proprietor's hand, but Clark had already stomped off.

'Let's go, Jack!' The innkeeper roared from the front hall. 'You coming or not?'

Dutifully, Jack ran to heed his master's command, tail between his legs.

'I want that dog.' Jill bit down on her back molars.

'You want every dog you see.' Michael poured himself a glass of bourbon.

'True, but I *really* want Jack. Mr Clark doesn't deserve such a sweet dog. He deserves something mean and vicious.'

While Michael laughed, Jill fantasized about smuggling Jack in her suitcase when it was time to leave.

A few minutes later, Mrs Clark entered the library with a second tray. 'Here's your tea, Miss Curtis.' She glanced from one face to the other. 'Oh, dear, you must think you've checked into a house of horrors.'

Jill jumped to her feet and took the tray from Mrs Curtis's trembling hands. 'We barely heard a word. Come, sit, and have tea with me.'

With that, the woman burst into tears.

Setting the tray on the hearth, Jill guided Mrs Clark to a chair, then poured two cups of tea. 'We don't think that at all.' She handed the woman a cup.

'Thank you, dear. Normally Roger isn't like this, but there's been so much pressure at the distillery.' She took a sip of tea.

'Like my partner said, every couple argues.'

'Are either of you married?' Mrs Clark gazed from one to the other.

When they shook their heads, she set down her cup and stood. 'In that case, I apologize if we spoiled any preconceived notions. Enjoy your complimentary beverages. When I see you tomorrow at breakfast, this tiff will be ancient history.' She walked from the room with her head held high.

During the bizarre *happy* hour, Jill ate three lemon scones and drank two cups of tea, while Michael gobbled half the sausages and consumed a liberal amount of bourbon.

'Still want to go out for pizza?' Michael asked once they both tired of staring at the fire.

'Nah, the scones filled me up,' Jill said with a yawn. 'I'm going to read in bed for a while.'

'Good idea. See ya in the morning. If it's OK with you, let's *not* start with Black Creek since Roger Clark owns the place.'

'My thoughts exactly,' she said, as they both climbed the steps to the second floor. 'Let's give Mr Personality a little time to get over his bad mood.'

TWO

Wednesday morning

Michael was first to break the ice as they left the B&B the next morning. 'That omelet and homemade pecan rolls were delicious, but Mrs Clark didn't say much at breakfast. And Mr Clark barely grunted as he hurried out the door.'

'Who can blame her for being quiet? She was embarrassed about crying in front of strangers.' Jill switched on the AC.

'She shouldn't have been. The neighbors probably hear my parents each time they argue. What's the big deal?'

'If you don't know, there's no point explaining. But I'll tell you one thing, Erikson. If Roger starts yelling at his wife tonight, he'll get a taste of real girl power.' Jill shook her fist at the windshield.

'Yeah, right. You're such a big talker.' Michael chuckled. 'Hey, one of the major bourbon producers has a visitor center in town with videos and a mock-up of the process. Want to start there and learn the basics?'

'Good idea. No way could I sample bourbon before noon, no matter how good it is. Let's do the visitor center, then lunch, then on to Founder's Reserve. That should fill the day nicely.'

'Considering how much guesswork goes into the aging process, bourbon masters must all be old and gray,' Michael said as they walked out of the visitor center and into the bright Kentucky sunshine.

'You're not kidding, but at least the video gave the general layout of a distillery and explained the necessary ingredients.' Jill slipped in behind the wheel of the car.

'Where should we eat? I'm starving.'

'Since the visitor center took longer than expected, let's just hit a drive-through and be on our way.'

'Fine, pull into that famous chicken place on the left. After all, when in Kentucky . . .'

On their way to the distillery, Michael munched on a two-piece crispy while Jill ate a grilled chicken sandwich. Then she switched off the AC, rolled down the window, and let her hair blow in the breeze. Twenty minutes later they reached the ornate entrance to Founder's Reserve. Jill paused in the turn-around to admire the stone mansion with a clay tile roof. 'Elegantly rustic – that's how I would describe the facade.' She jotted the phrase in her notebook.

Michael's opinion wasn't as kind. 'Looks to me they started with a log cabin and added on haphazardly at least a dozen times.'

Jill pulled into a parking space. 'What else can you do with a hundred-fifty-year-old family business? The place is gorgeous. Look at those private gardens. Any one of them would be perfect for a bridal shower or wedding.'

Michael craned his neck. 'Does look like there's money to be made in bourbon.'

Jill glanced at her watch and jumped out of the car. 'We'd better hurry to buy our tickets. The last tour starts in fifteen minutes.'

With tickets in hand, they followed a group into a high-ceilinged, oak-paneled room with heavy dark furniture and dozens of oil paintings. The stony faces of the well-dressed ancestors of the owners – the Shelby family, according to the nameplates – stared down on them.

'The Shelbys don't look like a pack of unschooled moonshiners to me,' Michael said next to her ear.

Before she could reply, a door in the paneling opened and a dark-haired man with high cheekbones entered. As he scanned the crowd, his gaze stopped on her. Jill's breath caught in her throat. 'And he doesn't look like any tour guide I've ever seen,' she whispered back, eliciting a smile from a woman with three little girls standing nearby.

'Good afternoon, ladies and gentlemen,' said the drop-dead gorgeous man. 'I'm Jamie Shelby, son of the seventh-generation master distiller here at Founder's Reserve. Since our regular guide called in sick, I'm afraid you're stuck with me today.'

Murmurs ran through the crowd. 'Called out the big guns, eh?' shouted someone from the back. 'We're in luck.'

Jamie Shelby unbuttoned his sport coat. 'For the next ninety minutes, the tour will be informal, so feel free to ask any question you like.'

'Do I have permission to videotape the tour?' Michael hefted his equipment bag to his shoulder.

The corners of Shelby's mouth turned down. 'You may shoot video in this room and the next and anywhere on the grounds, but not in the grain mixing or distillation areas. Sorry, but some of the processes you'll see are proprietary.'

Jill held up her hand. 'Am I allowed to take notes, Mr Shelby? I'm writing a piece on the Kentucky bourbon tours for several travel websites.'

'Of course. Founder's Reserve is honored to be included in your article. And please, call me Jamie.' Shelby offered a magnificent smile.

The youngest of the woman's three daughters raised her hand. 'Mister Jamie, do you want to be a mast'r distill'r someday?' she asked.

The creases around his eyes deepened as Jamie bent down to the child's level. 'Becoming the master distiller is my fondest dream, so I plan to work and study hard, just like you do in school. At the end of the tour I have something special for you while the adults sample our bourbon – fresh buttermilk and molasses cookies to eat during my final story and a bag of popcorn to take home.' He straightened to his full height. 'Who knows why I'm giving away corn today?'

The oldest daughter volunteered an answer. 'Because it's the main ingredient used in making bourbon?'

'Correct. We use only non-GMO corn, locally grown for Founder's Reserve. Now let's step into the next room to learn what other ingredients go into bourbon.'

'Shelby sure knows how to work a crowd,' Michael murmured as the group filed through the doorway.

'Maybe this isn't his first tour,' she hissed under her breath. 'I think Mr Shelby is very nice.'

While her partner hung back to shoot video, Jill joined the group at a display of recently harvested and milled rye and barley. While Jamie explained the constant need for new oak barrels and why limestone wells were used for their water supply, Michael hovered in the back of the room, waiting to video the displays after the crowd moved on.

Jill took plenty of notes during Shelby's tour and asked almost as many questions as the three little girls.

Michael finally caught up to the group in the distillation room. Thankfully, he'd stowed his video camera. 'What's going on in here?'

'They're cooking the grain mash until the liquid evaporates,' she said. 'What took you so long? Did you get any footage?'

He nodded. 'Some, but I don't understand how these processes can be *proprietary* if anyone can buy a ticket.'

Jill cringed, fearing Jamie might have overheard the comment. 'Behave,' she warned. 'Or you'll be sitting in a hot car.'

By the time they reached a cavernous warehouse, stacked high with oak barrels, most of the tourists looked tired and moved through the room quickly.

'Exactly how long does bourbon take to age?' Jill asked at the end of a row of barrels.

'There is no *exactness* to this stage, my lovely travel writer,' Jamie answered with a smile. 'Bourbon must age for a minimum of two years. After that, the master distiller tastes the barrels once a year. Upon his command, the batch is poured, filtered, and then bottled.'

'Your father has a huge responsibility.'

'He does, indeed.' Jamie's gaze drifted over Jill's head. 'I seem to be losing my guests' attention. Let's move to our final stop – the tasting room. Afterwards, I'll answer your questions all night. In fact, nothing would please me more.' He opened the double doors into a lounge with comfortable sofas and chairs. 'After you, Miss . . .'

'It's Jill. And I would appreciate that.' *Although I'm not sure my partner would.*

Once the adults had samples of bourbon and the girls had glasses of buttermilk, Jamie moved a stool to the center of the room. 'Now for the story I promised.' He waited for everyone to quiet down before he began.

'A long time ago, Waddie Boone – kinfolk to Daniel – started the first bourbon distillery in Kentucky. Isaiah Shelby grew corn north of the creek, while Tobias Cook – ancestor to the Clarks in this area – grew corn on the south side. Both farmers did quite well until one day a flood changed the course of the river. A big chunk of land that once belonged to the Cook farms now belonged to the Shelbys. My ancestor, Isaiah, said the sixty fertile acres were a gift from God. Tobias said nothing doing and crossed the creek with his sons to continue farming. This started a two-hundred-year feud that still continues today. Do you know what two things were always at the heart of their disagreements?' Jamie scanned the crowd, waiting for an answer.

'Bourbon,' said a voice in the back.

'Yep, that's one. What do you think is the other? Here's a hint: it seems to be at the heart of every book and movie ever made.' The future master distiller stared at Jill.

She swallowed a sip of bourbon. 'My guess would be romantic entanglements.'

'Exactly right. Love might make the world go round, but it has fueled plenty of high drama in these parts, including a few duels at dawn.' Jamie slipped off the stool and bowed to the audience. 'Thank you, ladies and gentlemen, for visiting Founder's Reserve, and for being so patient with me. Through those doors is our gift shop and retail store.' He gestured to the right. 'Please come and see us again.'

Everyone in the group clapped, while a few men shook Jamie's hand. Jill remained behind so Michael could shoot video in the sampling room.

After the last tourist exited, Jamie returned to Jill's side. 'I'm all yours. Why don't you ask your questions on the patio over a glass of our special reserve? I can have the hospitality manager send down a cheese and fruit tray.'

She laughed. 'Sounds lovely, but I can't. I rode with my videographer today.'

Color flooded Jamie's already-tanned cheeks. 'I meant the invitation for both of you.'

Jill covered her mouth with her hand. 'Of course, you did.'

'What's this?' asked Michael, switching off his camera.

'I would like you and Jill to join me on the patio for a bite to eat and a taste of something special. Jill has a few more questions.'

Michael pushed his glasses up his nose. 'Sounds great, but all that grain in the mixing room aggravated my allergies. I've got one nasty headache.'

'Can't you take a couple of ibuprofen?' Jill dug in her purse for the pill container. 'This is my once-in-a-lifetime chance to interview an eighth-generation master.'

'No, ibuprofen won't work. I need to take Benadryl and lie down.'

Jamie rubbed his jawline where a dark shadow had appeared. 'Are you sure you can drive?' he asked Michael.

'Yeah, I didn't drink the sample even though I wanted to. Alcohol would make my headache worse.'

'In that case, why don't I drive Jill back after we finish the interview? I'd love to get out of here for a while.'

Jill stopped looking for pills. 'No, I couldn't let you. Our hotel is in Roseville.'

Jamie grinned. 'That's not even thirty miles away – no big deal to those who live in the boondocks. Unless you don't trust me . . .'

'Don't be ridiculous. Anyone who can handle kids as well as you couldn't possibly be a serial killer. If it's OK with my partner, I accept the invitation.' Both of them focused on Michael.

'Of course it's OK,' he answered. 'But if you're not back in a few hours, I'm calling the sheriff.'

Jill laughed – but Jamie? Not so much as a chuckle.

'Let me lock up here and send a text to my hospitality manager. Why don't I meet you out front?'

'Great, Michael still needs to video the entrance and façade of the building.' Jill led the way through the gift shop.

'Do you really think this is a good idea?' Michael asked once they were alone. 'Haven't you had enough excitement for one day?'

Gritting her teeth, she plopped down on a stone bench. 'Like I said, this is my big chance for a one-on-one interview. Please, go shoot video while I finish my notes.'

When their host rejoined them fifteen minutes later, Michael was back from shooting the footage. Jamie extended his hand to Michael. 'Thanks for choosing Founder's Reserve today, Mike. And regarding your question about proprietary processes, our ticket sellers are trained to recognize other distillers. They would politely decline admission to our competitors. Bourbon is taken seriously in this state.'

So he had overheard Michael.

After her red-faced partner climbed into his car and drove away, Jamie offered her an elbow. 'I have the perfect spot for your interview.'

Jill linked her arm through his and Jamie escorted her to a multi-level terrace that overlooked a pond, gazebo, and manicured lawn straight out of a F. Scott Fitzgerald novel.

'What a lovely spot for a wedding,' she murmured.

'Glad you think so, as that's how we usually use the terrace. With the sun starting to set the deck might still be too hot, so why don't we sit under the arbor?' Jamie pointed at a bistro table and two chairs in the shade. A wrought-iron trellis covered in wisteria vines blocked the sun and provided complete privacy. Two snifters, a fancy decanter, and a tray of fruit and cheese waited for them.

Unnerved by how fast Jamie had organized the rendezvous, Jill pulled out her notebook and fired off a question the moment she sat down. Only after Jamie's third answer did she relax enough to eat a few grapes and a sliver of cheese. After his fifth detailed response without a hint of impropriety, Jill took a sip of bourbon. By the time she finished the glass, she'd jotted down more than enough background information.

'Well, that should do it. Thanks,' she said, tucking away her notebook. Then she noticed he hadn't touched his drink. 'Sorry, do you need more time?' She pointed at his glass.

'I'll enjoy mine after I take you back to Roseville. Are you ready? We don't want to worry your boyfriend.'

'Michael isn't my boyfriend,' she corrected. 'He's a work colleague and friend.'

'Nevertheless, we don't want him summoning the National Guard.'

As Jill pushed to her feet, a wave of light-headedness swept over her. 'Uh-oh, I should have eaten more from the tray.'

Jamie offered his arm. 'Would you like to hang onto me?'

'No, I'll be fine, but shouldn't we clean up our mess?'

'I have staff to take care of it.' Taking a firm grip on her arm, he led her to his car parked at the side of the building.

His assertive manner disconcerted her, but their conversation about college basketball and the ubiquitous weather helped her relax during the drive.

Halfway to Roseville, Jamie's phone rang. 'Sorry, but I need to take this,' he said after glancing at the display. 'Our head of public relations wouldn't call unless it was urgent. Good evening, Deanne. You're on speaker in my car.'

'Good evening, Mr Shelby. Sorry for the interruption, but your father wants to speak to you.'

'Tell him I'm on my way to Roseville but I'll see him before he goes to bed. Thank you, Deanne.' Jamie disconnected the call, turned into the next driveway, and skidded to a stop.

'Looks like the long, scenic route won't work for us tonight. What a shame.' He tapped Roseville into the car's GPS.

'I'm sorry I made you drive me home. I should've gone with Michael and come back another time.'

'Don't be sorry. Meeting you was the best part of my day. But I do hope you'll come back, whether or not you have more questions.' His smile could only be described as flirtatious.

Despite the fact Jill had had plenty of dates, the man's cool assurance and southern charm unnerved her. She spent the rest of the ride jotting down notes or fiddling with the radio.

But Jamie Shelby wasn't giving up easily. 'What do you say, Jill?' he asked after stopping in front of Sweet Dreams B&B. 'May I take you to dinner or sightseeing while you're a guest in our beautiful state?'

Jill knew Michael wouldn't like the idea. She also knew this was a business trip. But it would be the perfect opportunity to find out what goes on behind the scenes in a distillery. 'I would like that, Mr Shelby, providing there's enough time. I'm not sure how long we'll be in Roseville, but I'll give you my cell number.'

Jamie jumped out and opened her door. 'Call me Jamie,' he said. 'I'll call you tomorrow, in case you can break free from Michael for a few hours.'

Jill jotted her number and handed him the slip of paper. As she ran up the front steps, her feet barely touched the ground.

Her partner hadn't been included in the invitation. She wasn't misreading the handsome eighth-generation distiller's intentions this time.

Thursday morning

'Where to, your Majesty? Your wish is my command,' Michael asked as they climbed in the car for day two of bourbon research.

'Let's head to Black Creek,' Jill said. 'You barely said a word at breakfast. What's the matter?'

'Nothing's the matter. I was worried about you yesterday; that's all. You just met Shelby, yet you agreed to go out with him.'

'Stop pouting. Jamie behaved like a perfect gentleman. And I agreed to go out only if we have time.'

'Fine, just try not to fall in love.' Michael accelerated as they left the quaint village. 'In the meantime, let's take a quick tour at Black Creek and move on.'

Once they reached the distillery, a quick tour wasn't on the cards.

'I don't know what to tell you, folks,' drawled the young woman at the desk. 'The owner does the tour on Thursdays and he's not here. Right now nobody else is available.'

'Why don't you lead the tour, sweet thing?' Michael leaned over the desk to ladle on the charm. 'I could listen to you talk all day.'

Jill rolled her eyes. If a man talked to her like that, he'd get a knuckle sandwich.

But this particular teenager looked flattered. 'Oh, I couldn't,' she replied. 'I haven't learned all the facts. Maybe if y'all come back this afternoon, I can have Lois here. She normally has Thursday off.'

Jill stepped in front of her partner and smiled. 'Gosh, that is really sweet, but we need to catch a plane at noon. Couldn't we just wander around on our own? I'm sure we can figure out what goes on here.'

Lindy, according to her nametag, shook a thick mane of blonde hair. 'Sorry, tourists aren't allowed in the plant by themselves. Safety concerns and all that.' She produced a sympathetic expression.

Michael elbowed Jill to the side. 'Well, I won't tell if you don't. If the boss shows up, we'll say we sneaked in when you weren't looking.'

Lindy glanced left and right. 'Promise you won't get me in trouble?'

'I promise.' Michael drew an 'x' across his heart.

'OK, but you gotta leave by ten. That's when the production shift starts. And don't touch anything!' Lindy yelled as they headed down an arrow-marked hallway.

'We won't.' Jill waved and turned a corner.

Unfortunately, the process used at Black Creek wasn't self-explanatory after an hour of aimless wandering. 'So far we've learned nothing about small-batch production,' she moaned.

'And I've been too afraid someone will see my light to shoot video. We're getting nowhere.'

Jill checked her watch. 'The production crew will soon be here. Maybe we should come back another day.'

'No way,' he said. 'You keep moving along the arrows while I shoot video in this room. If either of us gets kicked out, we'll meet up at the car.'

'What if Mr Clark catches us?' Jill asked, remembering their host's temperament.

'Tell him you've been looking for him because of yesterday. Make something up. Look how well you lied to Lindy about an airline flight.'

'This is not a good idea.'

'For once, Jill, live dangerously. Neither of us wants to come back. Just follow the arrows. Eventually they should lead you out.'

Since arguing with him would be futile, Jill marched from the mashing and mixing room into an area filled with stainless-steel vats loaded with dials and gauges. She tried to discern differences in here from what she saw yesterday at Founder's Reserve but couldn't concentrate.

The sooner she finished the tour the better.

Tingles ran across her scalp and down her arms as she heard voices in another room. Jill bolted toward the arrow and through a doorway into a cavernous aging barn. Metal racks from floor to ceiling held dozens of barrels of bourbon. If one of the shelves gave way, she could be crushed to death. As she threaded her way through the maze of racks, blood pounded in her head while sweat dampened the back of her shirt. Her anxiety level felt more in keeping with a horror movie than a run-in with a distillery worker.

Spotting an exit sign at the end of an aisle, Jill broke into a run until something appeared on the floor halfway down the row. However, it wasn't *something* at all. It was a man – the proprietor of Sweet Dreams to be specific. Roger Clark lay flat on his back with his eyes closed and a purplish bruise on his forehead.

'Mr Clark!' She dropped to her knees next to him. 'You must have bumped your head and passed out.' As gently as possible,

Jill lifted him by the shoulders and placed his head in her lap. 'Wake up, Mr Clark. You've been knocked out.'

She heard only whimpering from over her right shoulder. Then Mr Clark's beagle crawled out from beneath a rack. 'Jack! What are you doing under there?' Jill held out her palm for the dog to smell. Jack approached cautiously, sniffed her hand, and laid down next to his master. When Jill looked back at Mr Clark, his head had lolled to one side and a pool of blood had soaked though her clothes. The master distiller hadn't bumped his head and passed out. He was dead.

It was then that Jill started screaming and she didn't stop until someone yanked her roughly to her feet.

'What on earth happened?' demanded Michael, his eyes wide.

'I don't know.' Mindlessly, Jill wiped her bloody hands on her soft pink T-shirt.

Distillery workers soon surrounded them, everyone talking at once.

'Who are you people?' shouted one voice.

'Did that lady kill Mr Clark?' someone asked.

'Hey, I told you two not to touch anything!' Blonde-haired Lindy pushed her way to the front of the crowd.

'For heaven's sake, somebody call 9-1-1!'

With an employee's desperate plea ringing in her ears, Jill lowered herself to the floor next to Jack and closed her eyes.

There should be a limit on how many times a person said 'I have no idea' during a given hour. But while the bearded sheriff questioned her in the back of his cruiser, she must have said it a hundred times. Jill couldn't explain why she had blood on her hands and down the front of her shirt enough to satisfy the man.

Michael, who was placed in a different police vehicle, also couldn't explain why they were snooping around when a huge sign read: *Absolutely no admittance unless accompanied by Black Creek personnel.*

Finally, after Sheriff Adkins checked with their boss at the news service, and since neither had confessed during the two-hour interrogation, she was taken to the ladies' room inside the distillery and handed a plain T-shirt. 'I'll need that shirt you're wearing, Miss Curtis,' Adkins growled. 'And I'll get those shorts from you later.' When she complied, they were released with a final warning: 'Don't leave town until I say so. Understand?'

'I promise we won't leave,' Jill said. 'Should you need us, we're staying at the Sweet Dreams Bed and Breakfast.'

Adkins's eyes bugged from his face. 'You're staying in the home of the victim?'

'Yes, but we didn't know he was going to be a victim when we checked in.'

The sheriff shook his head. 'Go there and sit tight. I might have a few more questions. Say nothing to Mrs Clark. I want to be the one to tell her the bad news.'

'Yes, sir.' On shaky legs, Jill joined her partner in his car.

'We can go back to the B and B?' Michael looked very pale.

'Yes, but I need to get upstairs without Mrs Clark seeing my shorts.'

He glanced again at her outfit. 'I'll run interference. No way should your relative see you, especially since it's her husband's blood. I don't care how long-lost she is.'

'We'll need to stay in tonight,' Jill added. Somehow she knew they hadn't seen the last of the sheriff that day.

THREE

N ick Harris of the Kentucky State Police walked out of the meeting with his boss with a bad feeling in his gut. Although he'd just been given an assignment his fellow troopers would kill for, Nick didn't like venturing into the unknown. He wasn't worried about the geographical area. He knew the rolling hills and fertile valleys of Nelson, Washington and Marion counties like the back of his hand. And he had more experience with murder investigations and violent crime than anyone at his post. But he'd never been much of a drinker and had never tasted bourbon in his life, despite being born and raised in the Blue Grass state.

Nick was being sent to assist local law enforcement with a suspicious death in Roseville. Maybe the death would be ruled murder and maybe not, but since the man died inside the area's fastest growing craft distillery, a second pair of eyes had been requested. Finesse would be needed on his part. In this area, saying the wrong thing about the Commonwealth's famous liquor could bruise more than a man's feelings.

Over the years, men had died over who made the best bourbon, dating back to the colonial period. Hopefully, what the county sheriff lacked in investigative expertise he made up for in bourbon knowledge. Nick glanced at the clock and opened his laptop. At least he had the rest of the afternoon to become familiar with Kentucky's top moneymaker before he hit the road to Roseville.

His father had always enjoyed a small glass of bourbon in the evening, claiming it settled his stomach and guaranteed a good night's sleep. Before his father had died, he had imparted two other rules to live by: never do less than your best at work, and marry a nice girl before the good ones get snapped up. Of Dad's three pieces of advice, Nick had only followed the maxim about hard work. He loved his job and had earned enough commendations to get a job anywhere. But he would die a happy man if he spent the rest of his life in Kentucky, even if he never found the right woman to marry.

After Nick learned all he could in the allotted time, he went home to pack a bag and water his plants. No telling how long he'd be gone, but at least the drive to Roseville was pleasantly uneventful. Nick spotted the husky, fortyish officer the moment he walked into the office.

'Good evening, Sheriff Adkins?' He stretched out his hand. 'Nick Harris from Kentucky Post number four.'

'That's me, but call me Jeff. Thanks for getting here so fast.' Adkins shook with a firm but professional grip. 'I'm eager for you to look at the crime scene, so let's talk on the road.'

Nick masked his immediate apprehension. 'The body hasn't been removed yet?'

'No, the body was moved to the office of the undertaker, who doubles as the county coroner.'

'You mentioned the deceased was the owner of the distillery. So his employees made a positive identification?'

'Yep, the production shift was just arriving when a tourist – actually a travel writer – found the body first thing this morning. Get this . . . she was found covered in blood with the dead guy's head in her lap. And the guy's dog wouldn't leave her side. Her side, not the deceased's. I cleared the room immediately and sent everyone home. Didn't need anyone else stepping in evidence. I questioned the writer and her videographer and took statements from the employees in the parking lot. I suspect Mr Clark – Roger Clark, the master distiller – died sometime during the night.'

'You didn't detain the writer so I could question her?' Nick asked.

'No, but I took her bloody shirt into evidence and ordered her not to leave town.'

Nick let the sheriff's oversight pass for the moment. 'No security guard on duty last night?'

'Yes, one was supposed to be.' The sheriff grinned from ear to ear. 'You are just as sharp as your commander described.'

Nick also let the praise pass without comment.

'But apparently he got sick to his stomach with *lower intestinal distress* and went home,' the sheriff continued.

'Abandoned his post, just like that?'

Adkins nodded. 'Elmer Maxwell. I talked to the guy's wife on the phone. Supposedly the guard called Mr Clark, who didn't pick up. Then he left a message for the production manager that he was sick and going home because "there was no human way he could stay on the job". That's a direct quote, Lieutenant Harris.' Sheriff Adkins punctuated his sentence with a roll of his eyes. 'I would fire the guy if he worked for me.'

'What about security cameras?'

'Black Creek has a few but none in the aging rickhouse.'

'I trust you took plenty of photos and had techs gather evidence?' Nick asked.

'Tons of pictures, but I'm the one who gathered the evidence, following standard protocols. It should soon be on its way to the state lab.' Adkins turned his focus briefly away from the twisty road. 'I called for assistance as soon as I saw the bruises on Clark's face, in addition to the deep gash on the back of his head. There was liquid on the floor, so theoretically Clark could have slipped and cracked his skull, causing brain hemorrhage and death. But it's hard to batter both sides of the head in a simple fall. Wouldn't you agree?'

'I would indeed. You were right to call and I'm happy to assist.'

'Good, because we're here,' Adkins drawled. 'Welcome to Black Creek Distillery.' He braked to a stop close to the front door.

Without a body, it didn't take Nick long to check out the crime scene. In fact, he wasn't sure why the sheriff had brought him here. Photos would have sufficed, along with the autopsy and crime scene evidence report. But he would gain nothing by insulting local law enforcement.

'Did you collect a sample of this?' Nick bent down to sniff the liquid.

'I sure did. It's bourbon, right?'

'That would be my guess.' He stood and brushed off his palms. 'Send a sample of Black Creek's bourbon to the lab to see if it matches the sample of this.'

'You think the killer might have brought a flask along?' asked Adkins.

'We shall see.' Nick walked slowly around the crime scene, making sure nothing had been overlooked. 'Did you take a sample of this?' He pointed at what looked like blood on the edge of a rack.

'Yep, got it. There was hair stuck to the dried blood too.'

Nick got down on his hands and knees. 'What about the blood over here?' He pointed at two tiny drops several feet from the body.

Adkins leaned over to inspect. 'Man, I can't believe I didn't see that.'

'There's a Styrofoam cup under the rack too.'

'I'll call a deputy to grab a sample right now. I'm fresh out of evidence bags.' He pulled out his phone and barked orders to whoever picked up.

'If the deputy's on his way, why don't we talk to the person who discovered the body? I trust you know where this travel writer is staying.'

'Yes, but I'd rather you question her at the station. She's staying at the B and B owned by Roger Clark.'

Nick stared at the sheriff, dumbfounded, not knowing which question to ask first. 'The travel writer who found the body is staying in the home of the deceased?'

'Correct, but let's not make it uncomfortable for the widow. The woman is a personal friend of my wife's.'

Nick nodded. 'What's the name of this place?'

'Sweet Dreams.'

He dropped his chin to his chest. 'That's where I'm staying! How *small* is this town?'

'We're not that small. What a coincidence.'

'Take me back to the station, Jeff. I want to read your report and study the photos while you pick up the witness.'

'Good idea. You and I are going to make a great team.'

In less than an hour, Sheriff Adkins ushered a petite blonde into the conference room. With her hair in a tight ponytail and huge tortoiseshell glasses, she looked young and scholarly.

'Lieutenant Harris? This is Jill Curtis from Chicago. Miss Curtis, this is Lieutenant Harris from the Kentucky State Police. From this point on, he'll be running this investigation.' Adkins backed out of the room and closed the door.

Nick rose to his feet. 'Pleased to meet you, Miss Curtis. Have a seat.'

'Investigation. Roger Clark was *murdered*?' The woman's face paled several shades as she wobbled on her high heels.

'Please, sit.' He pointed at a chair. 'We won't know that until the coroner completes his autopsy.'

She sat clumsily and clutched her bag to her chest. 'I hope that sheriff didn't say I was a suspect. Why would I kill Mr Clark? Are you going to keep me overnight? I learned on TV you could hold someone for twenty-four hours without charging them.' She was breathing so fast and hard that hyperventilation was a distinct possibility.

'Take a deep breath, Miss Curtis. I don't want you to faint.'

She did as instructed, then added, 'Thanks, and you can call me Jill.'

'All right. I know Sheriff Adkins took possession of the shirt you had on, but were you wearing that skirt this morning?'

'No, the shorts I wore are back at the B and B. Am I a suspect? Should I have a lawyer here?'

'Right now I consider you a witness, nothing more. But if you prefer to have a lawyer present during questioning, you have that right.' Nick waited, while she cleaned her glasses on her sleeve and continued to inhale and exhale deeply.

Finally, she looked him in the eye. 'No, Lieutenant Harris, I don't need a lawyer because I didn't do anything wrong. Ask me all the questions you want.' Jill pulled a notebook from her bag. 'Mind if I take a few notes? I'm writing a travel piece on the bourbon industry and your questions might come in handy for my article.' The last of her discomfort seemed to evaporate before his eyes.

Oh, great, Nick thought. *This writer has her sights set on a Pulitzer Prize while I try to conduct an investigation. And to ice the cake, we're both staying in the victim's house.*

Thursday evening

From her bedroom window Jill watched as the police car parked in front of Sweet Dreams B&B and the sheriff and Kentucky State detective climbed out and marched up the porch steps. Despite the fact the investigator was relatively handsome, Nick Harris gave her the heebie-jeebies. And it had nothing to do with the fact that he suspected her of murder.

What motive could she have in murdering Roger Clark, a man

she'd never met before Tuesday evening? Jill had felt sick to her stomach while washing Roger's blood off in the shower, even though the innkeeper's husband hadn't exactly been warm and fuzzy. At this moment, the hometown sheriff and his sidekick were telling Dorothy Clark the awful news, but all she could do was sit up here and wait. Jill wanted to go down and hold the woman's hand. Maybe brew a pot of chamomile tea to soothe her nerves. But as far as her innkeeper was concerned, she was just another rent-paying guest.

Her grandmother had explained she and Dorothy were first cousins, twice removed, whatever that meant. Jill lifted her damp hair off her neck and pulled her shirt away from her skin. Her bedroom was too warm even though the air conditioning was as high as it would go. What would it hurt if she tiptoed downstairs to a cooler spot in the house? But when she opened the door, Jill bumped into the starched, uniformed chest of a large man.

'Ouuff.' She gasped. 'What are you doing, Trooper Harris, eavesdropping?'

'Of course not, I was getting ready to knock.' Harris stuck his head into her room and glanced around. 'Who were you talking to? You're all alone.'

'Maybe I was thinking aloud,' Jill said, oddly defensive. 'But at any rate, what can I do for you?'

'I know Sheriff Adkins took the shirt you'd been wearing when you found Mr Clark's body. I would like your shorts or slacks too, along with your shoes.'

'The shorts are soaking in my bathroom sink.' Jill crossed her arms over her sleeveless dress.

Harris's gray eyes turned steely while he arched his back against the door frame. 'Why would you do that, Miss Curtis? It could be construed as tampering with evidence.'

'It only would be tampering if I did something wrong, which I didn't. If you don't soak bloodstains in cold water fairly soon, you might as well pitch the garment into the trash.' She lifted her chin indignantly.

Harris studied her like a bug pinned to poster-board. 'I'll need the shoes you had on or are those soaking too?' he said as he handed her a see-through evidence bag.

'No, I was going to scrub them outdoors when Mrs Clark wasn't home. I don't want her more upset than she already is. I'll get them.' Jill headed to the closet, but when she turned around, the cop was right behind her. *As though I might sneak down a hidden staircase or something.* 'Here are the shoes.' She held out the bag. 'I want them returned when you finish your investigation.'

He inspected the bag as he took it from her. 'Of course, I'll see to it personally.' Harris pivoted on one boot heel and headed down the stairs.

Jill stayed right behind him. 'I'll see you out, Detective.'

He stopped so abruptly, she almost lost her balance. 'You do realize I'm staying in this house too. My room is next to your videographer's. I believe he said his name was Michael Erickson.'

Her jaw fell open. 'The poor widow has to contend with yet another guest?'

'That was my reaction too. I assured Mrs Clark I would find somewhere else to stay in town, but she insisted I stay. She said she can't deal with an empty house right now. Having breakfast to fix will give her stability since the rug has been pulled from under her feet. Those were her exact words.' Despite being on a lower step, Harris managed to look down his nose at her.

'As soon as the sheriff leaves, I plan to volunteer my services to Mrs Clark. I can help with breakfast and at teatime and with housework.'

'That's very nice of you.' Harris's expression softened. 'Since I assume you'll be staying until after Mr Clark's funeral, I won't need to tell you not to leave town.' He tipped his hat, tucked the bag with her shoes under his arm, and strolled out the front door.

Pulling her focus off the trooper, Jill peeked into the living room. Sheriff Adkins had an arm around Mrs Clark's back while she sobbed into his shoulder. The tender, poignant scene made Jill feel even more like an intruder than she already did. For a moment she was uncertain what to do. Creep back upstairs? Seek out her partner to see if he had learned anything new online? March into the sitting room and admit she's a long-lost relative and take over the consoling?

Adkins's booming voice kept Jill rooted in place. 'Remember, Dot, if Jenny and I can help in any way, don't hesitate to ask.'

'Your wife has already organized the ladies' guild to prepare

the funeral luncheon, whenever that will be,' said Mrs Clark. 'You
go on back to work. If you think this wasn't a horrible accident,
you have a job to do.'

Jill slumped onto the hall bench, trying to become invisible.

Adkins spotted her on his way out. 'Miss Curtis,' he murmured
and tipped his hat, her second hat-tip of the day.

Jill counted to ten before entering the living room. 'Mrs Clark?'

The innkeeper was seated on the sofa with her face in her hands.
'Miss Curtis, how are you?' She peered up with red-rimmed eyes.
'Sheriff Adkins said you were the one who found Roger. How
awful for you!'

Jill closed the distance between them in a few strides. 'No, how
awful for you. I wished there had been something I could do.' She
perched on the arm of the sofa and reached for Mrs Clark's hand.
'I should've been arrested for trespassing.'

'Nonsense, you were trying to get a story. That's your job.'

'Trooper Harris said you'd appreciate your guests staying so
the house isn't empty. If that is the case, I want to help with
breakfast and teatime and house cleaning – anything you need.'

'Absolutely not. Fixing simple meals will keep my mind busy.'

'But you have to make . . . arrangements.'

One large tear slipped from beneath her lashes. 'Actually, the coroner is also the undertaker and one of my friends. Once the police
release . . . Roger, Mr Trehanny will make the arrangements with
my pastor. The luncheon will be handled by my friends at church.
Even our burial plots were bought and paid for years ago. See the
advantages of living in a small town?' Her lips formed a smile
while a second tear fell. 'There's nothing for me to do but pick
out Roger's outfit. And my husband only owns one suit.' Mrs Clark
squeezed her hand, then shakily pushed to her feet. 'You and Mr
Erickson came to Roseville with a job to do. Besides, I could
never allow a guest to run the vacuum.'

Jill inhaled a deep breath. 'I'm not really a guest,' she said
when her hostess was halfway to the door.

'What do you mean?' Mrs Clark paused and looked back over
her shoulder.

'Of course, we'll pay for our rooms, but I booked this place
for personal reasons. You and I have a common relative.'

'Who on earth would that be?'

'Emma Vanderpool. I believe Vanderpool was your maiden name and Emma was . . . is your first cousin.'

Mrs Clark strode back to the sofa. 'Emma! I haven't talked to her in ages. How are you related to Emma, young lady?'

Unable to gauge the woman's mindset, Jill braced for the worst. 'She's my grandmother.'

'You said *is*, so Emma Vanderpool is still alive?'

'She was when I left Chicago.'

'Oh, thank goodness! I was afraid one of us would go to the grave before we mended fences. Then we'd have to sort it all out at the pearly gates.' Mrs Clark released a chuckle. 'Did Emma explain the horrible transgression I committed against her?'

'No, ma'am, only that it was unforgiveable and that she never planned to set foot in Kentucky again.'

Mrs Clark's smile vanished. 'It was unforgiveable, at least for two eighteen-year-old cousins. At the time we'd been closer than sisters. Then I let hormones and emotions cloud my better judgment. I will write a long letter for you to deliver when you get home. After fifty years, Cousin Emma might be willing to forgive me.' She stood with great dignity and pulled Jill into her arms. 'In the meantime, welcome to my home, granddaughter of Emma Vanderpool. Even if it was just curiosity about a wanton woman that brought you here, I'm happy to meet you.'

'I meant what I said about wanting to help, Mrs Clark.'

'I won't have you calling me "Mrs Clark" now that we're related. And First-Cousin-Twice-Removed sounds like a bag of hot air.' She pressed a finger to her lips while considering. 'How about Aunt Dot? Dot is what my friends call me, and "aunt" respects the difference in our ages.'

Jill nodded. 'I don't plan to leave until your husband's killer is behind bars, Aunt Dot.'

Her eyes widened with surprise. 'Oh, my. I would like that very much, but I can't bear the idea of a cold-blooded killer prowling the streets of Roseville. I hope it turns out to be simply a bizarre accident.' She left the room with tears streaming down her face.

Jill was left alone in the formal parlor, wondering if her timing had again made a bad situation worse.

FOUR

T he last rays of a particularly gorgeous sunset fell on the uncut grass and peeling yellow paint of the home of Elmer and Janice Maxwell. Nick Harris and Sheriff Adkins climbed from the squad car and perused the residence of the irresponsible security guard at Black Creek Distillery. Enough toys and yard games were strewn across the property to mimic a day care center.

'Man, don't their kids put away anything when they're done?' Adkins groused. 'If these kids were mine, I'd bag it all up for the trash.'

Nick wasn't concerned about stuffed animals or board games left out in the rain. His focus fell on a 1966 Chevelle Super Sport convertible that was being restored to its original power and glory under an aluminum carport. Funny thing about vintage car enthusiasts – they often would let their kids go without shoes and the roof repair to consist of a well-placed bucket, so that they could buy the appropriate car part. Movement at the window caught Nick's eye as they made their way up the front steps. Something didn't feel quite right at this rural, middle-class home.

Nick pounded on the door while Adkins shouted, 'Elmer Maxwell. Spencer County Sheriff's Department. We'd like to talk to you.'

When the door opened, a very thin woman appeared with bleached blonde hair, very dark roots, and a bad complexion.

'What can I do for you, Sheriff? Elmer's sick in bed. I'm his wife.' The woman rubbed her forearms as though cold yet the temperature had to be in the eighties.

'Good evening, ma'am.' Nick forced a pleasant smile. 'I'm Lieutenant Harris. Sorry to bother you, but it's imperative that Elmer answer our questions himself. We promise not to stay long.'

Mrs Maxwell glared at Nick, letting her gaze travel from his polished shoes to the top of his head. When the cops didn't give up and go away, the woman finally stepped to the side. 'Fine, but I hope you don't cause a relapse.'

Nick crossed the threshold into a cluttered living room with worn carpeting the color of dirt. Almost as many toys were scattered in this room as outdoors.

Wearing striped shorts, black socks and no shoes, Elmer Maxwell sat in a recliner watching the ballgame, not in bed as his wife had described. 'Come in, Sheriff,' he greeted. 'What can I do for you? Take a load off. Just put those papers and magazines on the floor,' he directed when no other chairs appeared to be available.

The sheriff did as instructed, but Nick preferred to remain upright, keeping Janice Maxwell within sight at all times.

The sheriff took the lead, since he knew the man from previous run-ins. 'Were you aware that Roger Clark was found dead this morning in the main rickhouse?'

'Yeah, I got a call this afternoon from one of my buddies in production. Man, that sucks.'

'What exactly sucks, Mr Maxwell?' Nick asked.

Maxwell's brow furrowed. 'Roger slipping and fallin' like that. Goes to show just how easy everything can be over like that.' Elmer snapped his fingers to illustrate the brevity of life.

'You were supposed to be working security last night,' the sheriff prodded. 'When and why did you leave?'

He nodded his head enthusiastically, as though he'd been waiting for this question. 'My shift runs from seven in the evening to seven a.m. I always eat supper right before leaving the house, but last night Janice was at bingo with her mother. I dug around in the fridge for something to eat and found this casserole that looked OK to me. So I heated it up and chowed down.'

'That chicken and rice had to be two weeks old,' Janice said defensively. 'You shoulda given it the sniff test.'

'And you should clean that fridge out more than once a year,' shouted Maxwell. 'Before you put somebody in the ground.' The victim of food poisoning wasn't taking any sass from the little woman.

'Getting back to last night,' Adkins prompted.

'Well, I upchucked most of it in the men's room, but I still didn't feel right. So I called Mr Clark and left him a message when he didn't pick up. I also left a message for Gordon Clark. Gordy handles personnel and scheduling.'

'Then you just left without lining up a replacement?' Nick let his tone reveal his opinion on the matter.

'Hey, man. That's not how it works at Black Creek. I called Mr Clark and Gordy. It's up to one of them to find someone to fill in.' He took a gulp of whatever was in his plastic cup. 'I left another message this morning that I'm still sick.'

'So what happens now?' Janice demanded.

Nick half-turned to face her. 'You'll have to wait until Gordon contacts you to see if and when your husband should return to work.'

'And what are we supposed to do for money in the meantime? It ain't Elmer's fault that he got sick. We need sick pay or something to tide us over.' The wife's focus shifted to Adkins whom she thought might be more sympathetic.

But Nick provided the ready answer. 'Your husband will have only been off work for two night shifts. You shouldn't be in dire straits yet.'

The sheriff pushed to his feet. 'Elmer, did you see anything out of the ordinary when you arrived at work that evening or when you left to go home?'

'No, everything seemed to be right-as-rain in the plant.' Maxwell gazed up at them with bloodshot eyes.

'You locked the security room when you left the plant?' Nick asked.

Maxwell's forehead furrowed. 'Nah, I don't remember doing that.'

'We just stopped at the distillery before coming here and the room is locked. Do you have the key at home with you?'

'I guess it's in my uniform pocket, but that's weird.' Maxwell refocused on the TV screen.

'Could we have that key, Mr Maxwell?' Nick growled, unable to hide his impatience.

'No need to get nasty. The Reds just scored.' Maxwell swiveled around to his wife. 'Get that key out of my pants pocket.'

'Thanks,' Nick said after Janice complied. 'If you can think of anything *helpful*, give us a call.' He pushed aside an empty Coke can and laid down his business card. Then he strode out the front door and down the rickety steps to the squad car.

Later, on their way back to town, Adkins delivered a few pearls of wisdom. 'You know, Harris, you can usually get more flies with honey than with vinegar.'

'Sorry. You're absolutely right, but something about that couple rubbed me the wrong way. I won't let that happen again.'

The good-natured veteran lawman chuckled low in his throat. 'It happens. Don't worry about it.'

Friday morning

Jill needn't have worried about helping with breakfast that morning. From six thirty on, a steady stream of women arrived with home-made pies, cakes, bagels and muffins for breakfast, along with casseroles and salads for later in the day. Jill kept the coffee maker churning out pot after pot since most of the friends and neighbors remained on the porch to support Aunt Dot in her grief.

Jill carried extra dining-room chairs out as the crowd grew, then retreated to the kitchen. Despite having a family connection with the bereaved, she felt exactly like what she was: a stranger in Roseville.

'Wow,' said a deep voice behind her, startling Jill out of her reverie. 'Who brought all these goodies?' Michael pulled a mini muffin from the platter and popped it whole into his mouth.

'Who do you think, Erickson? Aunt Dot's friends in town. And stop sneaking up on people!'

'Who else could it have been? Either me or that state cop.' Michael reached for another muffin. 'Where is Lieutenant Harris this morning – sleeping in?'

Jill handed him a mug of coffee. 'Don't be silly. Harris was already gone before I came downstairs. He's got a killer to catch.'

'Yes, and his prime suspect sleeps down the hall.' This time Michael took two bites to finish the muffin.

Jill peered through the doorway to make sure their hostess was still surrounded by friends. 'Don't say those things where Aunt Dot could overhear you.'

'What's with the "aunt" stuff? You said she might be a long-lost relative – I thought you two were distant cousins at best.' He cut a large slice of coffee cake, which he proceeded to eat while leaning against the fridge.

'That's what she asked me to call her.' Jill pulled out a chair.

'Sit down and eat human-style. I don't want crumbs all over the floor.'

'Listen to you – a real mom-in-training.' Michael sat but didn't bother with the plate and fork Jill provided. 'So, can we go back to Black Creek Distillery today? I didn't have a chance to finish getting footage when I heard blood-curdling screams and had to take off running.'

She rolled her eyes. 'Roger Clark was just killed yesterday. I doubt the police have released the crime scene. And I'm sure they haven't started giving tours again. Remember, Uncle Roger had been one of the tour guides. Use your head.'

'I thought since you were blood-kin, Black Creek might cut us a little slack.' Michael licked his fingertips.

'I'll get you special permission from Dot, or perhaps you should charm adorable Lindy again. I'm on my way to the county library as soon as I'm no longer needed here.' Jill filled a carafe with fresh coffee.

'What on earth for? We've already got loads of story, especially if we throw in the murder of a master distiller. What we need is video.'

'We won't be saying a word about Roger Clark until the killer is found. I won't be a party to conjecture, innuendo and false news.'

Michael slumped into a chair. 'And I thought this assignment would be fun and easy. You're turning into a hometown bore instead of a journalist.'

'And you've turned into a . . .' Jill almost unleashed a word that would have earned her a mouth-washing from Granny. So instead she mentally counted to five. 'I'm sorry you feel that way, Michael. I want to research the two-hundred-year-old feud that Jamie Shelby told us about. Perhaps this murder is somehow related. Now if you'll excuse me, I'll check to see if the ladies need more coffee.' She set the carafe on a tray, along with the plate of muffins, and headed to the door.

'If you get a chance, pick up a pink housedress with roses and a pair of sensible pumps at Walmart.' Michael's laughter carried all the way to the porch, but Jill pretended not to hear. She had a job to do and a responsibility to Aunt Dot. The clothes she had on would do just fine.

After the group of ladies on the porch finished nibbling pastries and had had enough caffeine, they marched into the house. Two headed upstairs armed with buckets, sponges, and spray cleaner. Two marched into the kitchen where they began Swiffering and sanitizing countertops, while a buxom blonde headed for the formal parlor and library with a feather duster, despite Jill's loud protestations.

'Save your breath, Jill,' whispered Aunt Dot next to her ear. 'I already told them it wasn't necessary, but my friends listen worse than Jack.'

Jack. In all the excitement, she hadn't seen the dog since he'd crawled out from beneath the aging rack. 'Where is your dog?' she asked.

'He's moping on the loveseat in our bedroom, watching for Roger to come home. I tried coaxing him down with both kibble and biscuits, but he won't budge from his post. He always was Roger's buddy.'

'Mind if I try?' Jill asked. 'Jack seemed to take a liking to me.'

'I'd love it if you tried. There's his food bowl, still full from yesterday.' Dorothy pointed at the corner, then shrugged with despair. 'You might add a teaspoon of peanut butter. That's how we administer his heartworm pill.'

Jill picked up the bowl, stirred in a glob of peanut butter from the pantry, and climbed the steps to the master bedroom. As predicted, the beagle was on the loveseat with his head on the windowsill. From that spot he had a dog's-eye view of the driveway.

'Hi, Jack,' she greeted idiotically. 'It's me, Jill, from Tuesday night.' She sat down next to the beagle who thus far, hadn't acknowledged her presence. 'Don't you remember me?' Tentatively, she offered her hand for him to sniff.

After a few moments, Jack sniffed her fingers, then licked the finger she used to dispense the peanut butter. 'Do you like that, old boy?' His only response was to continue licking long after the sweetness was gone. 'I bet you miss your master.'

Incomprehensibly, Jack gazed up with his large brown eyes.

'Well, Uncle Roger put me in charge when he had to leave. And it's time for supper, young man.' Jill put the bowl of sweetened kibble under his nose.

Jack looked her in the eye and then began to eat. Perhaps it was pity for a masterless dog or pity for a husbandless wife, but Jill sobbed until the bowl was empty. Then she dried her eyes on her T-shirt and announced, 'Good boy, Jack. Now let's go for a walk.' To which the beagle trotted out the door and down the steps.

The walk around the block concluded her duties at the B&B that morning. Aunt Dot rejoiced that Jack wouldn't expire on her bedroom sofa. And Jill headed to the county library feeling down-right useful.

At the library, she had no trouble finding the correct person to talk to. On this sunny Friday morning, Roseville had only one librarian on duty.

'Hi, you look a tad lost,' said a tall brunette when Jill walked in. 'I'm Amanda Posey. Can I help you?' Smiles didn't come any bigger than the one on this woman.

'Jill Curtis, and I'm new to the area. Do you have any books with local history? I'm interested in a feud from two hundred years ago that involves bourbon.'

'That's an easy request. We have three books of local history and all three cover that feud. To my knowledge, all three are in the stacks. Shall I find them for you?'

'If it wouldn't be too much trouble, yes.' Jill grinned. 'When I took the tour at Founder's Reserve, Jamie Shelby spoke of a romantic feud that continues to this day.'

'Well, if anyone ought to know, it would be the town Romeo!' A look of shock crossed the librarian's face, as though the words had left her mouth without consent. 'Sorry, that didn't sound very professional. I'll get those books. In the meantime, please forget my biased opinion.' Amanda hurried to the non-fiction section and returned a few minutes later with three paperbacks. 'These were published by the University of Kentucky Press. They are the best source for Kentucky's colorful history on the regional level. I've read all three so I know the story by heart.'

Jill took the books from Amanda's hand. 'Thanks so much. I want to read everything about the bourbon industry.' She glanced around the sparsely populated room. 'In the meantime, do you have time to give me a quick overview of the feud?'

'I'd be happy to. Let's sit over there.' She pointed at an over-stuffed sofa in a sunny nook.

Jill took one end of the sofa, while Amanda sat at the other, then flipped through the first book until she found a topographical sketch. 'This is the infamous Black Creek, which is at the heart of the feud. Back in the late 1700s, Isaiah Shelby grew corn on the north side of the creek, while Tobias Cook grew rye on the south side. The creek had marked the property line between the two farms for decades. Then one summer it rained hard for five straight days and the flooded creek changed its natural riverbed. Isaiah Shelby claimed the additional sixty acres of fertile land as his own, claiming they were a gift from God. Tobias Cook, whose farm was much smaller to start with, claimed that God did no such thing. There were large boulders marking the original land grants which had stayed in place during the flood. So Tobias and his sons continued to cross the creek to work their land. All through the harvest, the Shelby sons harassed the Cooks until the Cooks had had enough. One weekend around Christmas, a terrible fight broke out in town between the sons of both families. Unfortunately, Tobias's oldest and favorite son ended up dead. After that Tobias Cook lost interest in farming. His other sons took up thieving and cattle-rustling to put food on the table, but they never left the area. Instead, they built their stills up in the hills where the law had a hard time catching them.

'By that time, Isaiah Shelby's grandsons were grown and had inherited the bourbon-making operation. The family plowed every dime of profit into buying up any available land in the area, including what had formerly belonged to the Cooks. Keep in mind, Isaiah and Tobias were long in their graves, but it must have looked suspicious when the Shelby homestead burned to the ground on Christmas Eve, killing the current Mrs Shelby.'

'Holy guacamole!' exclaimed Jill. 'I sure didn't hear all that from Jamie Shelby.'

'I'm not surprised. Both families pick and choose which parts they want to tell.' The librarian handed Jill the book with the map. 'That's the gist of it. By the twentieth century, the feud had pretty much been forgotten. But the bourbon tours at both Black Creek Distillery and Founder's Reserve have stirred up old hatreds.' Amanda shook her head. 'In my opinion, not exactly a good thing for the current generation who would rather forget the past.'

'So the Jamie Shelby I met on the tour is a descendant of Isaiah who claimed the sixty acres of land?'

'One and the same. Although I don't think much of Jamie, I must admit his family has worked long and hard to build Founder's Reserve into what it is today. And they came by every other acre through legal means.'

'Thanks, Amanda. That was one great story, but I had hoped the old feud might have something to do with Roger Clark's death at Black Creek. What's the connection between the Cooks and the Clarks?'

'Please call me Mandy, like the rest of my friends. Who's to say it doesn't? Roger Clark's great-grandmother was Henrietta Cook, the matriarch of the clan up in the hills. It was his father who brought their bourbon operation back into the *legal* realm.' Mandy jumped to her feet. 'I need to check the teenagers in the computer room. But these books should answer most of your questions. Nice meeting you, Jill. Stop in anytime to chew the fat.'

Jill knew she had only one shot at this and had to be quick. 'May I ask how you formed your low opinion of Jamie Shelby?'

Mandy glanced back over her shoulder with an expression indicating a line had been crossed. 'Sorry, history is one thing, but I don't want to gossip.'

'No, I'm the one who should apologize. I ask only because Jamie asked me out after my tour of Founder's Reserve. I was planning on going unless . . .' Jill left her sentence hanging in the air.

Mandy closed the distance between them. 'One of these days my big mouth will get me sued for slander!'

'Not because of me – you have my word.'

She perused Jill from head to toe. 'OK, I'll try to be fair and start with his good characteristics: Jamie is well-mannered, obviously attractive, spends plenty of money on his lady friends. The man would treat you very well.'

Jill pondered before asking, 'And his downside?'

'Notice I said *friends,* plural. Jamie will never be true to just one woman. While he was dating me – and we're talking for eight months while I fell head-over-heels – he was also dating Michelle Clark.'

'Clark! Is Michelle related to Roger?' Jill demanded.

'Come to think of it, I don't know. There are lots of Clarks and

Cooks in this county. Uh-oh, I hear those teenagers in the computer room. Gotta go.'

As the librarian scurried to rein-in some youthful patrons, Jill called her thanks and carried the books to the check-out desk. Since she didn't have a library card, she left a photocopy of her driver's license, the titles of the books, and her cell phone number. She had no desire to take up anymore of her new friend's time. Plus she couldn't wait to get back to Sweet Dreams B&B.

She found Aunt Dot in the living room, sipping tea next to a cold fire with Jack at her feet. The dog jumped up and wagged his tail when Jill entered the room.

'There you are, dear cousin. I brewed a full pot of tea, hoping you'd be back soon.'

Jill took the opposite chair and accepted a cup filled to the rim. 'Thanks, I could use this.' She drank half the contents.

'Have you eaten lunch yet? My friend fixed me a ham sandwich, but I could only eat half. I saved the other half for you. It's in the fridge.'

At the thought of food Jill's stomach rumbled since she wasn't used to skipping meals. 'Thanks, but you might want it later.'

'Don't be ridiculous. Someone brought over an entire party tray of cold cuts and cheese. Eat my other half so it doesn't go to waste.' Aunt Dot sounded like she wouldn't take no for an answer.

Jill's stomach didn't want to hear no either. She found the sandwich, added a handful of potato chips and some carrot sticks from the tray and returned to the library with a mounded plate.

'So, you were hungry.' Aunt Dot shook her head. 'Don't stand on ceremony in the house, young lady! Now that we're family I expect you to stop being so shy.'

'Yes, ma'am.' Jill devoured the ham and Swiss in four bites. 'Was there any news this morning about Uncle Roger?'

'Only that the coroner finished the autopsy. But until the medical examiner in Frankfort issues his findings, we can't schedule a funeral.' She set her cup in the saucer with a sigh. 'It still could be several days. I thought I might inquire of that nice Lieutenant Harris, but I haven't seen him all day. He must be taking his meals out, which is truly a shame. All that food in the fridge will go to waste if it's just you and me eating it.'

'I'll tell both Michael and the cop to start eating . . . or suffer the consequences.'

'Thank you.' Dot clasped Jill's hand and squeezed.

The gesture felt warm and comforting, yet it also filled her with regret. Jill hadn't seen her parents since Christmas and neither of them were the touchy-feely type. 'By the way, I met a nice librarian today,' Jill said in between potato chips. 'Amanda Posey loaned me three books and filled me in on the Shelby–Cook two-hundred-year-old feud.'

Dot shook her head. 'I told Roger that story would be better off forgotten. But he insisted it helped drive bourbon sales at Black Creek, especially since his specialty was rye bourbon. And liquor sales help maintain this white elephant of a house.' She flourished her hand through the air.

'Did your husband like Sweet Dreams B and B?'

'He did in his own way. But Roger loved to grouse about something – if it wasn't repairs on this place, it was equipment breaking down at the distillery.'

'Mandy the librarian also mentioned that Jamie Shelby used to date Michelle Clark.'

Dot shrugged. 'I don't keep up with who's dating whom in Roseville.'

'Was Uncle Roger related to this Michelle Clark?'

Her cousin studied her. 'Roger does have a niece named Michelle. She's his brother William's daughter. Of course, Michelle is a rather common name.'

'Do the brother and his family live up in the hills?'

'They do. What's this about?' Dot's forehead creased in confusion.

'Maybe Uncle Roger's death is tied to the old feud between the Shelbys and the Cooks.'

'There's a better chance it's related to aliens from space wanting Roger's proprietary recipes.' Dot reached down to scratch Jack's head. 'Need to go outside, old boy?'

'I'll be happy to take him for another walk.' Jill set her plate on the table.

'Thank you, dear. While you two are gone, I think I'll take a nap. One thing about doting friends . . . they sure can wear a person out.' Dot shuffled from the room, while Jill carried her plate to the sink with Jack by her side. The words 'another walk' hadn't gone unnoticed by the dog.

Jill loved walking in Roseville, especially through the downtown area. There were so many cute shops and restaurants to check out when she got a chance. Right now her determination to find a true killer wasn't allowing time to work on her travel feature, let alone go sightseeing.

Stopping at a coffee house with an outdoor patio, she ordered a double caramel latte for her and a bowl of cold water for her pal. Both libations were thoroughly enjoyed. On the way back, Jill found herself walking slower and slower, as though she didn't want her time with the droopy-eared beagle to end. How fair was that to Aunt Dot, whom she promised to help during these difficult days? Moreover, how fair was she being to Michael? This whole assignment, including staying at the home of an estranged relative, had been her idea. Not to mention she had found the distiller's body, making her suspect number one in his murder.

'Let's get some real exercise, Jack.' Jill and woman's best friend broke into a trot, covering the remaining blocks within ten minutes. Upon their arrival, she didn't have to hunt for her partner. Michael Erickson was sitting on the porch steps with a snifter of bourbon and a half-empty bottle. And he wasn't smiling.

FIVE

'Care to enlighten me as to where you've been all day?' Michael snarled. 'I've been waiting for you. The whole house appears to be empty.'

Jill sat down on the steps with the bottle between them and Jack by her feet. 'Did you drink all that?' she asked, trying not to sound accusatory.

'No, this is only my second drink. Don't try to change the subject. Answer my question.'

'Let's see.' Jill stretched out her legs. 'First, I served Aunt Dot's guests on the porch and helped her friends clean the house. It was two hours before the ladies put away their buckets and sponges and left. Then Aunt Dot mentioned Roger's dog hadn't eaten since the sheriff brought him home from the distillery. Jack keeps staring down the driveway, waiting for his master to come home. Sad, no?'

'Yes, it's sad.'

Jill knew Michael was trying his best to remain patient with her. 'Aunt Dot suggested that I stir peanut butter into his food to see if that made a difference. Well, the peanut butter worked and Jack ate every kibble in his bowl.'

'Any reason why Mrs Clark didn't try this herself?' he asked in a whisper.

'I don't think she and the dog ever bonded. He was strictly Roger's, but for some reason Jack likes me. So I coaxed him downstairs and out the door with a treat so we could take a walk.'

Michael's face screwed into a frown. 'You don't even like dogs.'

Now it was Jill's turn to be patient. 'No, but I happen to like this one. Plus I'm trying to help out Aunt Dot.'

'Go on with your story,' he prodded.

'Next I went to the library to find out more about the bourbon feud and I met a new friend – the librarian. When I came back with my books, I asked Dot what she knows about any current feuds between the two families. After we finished our tea, I took

Jack for another walk to downtown. And that brings us to the present moment.' Jill patted the dog's head.

Michael pressed his fingertips to his eyes. 'We're here with a job to do. There are several more distilleries on the circuit after Founder's Reserve and Black Creek. We need to finish up here and move on to the others.'

Jill lifted her chin defiantly. 'I'm not going anywhere until after Roger's funeral.'

Michael raised his palms in surrender. 'Yes, I know that. But the point is we haven't finished our work in Roseville.'

'I believe a feud between bourbon families can be an integral part of our travel piece. Readers and tourists eat that kind of stuff up.'

'Maybe so, but I was unable to shoot any video at Black Creek today. Lindy wasn't there because nobody is back to work yet. And the security guard didn't believe that I had permission from Mrs Clark.'

'You should have called me.'

'I did, three times throughout the day and left you three different voicemails. You failed to check your phone.'

Jill pulled her cell from her back pocket. 'Sorry. I switched it off when I entered the library, then forgot to turn it back on.' She tapped the screen several times. 'I won't do that again.'

'Great. In the meantime, try not to forget we're *partners*. Mrs Clark needs to make some calls so the security guard will let us inside Black Creek tomorrow.'

Anticipating Michael's reaction, Jill cringed. 'Uh oh, that won't work for me. I left a message for Jamie Shelby that I have more questions about Founder's Reserve. I'm driving out tomorrow to see him.'

'We have one car between us, remember?'

'Aunt Dot said I can use her car anytime. She has Roger's truck at her disposal. But before she goes to bed tonight, I'll ask her to make those phone calls.'

Michael shook his head like a stubborn mule. 'Nothing doing, Jill. We don't know anything about this Jamie Shelby. He could be the murderer for all we know. I don't like you being alone with him.'

'I won't be alone. On a Saturday, there will be throngs of tourists, plus all the employees of Founder's Reserve.'

'Somehow Mister-Tall-Dark-and-Rich will find a way to get you alone.'

Jill had been thinking the same thing, but refused to give in. 'Golly, Erickson, if I didn't know better I'd swear you were jealous.'

'Don't flatter yourself. I prefer women with gray matter between their ears.'

She chuckled. 'Honest, Mike. I believe this murder might be linked to that ancient feud. Did you know that Jamie used to date Michelle Clark? I believe Michelle is a direct descendent of the Cooks who burned down the old Shelby homestead, killing Mama Shelby.' Jill didn't mention this was over a century ago.

Michael blinked. 'There seems to be plenty you're not telling me, partner.'

'Only because there has been no time. Tomorrow I will make sure you have access to anywhere you want in Black Creek. I'll even try to get Lindy to be your tour guide.' Jill offered an exaggerated wink. 'Then on Sunday, you and I will spend the whole day together. We'll drive up the mountain to speak to Michelle Clark in person, along with her dad, William, who's the brother of Roger Clark.'

'Because you're just itching to meet more kinfolk.' He shook his head.

'No, because I want to see if Michelle's story matches what the librarian told me and what I'll hopefully learn from Jamie tomorrow.'

Michael downed the remaining bourbon in his glass, jumped to his feet, and picked up the bottle. 'Just once I'd like to win an argument with you.'

Jill stood too. 'This wasn't an argument, only a practical way to handle the assignment. Let's chow down in the kitchen. You have no idea how much food Dot's friends brought over.'

'If you're talking cucumber sandwiches and mini quiches, you and I are heading to a restaurant. No discussion, Curtis.'

In the kitchen, their hostess had just pulled out the sandwich tray along with several casseroles. 'Ahh, two of my three guests are here. We have homemade lasagna, sweet potato casserole, roast turkey, sliced roast beef, and several salads.' Glancing from her to Michael, Dot pulled the covers off the huge party tray and the lasagna.

'It's up to Michael, Aunt Dot. He's kind of a picky eater.'

Michael took one look at the party tray and meaty casserole. 'We're staying, Mrs Clark. I'll go get washed up.' He headed toward the lavatory.

'Jill, will you run upstairs to see if Lieutenant Harris would like to join us?'

'Of course,' she said after a brief hesitation. Taking the steps two at a time, Jill headed down the opposite hallway to the room next to her partner's. Just as she lifted her hand to knock, the door opened and before her stood the muscular and rather imposing state trooper.

'Good evening, Miss Curtis, what can I do for you?' Nick Harris looked just as surprised as she felt.

'How on earth did you know I was there?'

He looked about to say something then changed his mind. 'Just a lucky guess. What can I do for you?'

'Friends of our innkeeper dropped off a ton of food, and since the cops haven't released Mr Clark's body, she can't schedule the funeral.' As it occurred to her *he* was the cop who hadn't released Uncle Roger, Jill lost her train of thought.

'Go on, Miss Curtis.' Harris leaned against the door jamb.

'Mrs Clark doesn't want the food to go to waste, so she invited Michael and me to eat with her tonight. And she sent me up to fetch you.' Jill felt her cheeks grow warm. 'I mean, sent me upstairs to invite you.'

Harris stared at his well-polished leather shoes. 'That is very kind of Mrs Clark, but the coffee and pastries this morning were more than enough. Please thank her on my behalf.'

Jill kept the door from closing with her foot. 'Why can't you make a grieving widow happy by eating some food?' She didn't ask the question so much as she demanded an answer.

A tiny smile pulled up one corner of his mouth. 'Truly, I would love a home-cooked meal, but considering why I'm here, it's not a good idea.'

'Why not?'

'Because this is a homicide investigation and until I come up with someone better, the person who found the body and the bereaved spouse remain the chief suspects.'

That shut her up in a hurry. 'Oh, I see.' Keeping her foot firmly planted, Jill crossed her arms. 'I would hate to tell that to Mrs Clark, so why don't I make you a plate and bring it up later? I'll knock and leave. You won't have to set eyes on me again tonight.'

'That would be very nice. Thanks. Now I'd better get back to work.' He hooked his thumb at the open laptop on his desk.

'Good night, Trooper Harris.' Unnerved by the man's cool composure, Jill withdrew her foot.

Not until she was halfway down the stairs did she think of a few snappy comebacks: *You'd better get busy if a sixty-five-year-old woman and a travel writer are your chief suspects.* Or maybe: *If you really think one of us is a killer, why would you eat food touched by our hands?* When she reached the kitchen, Jill plastered on a smile and made up an excuse.

At dinner Michael ate enough to feed a village. Aunt Dot merely picked at her food, although she did share an amusing anecdote about the person who prepared each dish. Afterwards, the innkeeper fixed a tray for the hard-working cop who couldn't pull himself from his computer. This time Jill tiptoed as she delivered the meal.

Nevertheless, Harris opened the door as she bent to set his dinner on the floor.

'Thanks, Miss Curtis.' He took the tray from her hands. 'It looks like I'll have enough for several meals. What's under the foil?'

'Sliced meat and cheese, several pieces of bread, lasagna, potato salad, yam casserole and two kinds of salad. Since there's a fridge in every room, I recommend the hot food for tonight, and saving the cold cuts and salads for tomorrow.' Jill stepped back from the doorway.

'Look, I hope I didn't hurt your feelings. Even if I personally don't think you're a murderer, I must maintain police protocol.'

'Don't worry, by the time you catch the real bad guy, I will have recovered from your painful insult.' She gazed into his gray eyes and winked. '*Bon appetit,* Trooper Harris.'

The moment she reached her own room, her cell phone started buzzing in her pocket. 'Hello?' she asked, not recognizing the caller ID.

'Hi, Jill. It's Jamie Shelby. I got your message. Great minds must think alike. I'd planned to call you later about going out tomorrow night.'

'Can we get together for lunch instead? Mrs Clark might need my help in the evening.'

'Of course.' His voice was as smooth as his well-aged bourbon. 'What time shall I pick you up?'

'No need to drive to Roseville. I'd rather come to Founder's Reserve.'

'Shall I plan lunch for two or will your videographer be joining us?' he asked after a slight pause.

'Michael has to head back to Black Creek tomorrow, so it'll just be me.'

'Perfect. I would like to show you one of our old-fashioned stills in an area that's off limits to the general public, and I remember how grain bothers Mike's allergies.'

So much for having people around at all times. 'I'd like that, but please don't go to any trouble with lunch. A hot dog and Coke from your snack bar would be just fine.'

'You, Miss Curtis, won't be any trouble at all. Just tell the person at the front gate you're my guest. That way I can meet you out front with the golf cart.'

'Sounds like everything is settled. See you tomorrow.' Jill hung up, excited about seeing a still from a bygone era.

But that night Jill had trouble falling asleep. Could Jamie possibly be a murderer? He'd been with her for most of the evening. What would be his motivation? Roger Clark's distillery was much smaller and doubtlessly less profitable, judging by Jamie's Lexus and Roger's beat-up Ford pickup. If something was definitely going on between the two families, she planned to figure out what.

SIX

Saturday

The next morning Jill was up at the crack of dawn. She even beat Aunt Dot downstairs, so she had plenty of time to start the coffee and set out the last of the muffins, along with a spiced Bundt cake yet to be sliced. One of Dot's friends had created perfect seashell scallops all around the cake with buttercream icing. After Jill lined up plates, forks, and cups on the counter, she fed Jack his peanut butter-laced kibble and hitched him up for a run. Although Jack's spirit seemed willing, his short beagle legs had a hard time keeping up, so they dropped their pace to a fast walk and still managed to get plenty of exercise. When they entered the kitchen thirty minutes later, Nick Harris and Michael Erickson were at the table, drinking coffee and eating spice cake.

'Good morning, Miss Curtis,' said Harris, rising to his feet. The well-mannered cop had on running shorts and a T-shirt which showed off biceps usually seen only on workout shows.

Michael, however, ignored her and greeted only the dog. 'Hey, Jack. How's it going, buddy?' He scratched the dog behind the ears.

'Good morning, Lieutenant. I'm surprised you're hungry already, considering the size of last night's dinner.' Jill poured herself a cup of coffee.

'I took your advice and ate only the hot food. Then I made two big sandwiches, one for today with the pasta salad, and another for tomorrow with the potato salad. I haven't eaten that well since I went home at Easter.'

'Where's home?' Michael asked in between bites of cake.

'A small town called Lorraine, Kentucky, not that far from Louisville. How 'bout you?'

'Jill and I were both born and raised in Chicago, but she's taken quite a shine to Roseville. If Mrs Clark doesn't invite her to stay permanently, she might be forced to marry Jamie Shelby so she doesn't have to go back to the city.'

Jill felt blood rush to her cheeks as she glared at her partner. 'Have you been already hitting the rye whiskey or simply lost your mind?'

'I'm merely expressing an opinion on what I have observed.' Michael returned her glare. 'You're either smitten with small town life, or by an eighth-generation master distiller, who's waiting in the wings for Daddy to kick so he can inherit an empire.' He added a negative inflection to the final word.

'What's gotten into you? Could you at least save your venom for when we're alone? Trooper Harris will think Chicagoans are a pack of ill-bred jackals.'

Harris set down his fork. 'Michael and I were talking while you were out with the dog. I believe he's worried about you going alone to Founder's Reserve. Hence, his attitude.'

Jill turned her focus on the cop. 'Don't tell me you agree with this madman? I'm simply having lunch and getting more info about one of the oldest distilleries in Kentucky.'

'I don't agree or disagree. I'm just mediating between two work colleagues.' Harris's expression became unreadable.

'Thanks, Switzerland, but I have a job to do today and so does Michael. Mrs Clark made the necessary phone calls, so you can shoot all the video you need in Black Creek. She even asked Miss Lindy to serve as your guide at double her hourly rate, if she doesn't have anything else to do. I mentioned how you'd flirted shamelessly with her,' Jill added for a little revenge.

Michael's blush equaled if not surpassed her earlier one. 'Good, it'll be nice to spend time with a pleasant female for a change.' The videographer filled his travel mug from the carafe, grabbed the last muffin, and stomped up the steps.

'Do you two always spar like this?' Harris watched her over the rim of his mug.

'Only when we're not mudwrestling in the alley or taking aim at each other with slingshots.' Jill wrapped a piece of spice cake in a napkin.

'Brings back happy memories of growing up with three sisters.'

'Someday you'll have to share those with me, but right now I need to hit the shower and pick out my outfit. With any luck, I'll have a marriage proposal by sundown.'

Harris's deep laughter filled the kitchen. 'Just don't use up all the hot water,' he called after her.

Jill had no idea why she'd joked about a marriage proposal. Marriage was the last thing on her mind, no matter how rich and charming Jamie Shelby might be. He was certainly attractive. But a salt-of-the-earth, stand-up kind of guy he was not. And according to her grandmother, that was the only kind worth marrying.

Jill had finished showering and was back in her room when Michael left for Black Creek Distillery. She knew because he thumped his equipment bags all the way down the stairs. She'd wanted to say goodbye but by the time she threw on some clothes and reached the hallway, he was gone. All she could do was wave since her window wouldn't open, but Michael never looked up. Everything would be OK, though. They'd had far more serious spats than this, yet neither went to the boss to demand a new partner.

Jill dressed in a long print skirt and sleeveless blouse, checked on Aunt Dot, let Jack out in the fenced backyard, and left for Founder's Reserve. Since she'd fussed with her hair more than her normal two minutes, she kept the windows rolled up and turned on the AC. Why she'd primped so long for a man clearly not her type was a mystery. Despite everything she'd learned from the friendly librarian, she still felt flattered by his flirting during the tour.

As Jamie had promised, once she identified herself at the front gate, the guard directed her to park in the VIP area and told her Mr Shelby would join her shortly. Jill had barely locked Dot's car when Jamie pulled up in a golf cart. He jumped out wearing a polo shirt open at the neck, khaki Dockers, loafers with no socks, and a Panama straw hat.

'Who looks like a tourist today?' she teased.

'That's the look I was going for. I wanted the world to know I took the day off.' Jamie swept off his hat and bowed low. 'I'm one hundred percent at your disposal, ma'am. Your chariot awaits.'

Jill accepted his hand and climbed into the golf cart. 'Such manners – did you just graduate from charm school or did I time-travel back to the nineteenth century?' she asked, spotting the bouquet of flowers in the cup holder.

'Neither. My mama raised me to be a gentleman and some lessons are too ingrained to forget.' Jamie turned the key, and they headed for the paved path around the building and into the gardens. 'Those flowers are for you, but if you're too independent to accept such a blatantly sexist gift, we'll pass an abandoned cemetery along the way. We can spread them around there.'

She fingered a velvety petal. 'I usually make an exception for flowers, but an old cemetery sounds like an interesting angle for my travel feature.'

Jamie took his foot off the accelerator, letting the cart coast to a stop at the top of a rise. Jill gazed around at the cultivated gardens with gazebos and patios for parties and flagstone paths for strolling in the moonlight. Ahead of them lay nothing but cornfields and fenced pastures. She noticed a few cows lazily chewing their cud under a cloudless blue sky. 'Who's buried in this abandoned cemetery?' she asked. 'Native Americans chased off their land by the first white settlers? Or maybe some of the Cooks who tangled with the Shelbys one time too often? How about some tax revenuers from the Roaring Twenties or still-busters from Prohibition?'

'All great answers, but actually we don't know. My grandfather thinks they were a family who got sick while on their way west. Originally, there were two big wooden crosses and two small, but the names had worn off by the time Grandpa discovered the graves. Whoever they were, he fenced off the area and put up headstones.'

'That was very kind of your grandfather. May I see the graves?'

'Your wish is my command.' Jamie released the brake and pressed the accelerator to the floor.

Jill hung on for dear life as he barreled down one hill and up the next. Finally, in between cornfields, she spotted one lone oak tree atop a hill, surrounded by wrought-iron fencing. The outer wall of stones ranged in size from grapefruits to giant boulders. 'How did all these rocks get here?' she asked when the golf cart stopped next to the wall.

'Grandpa wanted to make sure the graves never got lost in the tall grass, so he brought the boulders here. Every spring when the fields are plowed, any large rocks that turn up are moved here.'

Jill glanced over her shoulder. They were no longer in sight of the distillery or other human beings. Despite all Michael's warnings, she and Jamie were utterly alone. She jumped out, grabbed the bouquet of flowers and headed to the gate. But after several attempts of pushing with all her might, the gate refused to budge.

'The latch has rusted shut. Allow me.' Jamie reached around her. With one good thump, the latch gave way and the gate creaked open. 'If that didn't work my reputation as a chivalrous gentleman would've been ruined,' he whispered in her ear.

Jill smelled his spicy aftershave and felt his hand at the small of her back. Unnerved, she divided the flowers and placed a handful on each grave. 'Unknown, but not forgotten.' She read the inscription on the largest headstone. 'Your grandpa sounds like a fine man.'

Jamie squatted to scrap dead leaves and dirt back from the children's graves. 'He was. I'm afraid "not forgotten" no longer seems to be the case since my grandparents died. I'll tell the groundskeeper to put this cemetery on his maintenance schedule.' Jamie didn't stop until all four gravesites looked presentable. 'If these graves had been trespassing revenuers or still-smashers, would it have made a better story?' Jamie dusted off his palms.

'I suppose I have an overactive imagination.' Jill followed him out of the cemetery.

'That's probably what makes you a great writer.'

'I'm not so great, but I hope to be someday, once I get a shot at investigative reporting. What do you want to be when you grow up?'

His smile showed a row of perfectly straight teeth. 'Once I take over the reins at Founder's Reserve, I plan to expand beyond the tried-and-true brands my dad refuses to deviate from. There's no reason why large-scale operations can't experiment with small-batch spirits. Most of the major breweries also make craft brews sold only on their premises or in draught kegs.'

'In other words, not sold in bottles or cans.' Jill carefully latched the gate behind her.

'Correct. Bourbon aficionados would have to come to the plant to taste the new offerings. That could bring people back once a season. Some small batches will hit and some will strike out, but we'll have the option of bottling the ones that people like.'

'Doesn't all bourbon have to age?' Jill tucked a lock of hair behind her ear.

'We could age the small batches for the minimum amount – two years. Of course, I've got plenty of kinks to work out in my master plan. So let's hope Dad stays at the helm for a long time. Then I'll have plenty of enjoyable days off like today.' Without warning, Jamie brushed her cheek with a kiss.

It happened so fast that Jill barely had time to react. 'Hey, cut that out! And what happened to the lunch you promised? I'm starving.' She marched back to the golf cart.

'I am too.' Jamie climbed up and patted the seat. 'Come on, soon-to-be Pulitzer-winning reporter. Let's head back. I promise no more stolen kisses until after we eat.'

Unfortunately no snappy retort came to mind, so Jill clung to the grab bar for dear life. Jamie didn't slow down until the distillery and other outbuildings were in sight. But the formerly-red barn where he parked looked deserted. Windows were obscured with dust and wild grapevines had taken over three of the four sides of the building.

'Is this where we're having lunch? What is . . . or rather, what was this place?' She approached the door cautiously.

Jamie lifted a picnic hamper from under a blanket and trailed after her. 'This building once housed our stills. Barrels once lined every wall, several rows deep. When my great-grandfather built the modern distillery you saw the first time you visited, this building was used for an occasional party or pig roast for our employees, for old time's sake. Of course, the original footprint of our current facility had been expanded during both my grandfather's day and my dad's.'

'My videographer noticed the original building had been added onto several times,' Jill said.

Jamie's lips pulled into a frown. 'Such is usually the case in a multi-generational enterprise. I believe it adds to Founder's Reserve's charm.'

His loyalty to the family business tugged at Jill's heartstrings. 'I agree,' she said, trying to make amends. 'I hope I didn't offend you.'

Jamie's sparkling smile returned. 'Not at all. You couldn't offend me unless you burned the flag or shot my dog.'

'No chance of either of those happening. What kind of dog do you have?'

'I have a springer spaniel. Mabel used to be a good duck retriever when my father and I hunted years ago. Then we both became too busy at work and in the meantime, Mabel got old. Now she enjoys an evening walk before bedtime or to sit by the fire with me. I'm still mighty fond of that girl.' Jamie unlocked the door and pushed it open.

Inexplicably, the story lifted Shelby's standing in Jill's mind by several rungs. Who could be annoyed with a man who loves his dog?

'I might have recently acquired a dog myself.' She stepped through the doorway into an 1880s saloon belonging more in Deadwood than a small town outside of Louisville. Gaslight chandeliers hung from open beams and a bar ran the length of the back wall, where one could belly-up but not sit down. The building had wide plank floorboards, round oak tables, and a spindled staircase that led to rooms in the shadowy balcony. 'Who worked up there – ladies of ill-repute in red corsets and fishnet stockings?'

Jamie smiled. 'That's the look Grandpa was after for this building, but no. Upstairs were just offices where everybody had to get their own coffee. No cocktail waitresses in stilettos. Like I said, we used this room for business meetings and employee parties.'

Jill spotted the antique liquor bottles lining the shelves above the bar. Unfortunately, they were so dusty labels were unreadable. 'Did your family ever rent this room out?'

'Nope, but our employees could use it at no charge. Plenty of retirement parties, baby and bridal showers, and even small weddings were held here over the years.' Jamie ran a finger through the dust on a table. 'Sorry, Jill, I didn't realize this place had become as neglected as the pioneer cemetery.' He pulled a checkered tablecloth from the hamper and spread it over the table.

She sat down on one chair. 'No one ever died from a little dust. What's to eat?'

'I like your attitude.' Jamie laid out plates and napkins, along with wrapped sandwiches, a bag of chips, and a tub of macaroni salad. 'I made the turkey sandwiches myself and bought the chips and salad at a deli. No corporate catering today, Miss Curtis.'

'All the better.' Jill pulled the lid from the macaroni, took a handful of chips, and reached for a sandwich.

'Tell me about this dog you acquired,' Jamie said after his first bite of sandwich.

'I guess "inherited" would be the correct term, but nothing has been decided yet. My uncle Roger's dog never bonded with Aunt Dot, but the beagle's taken a shine to me.' Glancing up from her sandwich, Jill noticed Jamie's expression had changed. 'What's wrong?'

'Roger and Dorothy Clark are your *aunt and uncle*?'

She laughed. 'They're not really my aunt and uncle – distant cousins would be more accurate. Mrs Clark is my grandmother's first cousin, which makes us first cousins, twice removed. But she and Granny have been estranged since they were eighteen years old. Dot didn't even know about me till I showed up on her doorstep.'

'Kinfolk are like money in the bank in these parts, so finding you must have made Dorothy happy.' Jamie scooped macaroni salad on both plates.

'I think so, especially since Roger's passing. I've been helping out around the B and B.'

'Any idea when the funeral will be?' he asked. 'My family and I would like to pay our respects.'

'No, but I'll let you know. The police need to finish their investigation.'

Jamie set his turkey and Swiss down. 'Investigation? I heard through the grapevine that Roger slipped on spilled liquid and cracked his skull on a metal rack.'

'As usual, the grapevine is wrong. To my knowledge, Roger's death was declared a homicide.'

'Well, that's a shame, because Sheriff Adkins just made things harder on Dorothy Clark.'

'It's not so much the sheriff as the big gun he brought in from the state police. Plus, the guy happens to be staying at Sweet Dreams just like Michael and me.'

'The world really is a small place.'

Jill could feel Jamie's eyes on her as she ate her macaroni salad. 'You've suddenly stopped eating. Penny for your thoughts, Mr Shelby.'

'I was thinking about you being a local gal, at least genetically. Who would have guessed?'

'Certainly not me. But I must admit, this part of the world has grown on me.' Jill focused on the green fields beyond the open doorway. 'Better not tell my partner, or Michael will drag me back to the Windy City by my hair.'

'Why would a videographer have such control over you?' Jamie pulled a flask from deep inside the hamper along with two shot glasses.

'He doesn't have control, but Michael has always been protective of me. Not that I need it,' she added, popping another chip in her mouth.

'Let's toast to Roseville's newest citizen.' He unscrewed the top and filled both glasses to the rim.

'If I drink that, I'll sleep the afternoon away instead of writing my story. But I will try a little. To your good health.' She lifted the glass and took a sip, the liquid scorching a path down her throat.

'And to yours, Jill.' Jamie finished his in one swallow.

'Speaking of local women, I heard that you once dated Uncle Roger's niece, Michelle Clark, his *real* niece.'

With a shrug, Jamie took another bite of sandwich. 'Yeah, I went out with her a few times. But it was more like hanging out than dating. I've known Michelle for years.'

'Hanging out like going to the DQ for milkshakes with a bunch of friends?'

He arched an eyebrow. 'Are you jealous, Miss Curtis? Because if you went on a real date with me, instead of merely researching the bourbon tours, you'd discover you have no competition.'

'How flattering.' Feigning a drawl, Jill fluttered her eyelashes. 'I was curious if dating was different here than in Chicago.'

'Let me think back.' He scratched his chin. 'Once when Michelle came to town, she called me and we shared a pizza. Another time we went to the movies because a doctor cancelled her appointment at the last minute.'

'When was the last time you saw her?'

He thought for a moment. 'I guess the last I saw her was for a fundraiser at Black Creek. You know, one of those charity events where you pay fifty bucks to walk through the door, but all you get are tiny bites of food and even tinier sips of bourbon. Michelle had invited me, but I shelled out the Benjamin for both of us.'

Jamie winked comically. 'I didn't mind. I knew lots of people there, and we both ended up having a great time.' Jamie looked inside the hamper. 'Would you like another sandwich? I made two each.'

'No, but lunch was delicious. Thanks.' She wrapped her scraps in the waxed paper. 'So all this talk about a major, long-running feud between the Shelbys and the Cook-Clarks . . . is it simply to boost sales at both distilleries?'

Jamie poured himself another drink and handed her a bottle of water. 'Not really. The feud was ongoing up until my grandpa's day. But my father and Roger Clark wanted to let it die. As you astutely assumed, we talk about it during tours to boost sales. That's pretty much the reason Michelle invited me to her uncle's fundraiser – to let the townies know our families buried the hatchet long ago.'

'So there's no possible connection between Uncle Roger's death and retribution for the past?' Jill asked.

'I hope you're pulling my leg. This is the twenty-first century, not the wild Wild West, despite my grandfather's choice of décor. Nobody in the bourbon business kills over a few acres of riverbed . . . or who has the best tasting reserve in a given year. There's plenty enough profit for all of us.' Jamie shoved the flask and trash into the hamper and folded up the tablecloth. 'Before your partner sends out the bloodhounds, I think I better get you back to the visitor's center.' His tone dripped with graciousness, but his expression had turned icy.

Jill took a last wistful look at the saloon from a previous era and followed him to the golf cart. She certainly hadn't been a model of politeness, but didn't want to add to her *faux pas* with a lame excuse. On the way back she considered how to apologize but thought of nothing clever by the time Jamie parked beside her borrowed car.

'Here we are, safe and sound.' He jumped out and walked around to her side.

'You have now entertained me twice, Jamie.' Shielding her eyes from the sun, she gazed up at him. 'And I've repaid your hospitality with rude innuendos in an attempt to fatten up my story about Roseville distilleries. I hope you'll accept my apology and agree to be my guest for dinner. Feel free to cast aspersions on me, my

family, and every ancestor who hasn't already disavowed knowledge of my existence.'

A slow grin spread across his face. 'I accept, as long as you
agree not to sensationalize your travel feature at Founder's Reserve
or Black Creek's expense. It's hard enough for bourbon to compete
with vodka, which can be distilled from any type of grain, starchy
fruit or vegetable, even grapes. Now they're making vodka in every
flavor from cranberry to bubblegum.' He released a weary sigh.
'The old masters are rolling in their graves.'

She shook her head sympathetically and unlocked her car. 'You
have my word that if I include the family feud, it will stay within
the historical context, much like you describe it during the tours.'

'Fair enough. Why not pick an evening next week and give me
a call?' Jamie opened her door, turned on his heel, and strode
toward his office.

'I will,' she called. 'Thanks again for lunch.'

Jamie stood and watched Jill's car drive away.

SEVEN

Saturday afternoon

On the way back to the B&B, Jill followed her instincts instead of using GPS. Soon she would know every twist and turn in the road between Aunt Dot's and Founder's Reserve. Michael wouldn't like the fact she'd made plans with Jamie for next week. Technically, she had all the research she needed, but considering her behavior, she wanted to make amends.

She found the innkeeper in the library, staring at a cold fire with an empty teacup. 'How about some more tea, Aunt Dot?'

'Sure, if you're having some.' She peered up blankly.

Jill filled both cups and took her usual seat. 'What's wrong?' It was a ridiculous question since the woman had just lost her husband.

Nevertheless, Dot answered, 'I heard from my friend, Joe Trehanny. Roger's body has been released by the police. We can proceed with the funeral. Joe will stop by later to pick up the outfit I selected.'

'If you wish, I can meet him at the door and give him whatever he needs.'

'No, Joe and I have been friends for a long time. I'll do it myself.' Dot sipped her tea and met Jill's eye. 'At least we worked out the details. Visitation will be at Trehanny's Funeral Home on Monday night. Joe said with the plant scheduled to start up again, employees wouldn't be able to take off Tuesday for the funeral.'

'The plant is starting up?' Jill sputtered. 'How is that possible without Roger?'

'Roger's right-hand man was his nephew, Gordon. Gordon came by shortly after you left to tell me the news. He said the employees can't go too long without a paycheck or it will cause hardship. So he notified the foremen to get everyone back on Monday.' A tear slipped from her lashes.

'I'll put a stop to this if you like,' Jill declared, sounding way too sure of herself.

'No, no, Gordon's right. People in this town need to work. His employees can pay their respects Monday night. Then Tuesday's funeral will be for family and friends. The church guild will serve lunch after the burial and the newspaper will print the obituary in tomorrow's edition. That takes care of everything.'

'What about flowers for the funeral home and the church?' she asked.

'Joe already ordered them.'

'Why don't I take you to the mall to buy a new dress?'

'Roseville has a dress shop, not a mall. I plan to wear the same black dress I wear to every funeral.'

'What can I do?' Jill pleaded.

Dot squeezed her hand. 'You can eat more leftovers with me later, you and Michael. Right now I'm going to take a nap, but I'll see you at six.'

Jill considered her options. She could check email or call her mom or re-do her chipped nails. Then the reality of attending a funeral on Tuesday popped into her head. She couldn't wear her jeans or shorts or pastel capris. Even her one skirt had pink and blue flowers. Grabbing Dot's car keys, Jill headed to downtown Roseville and its sole dress shop.

Once inside the sweet-smelling boutique, Jill stated her few but mandatory requirements to the helpful clerk: 'I need a dress in black, relatively close to a size eight, and not too short.'

'I have one that fits the bill!' The clerk marched into the back room. Five minutes later, she emerged with a hanger dangling from her finger. 'What do you think?' she asked.

Jill had to admit it met her requirements: the black dress was in a size ten with a hem stopping at mid-knee. Unfortunately, it also had a little white collar, a rope belt and puffy sleeves, which made it hideous.

Nevertheless, she handed the clerk her credit card. 'I'll take it.'

After checking her watch, Jill crossed the street to House of Flowers. After all, she was family, whether shirttail or not. 'I need to order flowers for a funeral,' she announced.

'Local or FTD?' asked a bored man while paging through a magazine.

'Local, the Roger Clark funeral at Trehanny's.'

The man closed his magazine. 'Yes, ma'am. Family or friend?'

'Family. I want something nice, second only to the widow's arrangement, with whatever you have on hand or can get by Monday's visitation.'

His eyes rounded. 'Do I have your permission to use orchids and African lilies like I will for Mrs Clark's arrangement?'

'You do.' Jill laid her credit card on the counter.

'The prices for those flowers change on a daily basis. I won't know how much to charge you until after I finish the arrangement.'

Jill circled her email address on her business card and set it next to her credit card. 'Run the card now and email me your final bill.'

'Of course, ma'am.' The proprietor wasted no time doing as she asked.

Jill returned to Sweet Dreams feeling grown up and like she'd accomplished something. She had just enough time to wash up and get down to the kitchen where Aunt Dot was already reheating casseroles.

'Ah, there you are, but where's your partner?' Dot took two more bowls from the refrigerator.

'I have no idea. I thought Michael would be back by the time I finished my errands. I can't imagine why shooting video would take this long.' Jill stepped into the hallway and tapped Michael's speed-dial button on her phone. But her call went straight to voicemail. After leaving him a scathing message, she took her usual place at the table.

'No luck?' Dot passed her a bowl of scalloped ham and potatoes.

'He didn't pick up, but I'm sure everything's OK. Sometimes Michael can be a perfectionist. If he doesn't join us while we're eating, I'll fix him a plate he can reheat later.'

'Will you fix one for that nice Lieutenant Harris, too?' asked Dot. 'Then we can finish off several bowls.'

'I would be happy to.'

While the two women ate dinner Jill brought up a tricky subject. 'I called my grandmother last night to see how she's doing.'

Dot swallowed a mouthful of potatoes. 'And how is Emma?'

'Fine, I guess, but she doesn't like the assisted living center that my mom found for her.'

'Oh, why not?' Dot's focus remained on her plate.

'She hates being surrounded by *old* people.' Jill grinned as she took another spoonful of beans.

'That sounds like Emma. Why can't she live on her own?' Dot finally looked Jill in the eye.

'Granny broke her hip last summer and went to rehab after the hospital. When rehab discharged her, my parents put her in Shady Grove Assisted Living since all her bedrooms were upstairs. Well, now Granny is better and insists she can live on her own. But my parents like knowing someone's around twenty-four-seven since they both work.'

'Can Emma walk around fairly well?' Dot asked.

'She says she can. She says she can even climb steps.'

'Your parents have no right to keep Emma a prisoner. Even *old* people have rights.'

'I was hoping you might say that. Got any advice for me?'

Dot opened her mouth, but closed it just as quickly. 'Emma wouldn't want me intruding in family business.'

'Even if it was to help her?' Jill lifted and dropped her shoulders.

'Even if. Emma Vanderpool was always a prideful woman.'

'Maybe you both are.' Jill reached for Dot's hand. 'Are you ever going to tell me what happened?'

Dot released a sound similar to a coyote's howl. 'It's very embarrassing. I don't want you to think poorly of me.'

'I promise, I won't.' As soon as Jill uttered the words, her mind began imagining the worst possible scenarios.

'I stole Jimmy O'Connor away from her. Jimmy was Emma's boyfriend and she really liked him. But I liked him too, secretly, since we were all in the eighth grade. Well, Jimmy started flirting with me at a football game that Emma couldn't be at because she had to babysit.' Dot paused to gauge her reaction.

Jill was having difficulty matching the narrative with the neatly coifed woman in pumps and Estee Lauder perfume. 'What kind of flirting?' she prodded.

'Oh, you know, the usual: switching seats so we'd be together, running his fingers up my back, holding my hand under the stadium blanket.'

Jill smiled. 'Sounds pretty innocent.'

'At first, yes. Then he followed me to the snack bar and kissed me under the bleachers. I should have pushed him away, but I didn't. I kissed him back because I had never kissed anyone before.'

Jill's face began to hurt from holding in laughter. 'Sorry, Aunt Dot.'

'Go ahead and laugh, but those were innocent times. Kissing meant you were practically engaged. Anyway, that night I felt so ashamed. I prayed all weekend that no one saw us and everything would go back to normal on Monday. I never wanted to hurt Emma.' Dot's face turned the color of ripe raspberries.

'But someone did see you two.'

Dot nodded. 'By the time the bus dropped me off, everyone at school knew. And what's worse, Jimmy told Emma he wanted to break up and date me. He just didn't know how to tell her.'

'Wow, not a very smooth move.'

'You're not kidding. Of course, I told him to get lost, but the damage had been done. No matter what I said or did, Emma hated me after that. In a few months, we both graduated and she moved to Illinois.' Dot rose to her feet. 'You see? Emma has every right not wanting me in her life. I can't be trusted.'

'You were eighteen. Granny needs to get over it.'

Dot patted her arm. 'Try Michael's number again. You're lucky to have such a good friend.'

Jill tried Michael's number with the same results. Short on options, she sprinted up the stairs to Harris's room and pounded on the door with her fist.

Nick yanked open the door almost immediately. 'Miss Curtis, is everything all right?'

'I wanted you to know Mrs Clark left dinner for you in the refrigerator in case you haven't eaten yet.'

'That's why you knocked as though the house was on fire?' He stared at her like she'd lost her mind.

'I'm worried about my videographer, Michael Erickson. He went to Black Creek hours ago to shoot footage and hasn't returned yet.'

'I thought the distillery was still closed.'

'It is, but Mrs Clark arranged for the security guard to let Michael in. It shouldn't have taken this long. I think we should check the place out.'

'I agree.' Harris crossed the room to where his holster and weapon hung on a hook. 'I'll ask Sheriff Adkins to meet us there. In the meantime, you get the security guard's number from Mrs Clark, along with any other contact numbers she might have.'

With growing trepidation, Jill watched him strap on his weapon before she ran downstairs. Five minutes later they were speeding toward Black Creek Distillery as fast as the narrow highway would allow with lights flashing. Neither the security guard nor Gordon Clark, Roger's nephew and right-hand man, answered their phones.

'I can't believe Mrs Clark only had the number for the guard who usually worked nights,' Harris muttered without taking his eyes off the road. 'Nobody can work twenty-four-seven, seven days a week.'

Jill gripped her seat with both hands as they rounded a corner. 'From what I gather, Roger took care of making bourbon at Black Creek, while Gordon scheduled the guards for all shifts. Mrs Clark handled the B and B and stayed out of distillery business. Roger and Dot might not have shared particulars with each other.'

Harris shook his head. 'That poor woman has a mess on her hands with his passing.'

Reluctant to reveal too much, Jill concentrated on reaching either the night watchman or Gordon Clark for the rest of the drive. When they arrived at Black Creek, she spotted Michael's car in the main parking lot while a second vehicle was parked at the loading dock.

'I'm going to try that door first.' Harris pointed at the employee entrance. 'You should wait in the car, Miss Curtis.'

'Nothing doing.' Jill jumped out and followed him through the unlocked door. 'I want to know if my partner fell asleep on the job.'

They found themselves in a hallway lined with bulletin boards, a timeclock and racks of timecards on one side, and employee lockers on the other. The hallway led to a messy room with plastic tables and chairs, with a glass enclosed office at the far end. A man with his back to them stared at a small television set, instead of the security monitors flashing images of various locations around the plant. Since the TV's volume had been turned as high as it would go, Jill and Harris could hear that the guard was watching major league baseball.

'I guess we know why he didn't answer his phone,' Harris

muttered. The state trooper looked so angry Jill thought he might pull out his gun and shoot the guy in the leg. Harris marched into the office and slammed his fist down on the desk. 'Excuse me, sir,' he drawled.

The guard scrambled to remove his feet from the desktop. 'Who the heck are you two and how did you get in here?' Indignation quickly replaced his shock.

'I am Lieutenant Nick Harris from the Kentucky State Police and this is Jill Curtis, who's writing a travel feature on the bourbon industry. She has Mrs Clark's permission to be here.' He sucked in a deep breath. 'We entered the facility through an unlocked employee door. Now, if it isn't too much trouble, we have a couple of questions for you.'

Mr Florio, according to his name badge, crossed his arms defensively. 'What can I do for you, Trooper?'

'Michael Erickson came here earlier today to take video of the distillery and still hasn't returned to Mrs Clark's B and B. Do you remember him?'

'Skinny guy, glasses, blond hair, carrying a bag that weighed as much as him?'

'Yep, that's him,' Jill snapped. 'Where is he?'

'I have no idea. I'm guessin' he took whatever pictures he needed and left.'

'Really? Then why is his car still in the parking lot?' Jill approached the guard with fisted hands.

'Look, lady,' he snarled. 'It's not my job—'

Nick didn't give the slacker a chance to finish. 'No, you look, Mr Florio. The security of Black Creek Distillery *is* your responsibility. They don't pay you to watch the Braves beat the Red Socks. When Sheriff Adkins arrives, tell him we're searching the building for Mr Erickson, unless that would overtax your abilities.' Nick didn't wait for the guard's reply. Instead he guided Jill through a set of doors into the hallway.

'Did you see all those security monitors?' she asked. 'Maybe one of those cameras caught Roger's murder on Wednesday night.'

'Sheriff Adkins and I already thought of that. We got the key from the guard who went home sick, Elmer Maxwell, even though he doesn't remember locking the room. All the tapes for Wednesday were blank, either erased or the cameras had been switched off.'

'How convenient. Either that guy erased them or looked the other way while someone else did.'

'That's our feeling too, but without proof our hands are tied.'

Jill pulled open the door to the area marked 'Mixing and Distillation'. 'As soon as we find Michael, let's beat the truth out of old Elmer.'

Room by room, the two of them searched for any sign that Michael Erickson had been there. When they worked their way down to the cavernous rickhouse, filled from floor to ceiling with barrels of bourbon aging to perfection, an ominous sensation of dread crawled up Jill's spine. 'This is the room where I found Roger Clark,' she murmured.

Nick hesitated just inside the doorway. 'If you'd like to stay here, I'll search and come back for you.'

'No, Michael is my best friend. He deserves someone who's not a coward.' Jill followed Harris down the first aisle of barrels, keeping pace with him until they'd searched the entire barn. There was no sign of the videographer. Underneath the sign, *Exit this way*, Jill scanned the parking lot from the window. Empty, except for one Styrofoam cup dancing in the breeze among the dead leaves.

'What now, Detective?' she asked.

'We retrace our steps at a slower pace. We must have missed something.'

And so they did.

They looked under displays, checked closets, and even searched each employee locker without a lock. In one of the first rooms on the tour, where grain was ground and mixed to specific propor-tions, Jill noticed a narrow catwalk running along two sides. Roger or one of his foremen would have been able to keep an eye on workers or a specific tour group unnoticed. 'Let's find the staircase that leads up there.' She pointed with her index finger.

'No one's up there, Jill. The catwalk has an open grate for a floor.'

'I know, but maybe there's a hidden nook we can't see.'

Harris nodded. 'I'll head to the right. You go to the left.'

Jill did as instructed but found nothing but a closet full of cleaning supplies.

'Over here, Miss Curtis.'

Jill bolted through a set of swinging doors in the direction of his voice, and almost smacked into Harris.

He stopped her progress with a steadying head. 'How did we miss this?' He pointed at a massive fake plant in an alcove, which hid an elevator. According to the buttons, a person could travel up to C or down to B.

'Looks like Roger didn't want tourists going in either direction.' Jill pressed both buttons, waited, and then pressed them again several times. Yet after a full minute, no elevator car arrived.

'The buttons don't even light up,' Nick observed. 'My guess is someone switched off the power.'

'You don't think . . .' Jill didn't wait for a reply. She pounded on the steel door with both fists. 'Michael!' she hollered at the top of her lungs. 'Are you in there?' She continued to beat on the door until Nick grabbed her arm.

'Take it easy before you hurt yourself. Let's listen and see if we hear anything.'

Jill swallowed down the lump of panic which had clouded her judgment. She pressed her ear to the metal on one side while Harris listened close to the floor at the other. 'Did you hear that?' she shrieked. 'He's in there. Hang on, Mikey. Help is on the way!'

While Jill tried to assure her partner, Nick was already on the phone with Sheriff Adkins. 'We're near the front entrance. There's an alcove off to the left. Get the fire department here on the double. We may need an elevator rescue. Are you still in the security monitoring room?' When Nick met her eye he frowned. 'Have Mr Florio show you where the main electrical board is. Make sure all breakers are on. I suspect someone switched the circuit to the elevator off.' Nick listened, nodded at her, and hung up.

'Let's find the electrical panel ourselves,' said Jill. 'If that creep, Florio, turned off the power with Michael inside I'll beat the tar out of him.'

'And I won't stop you. But Sheriff Adkins wants someone to wait for the fire department at the front door. Don't you think you should stay and keep your partner's spirits up? Let him know someone is still here?'

'Good idea. We're coming, Michael. Hang in there.' Jill pounded on the door and then listened. Unfortunately, she heard nothing in return.

How much air is in an elevator?
How long has Michael been inside?

Is there a vent to the open shaft?

Questions swirled through her mind until a ruckus in the lobby signaled the arrival of rescuers.

'Tell them to hurry,' she pleaded when Nick's head popped around the corner.

Then almost simultaneously, the up and down buttons lit up. 'The power is on,' she cried. Pressing both buttons, Jill heard the sweet sound of an elevator whooshing to her floor.

Two firemen, carrying oxygen and a defibrillator, pushed past her. 'We'll take it from here, miss,' said one. The two jumped into action the moment the door opened.

Despite Harris's firm hand on her shoulder, Jill craned her neck into the elevator and spotted Michael sitting cross-legged on the floor. Although his face was streaked with sweat, he looked no worse for wear. 'It's about time you missed me, Curtis,' he moaned. 'I could have starved to death in here. Plus an extra bottle of water would have been nice.'

With one on each side, the firemen hauled Michael to his feet. 'Are you all right, sir? Do you need medical assistance?' The fireman tried to slip an oxygen mask over his face, but Michael pushed it away.

'What I need is a more attentive colleague. Other than that, I'm fine.'

Jill elbowed her way into the already crowded elevator. 'Stop your whining. I missed you, didn't I? Now give me a hug.'

When the firemen released their hold, Michael wrapped an arm around Jill's shoulders. 'Better late than never, I suppose.'

Jill hugged him fiercely as hot tears flooded her eyes.

'Everything OK here, Lieutenant Harris?' The discombobulated voice of Sheriff Adkins floated into the elevator.

'I believe so, Sheriff,' Nick answered.

'How was I to know you got stuck in a two-story elevator?' Jill said to Michael, still hugging him tightly. 'I thought maybe you asked Lindy to go out for fast food with you.'

'It's three stories, Miss Smarty-Pants.' Michael pulled away from her. 'Now stop crying. I'm fine.'

'I saved you a plate of leftovers for dinner.' Jill wiped her face with a tissue.

'In that case, let's get out of here. I am starving.' Michael thanked and shook hands with each fireman and deputy. Then he turned to the two in charge. 'Thanks for responding, Sheriff Adkins, Lieutenant Harris. I'm in your debt. Who knew they would cut the power to the distillery while I was finishing my video?'

'The power hadn't been cut to the rest of the facility,' Harris said softly. 'But let's get you back to the B and B for a good meal and we'll sort this out later.' He aimed a meaningful glance at Jill.

'Come on, Erickson. We'll take your car, but I'll drive. Who knows how you'll act after food and water deprivation?'

Jill met the gaze of the Kentucky state trooper, then pulled her partner towards the front door.

Yep, something is definitely amiss in Black Creek Distillery.

Once they were back to Sweet Dreams and Michael was gobbling his dinner in record time, Jill turned to Nick. 'What are your thoughts?'

'That it's time to drive out to the Maxwell house. Would you like to tag along? You did promise to beat the tar out of him if Elmer doesn't cooperate.'

'You bet I do, as long as Michael doesn't mind being left alone.'

Her partner scowled. 'Go, I'm fine. As soon as I eat my share of the dessert, I'm going to bed. I'll see you in the morning.'

'It's great how you two look out for each other,' Nick said, once they were inside his car. 'I wish I had a friend like that.'

'I suppose, but usually Michael and I just drive each other crazy.' Jill relaxed against the headrest as she conveyed a few amusing stories.

When they reached the Maxwell house, all friendly banter ceased. 'You stay behind me, Jill,' Nick ordered. 'And let me do the talking.'

'Heigh-aye, Captain,' she agreed with a salute. But unfortunately no one was home to question. Although the front door had been locked, the back door stood ajar as Nick and Jill rounded the house.

'Elmer Maxwell?' Nick called, stepping across the threshold. 'It's Lieutenant Harris of the state police. We're coming inside.'

As the two made their way from room to room, they found kitchen cupboards open, something sticky spilled on the floor, clothes hanging from drawers and others strewn across the bed.

Nick squatted to rummage through papers on the floor. 'At the risk of stating the obvious, the Maxwells seemed to have left in a hurry.'

'That must move Elmer up your list of suspects at least several notches above me.' Jill leaned against the doorjamb.

Nick rose to his feet and dusted off his hands. 'It does look a tad suspicious. Let's go talk to the neighbors.'

They had no trouble finding a neighbor as they exited the house. Under the auspices of bringing in laundry, a middle-aged woman leaned precariously over the fence.

'Have they moved?' the woman hollered without bothering with introductions.

'So it would appear, ma'am.' Nick and Jill closed the gap between them.

'I knew it! I told my husband not to loan him money, but he did anyway.' The woman's face flushed brightly. 'Maxwell probably used it for the next race.'

'You're saying Elmer liked to bet the ponies?' Nick asked.

'Not just racehorses. Maxwell would bet on football, basketball, anything with odds. Too bad he never had much luck.' The woman stuffed her bedsheets into the basket with renewed fury. 'If you see that lowlife before we do, tell him we want our money.' With that the neighbor positioned her basket on her hip and stomped toward the house.

On their way to the car, Jill jumped in front of Nick and stopped. 'OK, Maxwell had a gambling problem, which means he was probably in desperate financial straits. Surely that moves him to the top of your list.' She crossed her arms.

Nick appeared to ponder the question. 'Maybe, but I'm not ready to rule you out quite yet.'

His smile and subsequent wink were so downright flirtatious, Jill had no idea if he was serious or not. And that gave her plenty to think about on the drive and while she was trying to fall asleep that night.

EIGHT

Sunday morning

Jill found Aunt Dot already sipping coffee and eating a cinnamon roll when she walked into the kitchen the next morning.

'Good morning, Jill,' Dot greeted. 'You're not going to church wearing that, are you?'

Jill glanced down at her Bermuda shorts and T-shirt, then at Dot's black silk dress and high heels. 'Good grief. Do I have time to change?'

'Yes, you do,' Dot said, beaming. 'And I'll save you a sweet roll.'

Jill bolted back up the steps. It wasn't that she never went to church. She attended every Christmas and Easter, plus whenever she stayed overnight at her parents' or grandmother's house. And Dorothy Clark being a churchgoer certainly didn't surprise her. But with the funeral scheduled for Tuesday morning, Dot would attend church two times in three days . . . and so would she.

After a quick perusal of her wardrobe, Jill chose the cotton skirt and blouse she'd worn yesterday to lunch with Jamie Shelby. Luckily, she hadn't balled it up and tossed it in the corner like usual. With a quick flick of the hairbrush, Jill coiled her long hair in a topknot and secured it with a clip.

'You look very sweet,' Dot declared when Jill returned to the kitchen. 'Mind eating your cinnamon roll on the way?' She grabbed her purse and headed out the back door.

'I don't mind at all.' Jill wrapped the roll in a napkin and followed Dot to the garage. 'Say, have you seen Michael this morning?'

'No, neither of my male guests is up yet.' Dot climbed into the car and backed carefully down the driveway. 'After the ordeal your partner suffered, he deserves to sleep in.'

Jill nodded while nibbling her breakfast. Thinking about her partner's 'ordeal' had kept her up most of the night. Yesterday had to be the worst day of Michael's life. Once he'd been liberated from the elevator, he had been questioned by both the state trooper and Sheriff Adkins. Then, after she'd taken him back to the B&B, Dot Clark had asked so many questions Michael had barely been able to eat his dinner. But he'd finally finished it, along with half a dozen cookies and a stiff glass of bourbon. It was after eleven when they'd finally said goodnight and gone to their rooms. Yet they still had no idea who had switched off the circuit breaker to the elevator. Baseball-fan Florio insisted he'd never left the security monitoring room.

'A penny for your thoughts,' said Dot, after several minutes of silence.

'I was wondering if you could write down the directions to William Clark's home,' Jill said.

'Are you talking about Roger's brother? Goodness, what on earth for? William's family lives up the mountain in a collection of ramshackle cabins. I've only been there once. After that visit Roger said they must visit us in Roseville.' Dot paused at the stop sign so long another motorist blew the horn.

'I want to make sure they know about the funeral on Tuesday.'

'I've already talked to Gordon Clark, William's son. He said he would make sure the rest of the family knew the time and place.'

'Good, but I'd also like to talk to Michelle Clark. This might be a longshot, but her relationship with Jamie Shelby might be why Uncle Roger was killed.'

Dot's expression revealed total confusion. 'Michelle dating Jamie Shelby? I find that hard to believe. The Shelby family is the richest in the county, while the Clark cabins aren't ramshackle in order to be chic.'

'I understand, but sometimes opposites attract.' Jill swiveled on the seat to face her. 'Could you possibly give me directions?'

'Roger stuck the directions in our phone book, so yes. But you shouldn't go alone and you shouldn't go unarmed.' Dot turned into the parking lot. The church was so close to Sweet Dreams they could have walked.

'Michael is coming with me if he's feeling up to it. And you were kidding about the "don't go unarmed" part, right?'

'Actually, I wasn't.' Dot switched off the ignition. 'Look, Roger's relatives are nice people for the most part. But they live up in the hills because they probably make moonshine. When people are involved in illegal activities, they get nervous when strangers drive up their road.' She grabbed her Bible from the back seat. 'We're here now, so let's discuss this later.'

Jill climbed out of the car. 'OK, but not in front of Michael. That boy rarely leaves the city so he won't understand William's need for privacy.'

Going to church in a small town was very different than in a big city. The congregation was small but very friendly. Everyone knew everyone including Dot, yet they wisely gave her some space. Not one person asked the ridiculous question: *How are you doing?* Most people either smiled sadly or hugged Dot without uttering a word. A few ladies curiously perused Jill but had the good sense not to ask who she was. Tuesday would be soon enough for introductions. The preacher's sermon involved surrendering our will and letting God take over our lives. Accomplishing that would be much easier at his age, somewhere around seventy, than at hers at thirty-one, Jill thought to herself.

His parting words to Dorothy Clark were: 'See you Tuesday. Together we'll get through this.' His promise brought a smile to her cousin's face, a smile that lasted all the way to the car.

'If you give up this crazy notion of heading up the mountain,' she said, 'I'll treat you to brunch at the best restaurant in town.'

Jill waited until they were inside the car to reply. 'I would love brunch, but today is the only day Michael is willing to drive up there with me. He thinks this will be a wild goose chase.'

'Chickens, not geese,' Dot said, switching on the AC.

'Excuse me?' Jill pivoted on the seat.

'My brother-in-law, Bill, raises chickens. I guess you would call them cage-free since they roam all over the place. He also has goats, several dogs, some rather vicious, a pet skunk, and an ornery. Do you still think this a good idea?'

'The drive will be beautiful, even if I turn around without getting out of the car.'

Dot drove home at a snail's pace. 'Roger keeps a handgun locked in the gun safe. Would you like to take it with you?'

'I've never fired a gun in my life and I'm certain Michael never has either. We'd be more likely to harm ourselves.'

'Then maybe you should take that nice state trooper, Nick Harris. He could handle himself around Roger's kinfolk.'

For a brief moment Jill mulled the idea of spending a leisurely Sunday with Nick Harris. He was handsome, competent, and had that marvelous gravelly voice. But the guy also considered her a murder suspect. Considering her recent luck with men, she'd blurt something so incriminating, she'd spend the next twenty years in jail. 'As appealing as that sounds, I doubt Lieutenant Harris would enjoy spending the day with me. Plus, if Roger's brother has an illegal still, he won't appreciate me bringing along the state police.'

'You have a point there.' Dot drove into the detached garage and turned off the car. 'Just promise me you'll be careful.'

'I promise.' Jill drew an X in the general vicinity of her heart.

'All right, I'll give you directions. But if you're not back by nine o'clock, I'm sending that handsome trooper up the mountain after you. Just think how embarrassing that would be.'

Jill and Dot entered a quiet kitchen with the exact same number of cinnamon rolls still on the plate. Proof that neither Michael nor Nick was up yet. The cop's sleep habits weren't her concern, but she was getting worried about her partner.

'Michael, are you awake in there?' Jill knocked hard enough to wake the neighbors.

'Yeah, I'm awake.' He yanked the door open fully dressed in pressed chinos and a plaid shirt. 'I've been up for an hour. Where have you been?'

'At church with Mrs Clark, but now we better hit the road if we're driving up the mountain.'

'This is your idea of spending the day together?'

'Just think how pretty the scenery will be. I'll pack some sandwiches and fill the gas tank. Wouldn't it be cool to shoot video of an old-fashioned still, just like on the History Channel?'

'You really think your relatives will let me photograph them?'

'Maybe, as long as you don't mention where they live or how they make a living.'

Michael grinned. 'This might be fun after all. I'll grab my gear and meet you in the kitchen.'

Jill loaded six sandwiches, fruit, and several bottles of water into a cooler. Once Dot gave her the directions, along with a worn-out county map, they were on their way.

'I can't believe you brought a ten-year-old map.' Snickering, Michael climbed in behind the wheel. 'The car has GPS, remember?'

'Laugh all you want, but Dot said GPS doesn't usually work up in the hills. By day's end, you'll thank me.'

And just like that, the smile vanished from his face. 'Hopefully you packed enough food in case we get lost. We might be stuck in the mountains for days.'

'That's what I like – a man with an adventurous spirit.' Jill settled back to study the scenery along the way. After they left the charming town of Roseville, they passed a few subdivisions of houses and farms of various sizes and shapes. Once the land became too hilly to grow crops, they saw cattle and sheep grazing and huge stretches of forest with an occasional house or trailer that may or may not be inhabited.

'Seems like a lot of hoarders live out in the country,' Michael murmured, breaking the silence.

'How on earth could you tell that? You've got to stop watching that show.' Jill heard the peevishness in her voice.

'Take a good look at the homes we pass. Some look like the homeowner has never thrown away *anything* ever.'

As much as she hated to agree, Jill soon saw what Michael was talking about. Most yards were neat as a pin with tidy flowerbeds, fenced-in vegetable gardens, and freshly mown lawns. Every porch had a rocking chair or glider where the weary could sit and sip something cool. But every now and then, they passed a home where *stuff* flowed out the front door, filled the entire porch, and expanded across the yard, where it was subjected to every type of weather. It looked as though every tool or implement used by past generations had found a permanent resting place on the property.

Jill refocused on the road as they snaked ever higher into the hills. 'I've been reading a lot about rural America. Apparently, most local townships don't offer trash pickup. People are on their own to haul what they no longer want to a landfill. Since a fee is charged to drop trash off at the dump, the poor have little incentive to do spring cleaning.'

Michael arched an eyebrow. 'That's a shame, because it detracts from the natural beauty of the area.'

'I agree. But if we find the same situation at William Clark's, don't bring it up, OK? We don't want to hurt anyone's feelings.' *Or catch a load of buckshot in our backside.*

Michael glanced in her direction. 'I'll be on my best behavior. You're the one who usually says the wrong thing at the wrong time.'

'True enough.' Jill pulled a bottle of water from the cooler and took a long drink. Then she found their location on the map. Between Aunt Dot's written directions and the map, it was time to pay close attention. The car's GPS had already shut down and rebooted twice due to lost signal. Soon the device gave up and turned itself off. However, thanks to Uncle Roger's forethought in saving the map and her eagle eye, Jill spotted the turn-off to the Clark homestead an hour later.

'Slow down and take the next right,' she said.

Michael stopped at a narrow opening in the trees. 'You can't possibly mean here. This isn't a road.' He pointed at a deeply rutted dirt lane.

'Yep, that's a private road. What we call a driveway back home.'

'You're sure there's a house at the end of this *private road*? But there's no mailbox or address sign.'

'The family probably picks up their mail at the post office when they go to town. And the only people who are welcome to visit already know where the Clarks live.'

'What about the fire department?' he asked.

Jill huffed out a breath. 'There is no fire department out here. The closest station is probably in Roseville. Any fire would burn itself out before fire fighters could get here. These people are on their own.'

'How do you know all this?'

'I read three books about this area when I couldn't sleep. Now turn in before someone slams into the back end of our car.'

Reluctantly, Michael turned and drove fifty feet with bushes on both sides scraping his car. 'At the very minimum, my paint job will get scratched up. That is if I don't break an axle in one of these ruts.'

'Your car isn't exactly in mint condition. Just go slow and try to miss the really deep potholes.'

And slow is how Michael went for the next twenty minutes until he reached a fork in the road. 'What do Roger's directions say to do here?' He dug two sandwiches from the cooler and handed her one.

'One of these roads is for logging, and the other leads to the house.' Jill tilted the paper several ways to get the best angle. 'Let's go to the right.'

'Because that's what the paper says?' He took a bite of roast beef and cheese.

'No, there's a rip in a critical spot. But the road on the right looks to be better traveled.'

'And those were Jill Curtis's last words before she was eaten alive by a grizzly bear.'

'Black bear,' she corrected. 'A black bear will have to do the honors. Grizzlies only live west of the Mississippi River.'

'You're starting to get on my nerves.' Nevertheless, Michael took the fork to the right.

Just when they thought the road couldn't get any narrower or steeper, the car plowed through some low-hanging foliage and ended up in someone's front yard. The Clark home was a rustic log cabin with a wide front porch covered by a roof overhang. Although the cabin had been added to several times, it still maintained a certain charm. There were no rusted farm implements or waterlogged toys lying around, no abandoned vehicles, and no broken windows that had been repaired with cardboard. A stone path led to the front steps, while a scraggly rosebush climbed up a painted trellis. It was a shame few people saw the historic homestead of the Cook descendants.

While Jill had been assessing the exterior ambience, their presence had not gone unnoticed. Suddenly, a raspy cough drew her attention to someone sitting in the shadows of the porch.

'Excuse me, sir,' she called. 'I was admiring your home and didn't realize anybody was outside.'

'Yep, that was pretty apparent,' said a hoarse voice.

'My name is Jill Curtis and I'm a distant cousin of Dorothy Clark. She provided me with directions here.'

'Uh-huh,' said the unseen man as if none of this was news to him. 'I had a feelin' you'd find your way up here.'

'May I step onto the porch, sir?' Jill asked, regretting her decision to come unarmed. By now Michael had parked the car and joined her.

'Might as well, seein' that you came all this way. My son told me you turned off the county road half an hour ago. Never saw anybody drive that slow. Figured you musta run outta gas.' The man laughed heartily, which triggered another raspy cough.

'This is my business partner, Michael Erickson. He's from Chicago, same as me. We're not used to roads like this.'

The man in the shadows uttered a foul word. 'Nothing wrong with my road. 'Course, nobody in their right mind comes up here without four-wheel drive. So what does that make your partner?'

Jill couldn't keep from smiling as she approached the steps. 'An excellent point.'

'Tell your partner to stay where he is since he ain't kinfolk. You, Jill Curtis, can come up here and state your business.'

Nobody had to tell Michael Erickson twice. He turned on a dime and headed back to the car, while Jill climbed the steps with growing trepidation.

On the porch sat a sinewy old man in a wheelchair. His face was deeply tanned and pitted from a long-ago ailment, while his white hair hung in a single plait down his back. His overalls were clean but worn threadbare with ripped knees like teenagers pay extra for.

'Stop staring at me, gal, and sit down.' He pointed at a webbed lawn chair.

'How do you do, Mr Clark?' As Jill extended a hand, she spotted the outline of someone behind the window's thin curtain.

'I'm fine. Call me Will. Then tell me why you wanted to meet me. If you're Dot's cousin, you were Roger's kin through marriage, but you're not my kin.' The man shook her hand, then perused Jill almost as thoroughly as she did him.

'That is correct, but I wanted to make sure you knew about the passing of your brother.' Jill took the chair on his right.

Will's face paled slightly. 'Yeah, I know Roger was murdered, right there between the racks. And the cops still don't know who done it!'

'That's correct. But I assure you Sheriff Adkins sent for a state police investigator who's bound and determined to find the killer.'

'We'll see 'bout that. Now why else did you come?' He squinted at her.

'Your sister-in-law said you used to distil bourbon the old-fashioned way. Since I came to Kentucky to write an article about the bourbon industry, I was hoping you'd let me photograph your old still. I promise I won't use your name or address.'

At first Will chuckled, then he broke into a down-and-out howl of laughter. 'Well, at least you ain't no liar, Miss Jill Curtis from Chicago, Illinois.'

'I try my best to tell the truth, Mr Will Clark.' She leaned back in her chair.

'That's a good rule to live by, but my answer is no. No photographs of me or my house or my *former* still. I ain't no tourist attraction. So it looks like your chicken-livered partner drove you all the way up the mountain for nothin'.'

For one brief moment, a frisson of panic shot up Jill's spine. Should she have taken Aunt Dot's advice? Had she dragged her partner into another situation that could threaten life and limb?

Perhaps Will smelled her fear or perhaps he simply took pity on her, but his expression turned benign. 'Unless you're in the mood to sample real mountain cookin'. My daughter always sets a fine table for company.'

'Would that be your daughter Michelle?' she asked.

'Before she passed, my wife only gave me one daughter, but she stuck me with three worthless sons.' Will broke into another peal of laughter.

With that the screen door opened and a boy of nine or ten emerged. 'Oh, Pa, don't say things like that to this nice lady. She'll think you're serious.' The boy perched on his father's knee. 'Hi, I'm Justin.'

'And you're adorable!' Jill's declaration brought an immediate blush to Justin's cheeks. 'I'm Jill, and I'm kinda your cousin, twice removed, then twice removed by marriage.'

The boy smiled. 'We just call that "cousins" in these parts.' He stuck out his hand to shake.

Jill was so moved by his friendliness she jumped up and hugged him instead. 'I'm so pleased to meet you,' she said.

'Does all this huggin' and carrying on mean you're staying for supper?' A young woman with dark, almond-shaped eyes and thick auburn hair appeared in the doorway. She was very beautiful and very pregnant.

'Are you Michelle?' Jill asked.

'Who else would I be? Ma's dead,' she said without a hint of a smile.

'Mind your manners, missy,' Will warned.

'Just want to know if the fancy writer was stayin' or not?' Michelle softened her tone.

'I would love to, if it wouldn't be too much trouble and if my videographer can eat with us too.'

'Fine by me, if it's fine with Pa. I always cook plenty.'

With three sets of eyes on him, Will nodded affirmatively.

'You eat wild game or not?' Michelle asked. 'Lots of city folk don't eat game.'

'No game for me, but a plate of veggies will do nicely.'

'I got some dried beef left. We'll eat in fifteen minutes, Pa.' She vanished from the doorway.

'Michelle can cook an entire dinner in fifteen minutes?' Jill asked, not hiding her shock. 'I have trouble when I have the whole afternoon.' She settled back into her webbed chair.

Will, with Justin back on his knee, smiled. 'Don't give her too much credit. We all knew the moment you turned up the driveway. Michelle was ready to start Sunday dinner anyway. She just didn't know whether to add some fresh venison or that old dried jerky from last season. Don't blame me if you break a tooth.'

Maybe it was because he made her feel so welcome, or maybe it was because he hadn't shot her and Michael on sight as trespassers, but affection for William Clark soon filled every inch of Jill's heart. 'So there's hope for me yet?' she asked, with her face in her hands.

'Oh, you'll learn to cook when the time is right. Just make sure you marry somebody with a lick of sense. Now tell me what's gonna happen at the funeral. I ain't never been to a city funeral.'

Jill smiled at Will's reference to Roseville as a *city* and explained what to expect on Tuesday. When Michelle announced dinner was ready, Jill went to look for her partner. She found Michael under a tree, reading the owner's manual for his car.

'Here, I thought you forgot all about me,' he said, glancing up from the manual.

'Of course not, but I had to get a few preliminaries out of the way.' She leaned one shoulder against the vine-covered tree trunk. 'We have both been invited to Sunday dinner with the Clarks.'

'You really want to eat here? What's on the menu – frog legs or maybe fried possum?' Michael leaned back on his elbows.

'No possum tonight. It'll be some kind of beef stew. And I absolutely want to stay. Aunt Dot said the original part of the cabin was built in the 1700s and, to this day, the Clarks live totally off-the-grid.'

'Can I take a few pictures inside?'

'You can ask William, but make sure you treat everyone with upmost respect.' Jill offered a hand to pull him up. 'If you can't behave, you can stay out here and finish the sandwiches.'

'What's the worst thing that could happen?' he muttered, loud enough for her to hear.

Jill thought it prudent not to answer that question. After all, Michael would probably be tougher than last year's jerky.

'Come on in. I'm Justin.' The boy held open the screen door as they climbed the steps and crossed the porch.

'This is Michael Erickson, my videographer,' Jill said. 'Michael, this is Mr William Clark and his daughter, Michelle.'

After the men shook hands, Will hooked his thumb over his shoulder. 'And that's my eldest son, Billy.'

Jill locked eyes with a wiry but muscular man leaning against the sink. Like his sister, Billy's expression revealed disdain or distrust or both.

'Hi, Billy,' she said.

Billy responded with a slight lift of his chin.

'I've not met your third son yet . . .?' Jill directed her question to Will, hoping to get a little more information on the family dynamics.

'Yes, my middle son, Gordy, stays with a friend in town most of the time. He works at Black Creek Distillery.'

'Yes, Gordon. Aunt Dot said he was Roger's right-hand man.'

Justin shook his head. 'You better not call him "Gordon". Gordy hates that name.'

'Thanks for the heads-up.' Jill ruffled the boy's hair.

'With that settled, let's sit down and eat.' William rolled his chair up to the head of the table, while Michelle sat closest to the stove.

Jill waited to see where Billy and Justin would sit, then she and Michael took the two remaining chairs.

Michelle set a cast iron pot in the center of the table. 'This is beef stew with carrots, potatoes, turnips, and onions. If there's something you don't like, just push it to the side of the plate. Justin will feed it to the hog later. That's wilted spinach with a hot bacon dressing and we'll have cornbread soon as it cools enough to slice.' She pointed at a red ceramic bowl and a bread board with a tub of butter. 'Now hand me your plates. This kettle is too heavy to pass around the table.'

Justin tried to give his sister his plate, but Will slapped his arm. 'Company first, boy.'

'Sorry, Jill,' he said.

'No harm done.' Jill passed down her plate along with Michael's. Once all plates had been filled, Michael stabbed a carrot and popped it into his mouth. Unfortunately this was just before Will bowed his head and said grace, much to Michael's embarrassment.

As Jill passed around the bowl of greens, Michael tried a piece of meat. 'This is real good. Thanks for including me.'

'You're welcome,' Michelle murmured.

'Say, Mr Clark, Jill tells me part of your house dates back to the eighteenth century. Mind filling me in on your family's history?'

Will set down his fork with a clatter. 'I got a rule – no jawboning at the table. We sit down, we eat our meal, we get on with the day. If you want to chit-chat, we can do that later on the porch with a cup of coffee or glass of whiskey.' He hacked off a hunk of cornbread and passed the board to Michael.

'Yes, sir.' Michael cut off a piece and passed the board to Jill.

And so they enjoyed a quiet but delicious meal with the only sounds being the clatter of cutlery and one small burp from Justin. When they finished, Jill stacked the plates and carried them to the kitchen sink. Michelle was already transferring the stew into a smaller pot. There was no cornbread left and she scraped the tiny amount of greens into a bucket, presumably for the hog.

'Truly, that was a delicious meal,' Jill said when Michelle finally met her eye.

'Thanks, I started cooking when I was eight or nine. I used to love helping Mom. Now it's not much fun once it's your duty every day.'

'I'm ashamed that I don't know how to cook.'

Michelle studied her for a long moment. 'Don't be ashamed. When you have a family, you'll learn to cook. It's not that hard. Just remember: once you start, folks will expect you to do it all the time.' She winked playfully.

'Sounds like good advice.'

'Right now, I gotta check the chickens. Make sure they're in for the night.'

'Mind if I walk with you? There's something else I wanted to ask you.'

'Suit yourself.' Michelle slipped off her flip-flops and pulled on high rubber boots.

Halfway to the henhouse, Jill mustered her courage. 'I see you're expecting. When's the baby due?'

'In three months and no, I'm not married.' She kept her focus on the dirt path.

'Such is the case with lots of new mothers. I have no reason to judge you.'

'Tell that to old Will Clark. Daddy called me just about every name in the book.'

'Parents have a tendency to overreact. He'll soften once the baby gets here.'

Michelle stopped abruptly and set down the basket. 'This isn't what I planned for my life – to raise a baby in a log cabin with three brothers and a stubborn father. When I told this guy I loved him, he said he loved me too and wanted to take care of me. He talked about us getting an apartment in Roseville. When I told him the good news, he handed me five hundred bucks to "fix the situation". That was his idea of taking care of me. I threw the money in his face.' She spat in the dirt. 'If I had told Gordy or Billy what he said, one of them would have put that man in the ground.'

'It's normal to want to trust people you love.' Where Jill was getting this relationship insight, she had no idea.

'That's what I get for trusting a rich guy. I should've stuck with guys from around here. I hate it when Daddy is right.' Michelle picked up the basket and took a few steps. 'Are you comin' or not?'

When Jill heard the words 'rich guy' her legs turned to jelly. 'Your baby's father is Jamie Shelby?'

'Yeah, how could you possibly know him?'

'I'm writing a travel article on the bourbon industry. When Michael and I visited Founder's Reserve, Jamie gave the tour because someone was out sick. And I interviewed him two more times on the distillation process.'

'Ha!' Michelle squawked. 'That never would've happened if you were toothless or gray-haired. Watch your step, cousin, or you'll end up like me.' She patted her rounded belly.

'I'd be more likely to bash that rotten scoundrel over the head with a stick.'

Jill's outburst brought a smile to Michelle's face. 'You'd do that for me? That is so sweet.' She continued toward the henhouse.

'Wait up.' Unfortunately when Jill tried to catch up she stepped in a pile of dung and let out a screech.

'Sorry 'bout that,' Michelle said, unable to stop laughing. 'That's the hazard of free-range cows and goats. Go back to the cabin and wash off your shoe with the hose. Just don't leave until I get back. I'll give you fresh eggs for Aunt Dot.'

Jill did as instructed then circled the house in the direction of voices. She found Michael, Will, and Justin sitting on the porch. The boy had a glass of milk while the men had glasses of something dark amber.

'Hey, Jill,' said Michael, brimming with enthusiasm. 'Did you know that your cousin harnessed the wind for his water well? It pumps water to both the kitchen and the bathroom. And there's a hand pump in the kitchen in case there's no wind, which isn't very often up here.'

'Shucks, boy. Have you been living under a rock? Windmills have been around for hundreds of years.' Will poured Jill a small glass of bourbon.

'I ask myself that question on a regular basis,' Jill said. 'And I must pass on the bourbon. It's my turn to drive.'

'Just try a tiny sip, Jill,' Michael coaxed, his excitement still soaring. 'It's so smooth. They use propane for the stove and refrigerator, plus Will has a diesel generator for emergencies. Living off the grid is pretty cool.'

'I think so too, but you couldn't live without television or internet.' Jill sipped the tiniest amount and started to cough, triggering laughter from the three males.

'There's coffee on the stove. Help yourself,' said Will. 'That shouldn't be as strong.'

'Sounds good. Thank you.' Jill entered the dim cabin, still warm from the cooking stove. For a few minutes she wandered around the living room and kitchen, admiring the simple efficiency of their lifestyle.

'You about done snooping around, Jill from Chicago?' said a voice from a dark hallway. Billy Clark stepped into view, minus the shirt he'd worn at supper. He had a multitude of tattoos and a long scar down the side of his neck. Every muscle in the man's chest and arms rippled as he walked towards her.

'Sorry, just coming in for some coffee.' Jill took a step back.

'The pot is on the stove.' Billy pointed with a dirty fingernail.

'You can't blame me for being curious. You would be too if you visited my apartment.'

'That ain't ever gonna happen.' Billy lit a cigarette and blew a stream of smoke in her face.

'Stop that!' Jill fanned the smoke away. 'Why are you hot under the collar? I didn't mean any disrespect.'

'Fine. Then go on your way, city girl. Forget all about us. I 'specially don't want you worrying about Michelle. Up here on the mountain, we take good care of our own.' Billy took another drag on the cigarette. Although he blew the smoke down toward the floor, there was no mistaking the look in his eyes.

'Got it. I guess I'll skip the coffee.'

'You have to leave so soon?' Michelle entered the kitchen with a basket brimming with eggs.

As Billy vanished back into the shadows, Jill plastered on a smile. 'I'm afraid we must. We want to get back before it's dark. We're not familiar with these roads.'

Michelle handed her the eggs. 'Tell Aunt Dot I'll get the basket back on Tuesday. See you then.'

After giving Michelle a clumsy hug, Jill collected her purse and her partner, bid everyone goodbye and hightailed it down the Clark's private road, at least as fast as the ruts would allow. She would fill Michael in on what she learned from Michelle, but she decided to omit Billy's thinly veiled warning to mind her own business. After all, he could just be super protective of his sister.

Or he might want to take matters into his own hands with the Shelbys.

NINE

J ill needn't have worried about conversation on the way back to Roseville. Michael had been so impressed with William Clark and, not having any bills other than real estate taxes and food they couldn't hunt, raise or grow, he talked exclusively about that.

'Just think, Jill. No water bill or sewer charge, no electric or heat bills, or credit cards. They don't pay homeowner's or health insurance, and have only minimum liability insurance on one car used to get to town. All other vehicles are listed as "off-road". No cable bill or satellite dish. If they can't pay cash for clothes or staples, they just plain don't need it.'

'You would die without the Weather Channel,' Jill said. 'And what if one of them got seriously ill?'

'I asked Will that. He said the state's Medicaid fund will pay to deliver the baby or if Justin got sick. And the adults? Will said they drank unfiltered cider vinegar every day and none of them *ever* get sick. One fell off a roof and needed stitches, so they made payments to the doctor until the bill was paid. Better than paying for health insurance each month whether you need it or not. I'm totally impressed with your family.'

Jill took her eyes off the road long enough to make sure Michael was still in the passenger seat. 'They're not technically my family. And although I respect their choices, that lifestyle wouldn't work for you.'

'I don't know 'bout that . . . Cousin Michelle is awfully cute. Maybe she'd settle for me as a husband instead of Jamie.'

Jill swerved to miss a tree. 'You're kidding, right?'

'Calm down. Yes, Curtis, I'm kidding about moving to the mountains. But I do like Michelle. That woman is no-nonsense.'

'I like her too. That's why I want Jamie Shelby to get his just comeuppance.'

'*Just comeuppance?* Your kinfolk are starting to rub off.'

Jill rolled her eyes. 'I'm serious. When we get back to town, we need to talk to Lieutenant Harris. Poor Roger might have died defending Michelle's honor with Jamie. For all I know, Jamie went to Black Creek after dropping me off. Michelle was Roger's goddaughter. Maybe Nick will be willing to meet us at the pizza shop. I'd rather talk someplace where Aunt Dot won't overhear us.'

Michael released an exaggerated yawn. 'Chat with the state trooper by yourself. Maybe it was the moonshine or maybe all that clean mountain air wore me out, but I'm going to bed. Besides, you're the only one convinced romance is at the bottom of this murder.' Michael leaned back in his seat and closed his eyes. He was sound asleep and snoring within minutes.

Jill had the rest of the drive to ponder Billy's behavior. That man truly didn't want her meddling in his family's business. But he couldn't be behind Roger's murder. What would he have to gain by his uncle's death?

When she reached the outskirts of Roseville she gave Nick a call. 'Hello, Lieutenant Harris? Jill Curtis.'

'Yes, Miss Curtis. I recognized your voice. What can I do for you?'

'I was wondering if we could meet at the pizza shop tonight or someplace else if you prefer. I have information you might find useful.'

'I just ordered a pizza to be delivered here. Why not join me in the backyard?'

'Oh, I had hoped to talk where Mrs Clark won't overhear us.'

'No problem. I just had a cup of coffee with her. She said she's retiring to her room to read. Tomorrow will be a long day for her.'

'In that case I'll join you. Mrs Clark's room is in the front of the house.'

'Cut out the *Mrs Clark* stuff. I know you two are related. You should realize that when suspects lie or omit details, it only makes them look guilty.'

Jill could imagine steam coming from Harris's ears. 'You can't possibly still think I killed Roger. What would be my motive?'

'Why wouldn't you still be a suspect? Maybe *Auntie* Dot asked you to come on down to help get rid of an abusive husband. Plenty of people in town said Roger wasn't very nice to his wife or his employees.'

'First of all, she's not my "aunt". We're cousins twice-removed. My grandmother is her first cousin. Aunt Dot is simply a respectful address. And secondly, we never set eyes on each other until I showed up with Michael. She hasn't talked to Granny in fifty years. And thirdly, Dorothy Clark is the sweetest, kindest woman I've ever met. She wouldn't hurt a fly.'

'That's pretty much what Sheriff Adkins said too. So that's why I'm willing to share my deluxe pizza with you and see what you have to say. Should I expect Michael too?'

Jill closed her eyes and counted to three. 'No, just me. Michael's hitting the sack. See you in ten minutes.'

'Do you like red or white?' he asked.

'Red or white *what*?'

'Wine. Your videographer said you only drink wine that comes in cardboard boxes. So I bought a small box of each at the drug store.'

'You had this all planned?' This time she had to count to five. 'I prefer white, but red goes better with pizza, so you choose. Goodbye.'

When Jill pulled into the driveway of Sweet Dreams B&B, Michael made a sandwich, grabbed half a dozen cookies, and went straight to his room. Jill let Jack out into the fenced backyard and spotted the trooper at a picnic table with a bright tablecloth, two wine glasses, a huge pizza box, and two glowing candles.

Sucking in a deep breath, Jill followed Jack to the table. 'Candlelight, Lieutenant Harris? Yesterday you thought I was a murderer.'

'Don't get too excited. The candles were Mrs Clark's idea because they repel mosquitos. I would've preferred paper cups, but our innkeeper insisted on the crystal. Shall we start with the red?' Harris unscrewed the plastic top.

'By all means. At least the Roseville drug store carried a decent variety of boxed wine.' Jill placed a slice of pizza on her plate. 'How did you know I love black olives?'

'Michael. You shouldn't leave the two of us alone together if you don't want your secrets revealed.'

Jill tasted her glass of dry red. 'This tastes perfectly fine to me. I don't know what all the fuss is about.' She took another sip. 'So, how is the case coming along?'

'Great, we've discovered some interesting facts about Black Creek's master distiller. And results from the fingerprints on the bourbon rack should be back tomorrow. Which of course I won't be at liberty to share with a travel writer from Chicago.' Nick took a huge bite of pizza.

Jill frowned over her slice.

'This is a police investigation. There are strict protocols I must follow. So if you were expecting some type of *quid pro quo*, I can't reciprocate.'

'I wasn't expecting anything, but before you lock somebody up and throw away the key, you should listen to what I found out.'

Nick washed the pizza down with a swallow of wine. 'You have my full attention.'

'The local librarian told me that Jamie Shelby had been dating Michelle Clark the same time they were dating. So Amanda, the librarian, broke up with him.'

'Although being a two-timer is deplorable, it's not a police matter.' Nick refilled both of their glasses.

Jill glared at him over her sunglasses. 'Just hear me out. When I questioned Jamie about his relationship with Michelle, he said it was no big deal and that they had been *just friends* for years.'

'You actually asked Shelby about this?' asked Nick, looking dumbfounded. 'This story keeps getting better and better.'

'Well, yes. We were on a date at the time.' Jill chewed her next bite slowly. 'In case you weren't aware, Michelle Clark was Roger's niece and goddaughter. I went to meet Michelle and the rest of William Clark's family today. They live up in the hills.'

'But you're a distant relative of Dorothy's, not Roger's.' He studied her over his wine glass.

'Correct, but the Shelbys and the Clarks have been feuding for years. Roger's murder might be connected to a recent flare-up of hostilities, *if* you would let me finish.'

Harris's smile softened the features of his usually serious face.

'I happened to notice that Michelle was pregnant, which matched up to when the librarian was also dating that snake-in-the-grass.'

'And now *you* are dating the very same snake.'

'I'm only pretending to like Shelby in order to get information.'

Jill shook her fist at the trooper. 'And if you interrupt me one more time, buster, you'll get a douse of Chicago justice.'

Nick appeared to be biting his cheek as he dished out more pizza.

'I asked Michelle about the baby's father and she confirmed it was Jamie Shelby. She said she loved him and that he loved her and had promised to take care of her . . . right up until she got pregnant. Then he tried to give her money to take care of the problem. Michelle threw the money in his face. At which point they broke up.' Jill took another bite of pizza.

'We already concluded that Shelby behaves deplorably. How could this possibly relate to Roger's murder?'

'Before I left their farm, Billy Clark told me to butt out of Michelle's business, because the Clarks always take care of their own.'

'So if Jamie-the-snake goes missing, Billy Clark will be our ready-made suspect. I suggest you stick to your bourbon story and leave the investigation to me and Sheriff Adkins.'

'Consider this. After Jamie dropped me off at the B and B—'

'Dropped you off?' Nick interrupted.

'Yes, after our tour Jamie invited me to continue our interview on the veranda over drinks and appetizers. Then he drove me home since Michael had already left with the car.'

'Yet another date with the snake!'

'Please, let me finish. Roger Clark could have asked Jamie to stop by the distillery for a man-to-man chat after he dropped me off. You know . . . do the right thing by my goddaughter. When Jamie refused, Roger might have thrown a punch and they got into a fight, which ended badly for Roger.'

Nick rubbed the back of his neck. 'Altogether feasible. But since not one shred of evidence puts Jamie at Black Creek that night, the sheriff and I are forced to work with what we have.' He wiped his mouth with his napkin. 'Tell me, wasn't that fabulous pizza? And this wine wasn't bad at all. Shall we crack open the other before we call it a night?'

His smile looked so earnest Jill couldn't refuse. 'Yes, the pizza was delicious. Thank you. And I'll have one glass of white as long as you at least consider my theory.'

'It's a deal. Until the moment we make an arrest, your theory will never be far from my mind. Now, let's talk about you, Jill. What is there to do in Chicago for fun?' Nick threw the remnants into the flowers and refilled their glasses. 'And may I take your picture to remember this special night?' He pulled out his phone.

Jill allowed him to photograph her smiling, frowning, and looking aloof. They then spent an enjoyable hour discussing sports, college and pro, their favorite types of restaurants, and just before they finished the second little box of wine, their worst dates ever. Since both of them were single and neither would be driving anywhere that night, what was the harm?

Except for the fact she was starting to really like Nick Harris and from every indication he really liked her too. That didn't bode well for her long-range career plans. Plus, he hadn't ruled her out as a murder suspect.

Monday morning

Nick woke up early Monday morning with a dull headache, a dry mouth and a big regret. He seldom drank wine and when he did, he never drank four glasses. Two aspirin with a large glass of water should take care of the after-effects of over-imbibing, but he never should have drank so much with Jill Curtis. Even if she was no longer a suspect, she still wasn't laying all her cards on the table. And he knew better than to get close to somebody connected to the case. Too bad she was so darn cute. And funny. And easy to talk to.

Nick showered, dressed and left the B&B as fast as possible. He hadn't talked to Sheriff Adkins all weekend and he wanted to compare notes before the sheriff got busy with department business. Luckily, when Nick arrived in the kitchen, the coffee was ready, but neither Mrs Clark nor any of the other guests had come downstairs. After filling his travel mug, Nick bolted out the door to his car. He had no idea why he was so reluctant to face Jill. Nothing had actually happened last night, but if shameless flirting and suggestive innuendoes were crimes, they could have been arrested on the spot.

When Nick arrived at the Spencer County Sheriff's Department, Jeff Adkins was just settling behind his desk with an apple, hard-boiled egg, and carton of milk. 'Good morning, Lieutenant Harris,' he called.

'Good morning, Sheriff. No donuts? If you continue to eat like that you'll ruin a perfectly fine cliché about cops.' Nick sat in the opposite chair.

Adkins laughed good-naturedly. 'No chance of that happening with my deputies. How about an egg or piece of fruit? My wife always packs extra.'

'I'll take an apple if you don't mind. Everything quiet in Roseville over the weekend? I went home to water my houseplants and do some laundry.' Nick bit into the crisp apple.

'Just your normal mailbox bashing on Saturday night, along with two complaints for loud music at backyard cookouts. Summer parties start out tame with volleyball and horseshoes and marsh-mallows roasted over a campfire. But once the kids go to bed they build the fires into raging infernos, turn up the music, and bring out a bottle of bourbon. One year some fool tried to jump the bonfire with his Harley and suffered third-degree burns.'

'I should ask for a transfer to your district. I like the crime better in your neck of the woods.' Nick finished his apple and tossed the core in the rubbish can.

'Except when we got ourselves a first-degree murder.'

Nick met the sheriff's gaze. 'We should get the crime lab and medical examiner's reports today. Hopefully, they'll point us in the right direction.'

As Adkins finished his healthy breakfast the fax machine started to whir. 'Speak of the devil. That's probably what we've been waiting for.' Adkins jumped from his chair and handed Nick the first several of multiple sheets.

Nick skimmed and read the key points aloud. 'All of the blood evidence found at the crime scene was Roger's, along with most of the fingerprints. No match in the database for the partial print found smeared in blood. Of the two other prints found on the racks – one belonged to the worker who recently filled the rack and the other belonged to Jamie Shelby. His prints apparently were on file from a DWI arrest back in 2015.' Nick skimmed the rest of the report and handed it to Adkins, trying not to fixate on what he'd learned from Jill last night. 'So why was Jamie inside Black Creek Distillery?'

'That's a very good question.' Adkins downed the rest of his milk. 'Now we have a good reason to bring the guy in for ques-tioning. Would you like to do the honors or should I send two of my deputies?'

'Send the deputies. I want to go over every detail of the forensics to be fully prepared for Shelby. Plus we still need the medical examiner to make an official determination of homicide.' When the sheriff walked out of the office, Nick started thinking about what Jill had said. *Could Roger Clark have invited Jamie there to talk and things turned ugly?* Everyone knows how competitive bourbon masters could be. Maybe Jamie getting his goddaughter pregnant had pushed Roger over the edge.

Suddenly the fax machine whirred to life again, spitting out the Kentucky Medical Examiner's report with determination of death. As Nick and the sheriff had expected, Roger Clark had not died by natural causes or accidental occurrence. It was murder, either first or second degree. The bruising on Clark's face and upper torso were consistent with blows made by a fist, while the blow to the forehead was consistent with hitting the edge of the rack. However, a simple fall wouldn't have caused such a deep facial laceration. In all likelihood, Roger Clark was pushed into the rack by either someone very strong or a person in a rage. Clark had probably been rendered unconscious by such a blow. However, that deep laceration hadn't killed him. Someone had cracked Clark's skull while he lay helpless on the floor, most likely with a heavy tool found in the distillery or brought by the killer. Either way the ME declared the death a homicide.

Nick leaned back in his chair, pondering the conclusion. Hard to imagine someone generating enough hatred to kill from either business dealings or an unexpected pregnancy. Someone as rich as Jamie Shelby could afford to support his child without marrying the baby's mother. Although it didn't match his personal convictions, this happened all the time.

Nick went in search of a cup of coffee. Just as he got back to his desk, Sheriff Adkins walked in with the heir to the Founder's Reserve fortune.

'Mr Shelby, this is Nick Harris from the Kentucky State Police. Lieutenant Harris, this is Jamie Shelby of Founder's Reserve. I explained to Mr Shelby that he's here for questioning and not under arrest. However, I advised him that he may have counsel available if he wishes.'

Jamie strode to the nearest chair and sat without being invited. 'My, I'm surprised to see they called the cavalry to Roseville.

From what I heard, poor old Roger slipped in spilled bourbon and whacked his head. That wannabe distiller was usually half in his cups most of the workday.'

Maybe it was his attitude or maybe it was the expensively tailored suit. Or maybe it was on general principles, but Nick hated Jamie on first sight. 'By all means, Mr Shelby,' he murmured. 'Have a seat.'

Jamie lifted an eyebrow. 'Excuse me, Lieutenant. I thought I was here as a *courtesy* to your investigation, to provide distillery information of a general nature. After all, my family and the Clarks have been friends for a long time.' He smiled at the sheriff who hung back in the doorway.

Switching on the tape recorder, Nick chose his words carefully. 'I appreciate that, sir. But just so we're clear, Mr Clark didn't die by slipping on spilled liquid or any other accidental means. I'm conducting a murder investigation, so I'll ask you again and record your response: would you like an attorney present during questioning?'

Shelby crossed his legs. 'Absolutely not, only guilty people need attorneys. Ask me whatever you like.'

'We've just learned that Michelle Clark, Roger Clark's niece and goddaughter, was pregnant with your child.'

'Only a DNA test can prove whether or not that's true, which I will demand if Michelle expects any sort of financial support. Michelle and I have been friends for years, during which we've both had plenty of lovers.' He grinned smugly.

'So you don't deny being intimate with Michelle Clark?'

'I do not, but I thought this was a murder investigation, not family court.' He aimed a confused expression at Adkins.

'Correct,' said the sheriff. 'But we wanted to verify any gossip or conjecture that could be connected.'

The sheriff's choice of words triggered a laugh. 'Excellent, since we know how small-town folks love to gossip.'

'I learned from the widow, Mrs Clark,' Nick continued, astounded by the man's self-confidence, 'that Roger occasionally made appointments in the distillery after hours, especially if he wanted to discuss sensitive matters. Perhaps his niece expected you to marry her, so Uncle Roger asked you to stop by Black Creek after the production crew left.' Nick glanced at the sheriff to see if he wished to take over the questioning. Judging by his expression, he did not. 'If Clark insisted that you do the right thing, you two could have gotten into a fight, especially if you insinuated Michelle had multiple lovers.'

Shelby ran a hand through his hair. 'This is starting to sound like a bad made-for-television movie. Any of that could have happened, but I assure you it didn't. Roger died last Wednesday, I believe. I wasn't at Black Creek the night Roger died. I was at my own distillery late that day because our tour guide called in sick and I had to fill in for her. There was a very pretty travel writer in the last tour who wanted to ask more questions. Since Founder's Reserve loves to promote positive publicity, I invited the writer for drinks and canapés on the patio afterwards. Once I answered all her questions I drove her back to her B and B.' Shelby glanced at his watch.

Nick felt his breakfast sour in his stomach. 'And this travel writer will verify this?'

'Oh, I'm sure she remembers me. Her name is Jill Curtis and she's staying at the Sweet Dreams B and B.'

'About what time did you drop off Miss Curtis?'

Shelby gazed at the ceiling for a long moment. 'I'm not sure . . . maybe eight or eight thirty. And to save you from asking, I got a call from my father during the drive to Roseville. I drove straight back to Founder's Reserve where I was seen by several people. I spoke to my father, then a few friends dropped by and I ended up talking late into the night on the back terrace.'

Sheriff Adkins finally pushed away from the doorjamb. 'We've got one troubling detail to clear up, Jamie. Your fingerprint was found at the crime scene on an aging rack, fairly close to the body of the deceased. The Shelbys and Clarks aren't known to socialize in the same circles.'

'Why was my print on file at the sheriff's department?'

Although Shelby asked the question of the sheriff, Nick provided the answer. 'It went into the database when you were arrested for a DWI a few years ago. How do you suppose it ended up several feet away from Roger Clark's body?'

Shelby rubbed his clean-shaven chin. 'I must have grabbed the rack during the party at Black Creek. Michelle Clark had invited me to her uncle's fundraiser. At one point we ducked into the warehouse for a little private time. We're all men here. I think you can read between the lines.'

Nick clenched his fists under the desk, but Adkins spoke first. 'In her uncle's distillery? What's the matter with you, boy?'

Anger sparked in Shelby's dark eyes. 'First of all, Sheriff, I'm not a boy. And secondly, the tryst among the barrels had been Michelle's idea. It was quiet and dark and nobody saw us.'

Nick swallowed the bad taste in his mouth. 'When was this fundraiser?'

'Roughly a month ago. But the invitation is still on the office bulletin board if you need an exact date.' Shelby swiveled the chair to face Adkins. 'I assure you, Roger Clark didn't know what Michelle and I were up to at the cocktail party. And I didn't see him the night he died. So can I leave now?'

'Yes, Mr Shelby, we're done, at least for now.'

He rose to his feet and straightened his tie. 'If there are any additional questions, direct them to my lawyer, because this' – he drew a circle with his finger – 'was humiliating.' Shelby stomped from the office.

'There goes his vote for my re-election,' Adkins joked. 'But his alibi sounds pretty solid. It's possible for a print to last that long.'

Nick glanced over notes in the file. 'According to the widow, Roger came home from work on Wednesday around six o'clock, wolfed down his dinner, and went back to the plant. He'd been doing that a lot lately, but Mrs Clark didn't know why. He wasn't home yet when she retired for the evening and still hadn't returned when she woke up Thursday morning.' He tapped the pen tip against the file. 'Don't you think it's strange that Mrs Clark didn't call the police when her husband was still MIA Thursday morning?'

Adkins needed no time to ponder his response. 'Nope, you never met the deceased, but I did. Roger Clark was not a warm, fuzzy kind of guy. If Dot sent in the hounds after him, and it turned out he was just sleeping off a bender in his office, he would have blown his stack.'

'You're saying Clark had a drinking problem?' Nick asked.

'Oh, yeah, but that's not what killed him. Could the ME narrow down the time of death?'

Nick picked up the report. 'He estimated Clark had been dead approximately twelve to sixteen hours when Miss Curtis found

his body, which puts his time of death between seven and nine
p.m. Wednesday evening.'

'Which might rule out the upstanding Jamie Shelby as a suspect.'
The sheriff drew the obvious conclusion.

'Yeah, I'd better check into the timeline of his alibi. Too bad.
It would be great if Shelby had to spend a few nights in lockup
just for being a jerk.'

'Can't argue with you there.' Adkins strolled to the window to
gaze out on parked cars, a tasteless office building and a dilapidated
billboard in the distance. 'Don't you find it strange that Miss Curtis
found the body *and* provided Shelby with an alibi? That woman
just blew into town and checked into the deceased's B and B.
Then she informed the widow that she's a long-lost relative. Way
too many coincidences, don't you think?'

Nick studied the back of the sheriff's head. 'There are not many
places to stay in Roseville. Plus I called her boss at the news
service – her story checked out.'

'Yeah, I know. But I think you should verify this so-called
family connection. Dot Clark had never heard of this woman
before. And see if you can find anything connecting Jamie Shelby
to this Jill Curtis. All too neat and tidy in my book.'

'I'll get right on it, Sheriff,' Nick murmured, mildly annoyed.

'Sorry, Lieutenant,' Adkins said over his shoulder. 'Didn't mean to
start issuing orders. This is your case and I have complete confidence
in you. It's just that tomorrow we bury the husband of my wife's best
friend and we're a long way from knowing who put him in an early
grave. Nice guy or not, Roger Clark didn't deserve what he got.'

Nick laced his fingers behind his head. 'It's OK, Jeff. I get it.
If Jill Curtis is hiding something, I'll find it. And I will enjoy
digging up the dirt on Jamie Shelby.'

Adkins left Nick's temporary office. When he strolled back in
two hours later, neither of them was smiling.

'Tell me you found something.' The sheriff set a cup of coffee
on Nick's desk.

'I found nothing connecting Miss Curtis to anyone at Founder's
Reserve Distillery. I don't believe the woman has ever set foot in
Kentucky until now. From Mrs Clark I learned the relative they
have in common is an Emma Vanderpool, who is Mrs Clark's first
cousin. Then I spoke with Mrs Vanderpool who lives in assisted

living in St. John, Illinois. She verified that Jill is her granddaughter and that she was born in a small town outside of Louisville. She indeed has a first cousin living in Spencer County. I found nothing on Jamie Shelby that you don't already know . . . DUI, two drunk and disorderlies while attending University of Kentucky, where he finally flunked out in his junior year. One charge of felonious assault with a deadly weapon, but the charges were later dropped. Wonder how much that cost dear old dad to make it go away?' Nick tossed his yellow tablet across the desk and picked up the coffee.

Adkins slumped in the opposite chair. 'Two of my deputies caught an interesting call while on patrol. Malicious vandalism out at Founder's Reserve. Sometime last night or early this morning someone spray-painted: *You ain't getting away with murder this time, Shelby* on the side of Founder's rickhouse.'

Nick straightened in his chair. 'And no one saw it until now?' He glanced at his watch. 'It's almost noon.'

'Apparently not. When one of the workers did spot the graffiti, they reported it to their supervisor, who then reported it to his boss. Finally, Jamie Shelby made the call to dispatch once he returned from our little interview. How's that for coincidence?' Adkins shook his head. 'According to the deputy at the scene, the number-one-son was fit to be tied. I instructed the deputy to send you photos and a copy of his report when he's done.'

Nick nodded. 'What do you suppose was the first murder – the Christmas Eve fistfight that killed one of Cook's sons?'

'So you heard about the old feud.' Adkins stared at the ceiling. 'I doubt that's what they meant. It was so long ago. Nobody cares about ancient history except for librarians, history teachers and a few geeks.'

'You have other unsolved murder cases lying around?'

'No, but who knows what the artist meant by the wording. Unfortunately he or she didn't leave the paint can behind with plenty of fingerprints. Shelby said this was the second vandalism in two weeks. His father, Owen Shelby, refused to report the first incident.'

'What happened? More graffiti?'

'No, someone dumped over several huge potted plants on their terrace. Made quite a mess. Owen Shelby thought it related to an incident at a recent wedding reception at the facility. One of the guests had too much to drink and picked a fight with one of the groomsmen. Security guards hustled the man into a taxi and off the premises. The guest actually took an Uber back to the reception to pick up where he left off. This time security locked the man in a storage room and didn't release him until the next morning, madder than a wet hen. He threatened to bring a lawsuit and blah, blah, blah. Nothing came of his threats, but the senior Mr Shelby chose not to make an issue about the potted plants. Bad publicity might hurt their wedding bookings.'

Nick pushed to his feet. 'I think I'll take a drive out to Founder's Reserve. See the graffiti for myself. Then I've got a few questions for Miss Curtis.'

'Don't forget tonight's the wake for Roger Clark at Trehanny's. Never know who might show up at these things.'

'With any luck, one of his employees will throw themselves at our feet and confess. That's what we could use right about now.'

'Does that happen a lot in Louisville, Lieutenant? I can't remember the last time anybody confessed to anything in Roseville.'

TEN

Monday evening

Jill had spent the day sticking close to Sweet Dreams Bed & Breakfast, on the off-chance Aunt Dot needed her help. However, between Mr Trehanny's expertise with tasteful funerals, the ladies' guild of the Roseville Episcopal Church, and Dot's wide circle of friends, the house was spotless and the food prepared. Everything was ready for tonight's wake and tomorrow's funeral. Uncle Roger would get a proper, southern-style send-off.

Instead she had typed, edited and proofread the first two installments of the Kentucky Bourbon Tours. Then she helped Michael edit the video footage which would bring her clever narrative to life. With little else to do, Jill put on her new black dress and black high-heeled sandals and nursed a cup of tea in the kitchen until it was time to leave.

'Good evening, Jill,' Nick said as he rounded the corner from the stairwell. 'I didn't know anyone was still home.'

'Why wouldn't we be, Mr Harris?' She leveled an icy glare. 'The funeral home is only five minutes away. We don't need to be early to get a good seat.'

Nick paused in the middle of adjusting his tie, as though her flip comment caught him by surprise. 'I thought we'd gotten along well last night. In fact, I'd describe our pizza party as rather splendid. Yet this evening I seem to have fallen from favor, despite the fact we haven't seen each other all day.' With the crooked tie forgotten, Nick sat down beside her, his spicy aftershave assaulting her senses.

'Today I realized I'm still one of your suspects, if not your primary suspect.' Jill walked her cup to the sink to put some distance between them. 'What were you playing at last night? Were you hoping I'd drink too much and let some crucial detail slip that you could hang me with, literally and figuratively?' She dropped her voice to a whisper. 'Dot said you asked her about the relative we *allegedly* have in common. Sounds like you don't trust me. What's next? Are you going to call my Granny Emma?'

Nick's gray eyes locked with hers. 'I already did. Mrs Vanderpool confirmed you were her granddaughter and that she had a cousin who lived in Spencer County she hadn't seen in decades.'

Jill's mouth fell open wide enough to catch flies. 'How could you, Nick? You act like we're friends, then you sneak around behind my back. Some things are none of your business.'

A tic appeared in Nick's right cheek, but his voice remained soft and in control. 'This is a murder investigation. It's my job to verify every detail in this case. It was the only way I can rule you out as a suspect.'

She shrugged. 'You should be able to tell by my character that I'm no killer.'

'If only it were that easy,' he said. 'Beautiful women can be killers. Nice girls who take their aunts to church on Sunday can be killers. I can't rule someone out just because they charmed me one night in the moonlight.'

Jill braced her hands on the table. 'Now I'm confused. Am I beautiful or nice or am I simply charming?'

'What you are is an exasperating woman.' Again the cop didn't bat an eyelash.

'Well, good, because that particular feeling is mutual,' she sneered, feeling a tad juvenile.

'Look, Jill, I had no choice. Sheriff Adkins pointed out all the coincidences in this case: you showed up in town and announced you're Dorothy Clark's relative.' He held up one finger. 'You found the body, and you're staying in the home of the victim.' Nick extended his second and third fingers. 'Then today I identified a fingerprint found close to Roger Clark's body and brought the man in for questioning. But he has an alibi for the time of the murder. Guess who that would be?' A fourth finger popped up.

Jill swallowed her irritation with the handsome detective. 'I told you Jamie Shelby drove me home after the tour. His print was found at the crime scene?'

'It was. And I thought you took a tour, had one drink and a snack and went home.' Nick stretched his legs out under the table.

'Well, he was with me Wednesday afternoon and early evening until maybe eight or eight-thirty.' Jill reiterated facts Harris already knew. 'But that doesn't mean he couldn't have stopped at Black Creek on his way home.'

'You've been spending a lot of time with Mr Shelby. So tell me, what are *you* playing at?'

Jill knew by his tone Nick wasn't talking solely about the case. 'I must admit Jamie is a handsome man, assuming he's not a murderer. But if he is involved in this mess, I might be in a good position to discover how. He likes me so I can use his trust to my advantage.' She grinned. 'Goodness, Detective, you sound a tad jealous.'

Nick blushed as he pinched the bridge of his nose. 'You need to step back. I have the sheriff, along with several deputies and the full resources of Kentucky law enforcement. I don't need a travel writer and her videographer getting in my way.'

Jill's head snapped around. 'Getting in your way? I'm the one who told you Michelle Clark, Roger's goddaughter, was pregnant by Jamie. That little tidbit could be connected to the murder.'

'We don't have one shred of evidence tying Michelle to the crime. You and Michael jeopardized yourselves by going up the mountain to confront the Clarks. That could have ended badly.'

'But it didn't. And the fact someone cut the power while Michael was in the elevator proves we're getting close to the truth.'

Nick exhaled a sigh. 'A smart person would've taken it for what it was . . . a warning. You and Michael are in danger. You should return to Chicago immediately after Roger's funeral.'

'So I'm beautiful, kind, charming, and *stupid*? Wow, Lieutenant Harris, you really have a way with words.' Jill's fingers curled into fists as she sprang to her feet.

'That didn't come out how I intended.' Nick held up his palms. 'You're right, Jill. Something is going on at Founder's Reserve that we don't understand. Today someone vandalized the building where they age the bourbon. Apparently, it was the second time they had been vandalized. I don't want you getting hurt. You can always come back to Roseville after we put the killer behind bars.' Harris placed a condescending hand on her shoulder.

It was a fatal mistake as far as Jill was concerned. She batted his hand away as though a hairy spider had dropped from the ceiling. 'Oh, this is priceless. Sheriff Adkins ordered us not to leave town under no uncertain terms. Now you advise we should hop on the next boat, train, or plane going north. Who exactly is in charge here?'

'No boats go to Chicago,' he said softly.

Jill pressed one recently polished fingernail to her lips. 'I am grateful for your concern, Nick, especially since I'm cognitively impaired, as was recently pointed out. But I promised my first cousin twice-removed that I would stay until her husband's killer was caught. You do not have the authority to order me back to Chicago. So if you'll excuse me, I hear my aunt on the stairs. I have a wake to attend.' Jill circumvented the hulking cop as though he were a mossy statue in the center of town.

For the rest of the evening, Jill stood with Aunt Dot next to the open casket of her husband. She tried not to look at the heavy make-up obscuring the cuts and bruises on Roger's face. She supported Dot's arm whenever the woman wavered from fatigue or under a Black Creek employee's outpouring of grief. Jill tried not to notice Gordon Clark's blatant glares in her direction, as though she were personally angling for his job. And she flat out ignored Nick Harris and Sheriff Adkins who lurked in the back of the funeral home, who studied each mourner who passed through the line while jotting details in their little notepads.

Nick had tried to engage her in conversation when he initially paid his respects to Dot Clark. But Jill had delivered a witheringly cool, 'Thanks for coming, Officer Harris. Be sure to sign the guest book before you leave.'

Nick hadn't tried to talk to her again that evening. And his car wasn't in its regular parking spot when she finally reached her bedroom, weary beyond words. Whatever flicker of attraction she'd felt last night – and was certain he had felt too – was long gone. Distrust and heavy-handedness killed romance just as handily as a whack to the back of the head.

She had more than just Roger to be sad about.

Tuesday morning

In keeping with the day's somber mood, Jill opened her bedroom shade on steady rain and a dreary landscape. She lifted her one black dress from the back of the chair and shook out the wrinkles. Hopefully, no one would notice it was the same dress she'd worn last night.

As a wave of sorrow crept up her throat, Jill grabbed the

windowsill to steady herself. Was her grief for Roger Clark, a man she'd met only once and formed a rather negative opinion of? Even if Roger hadn't been especially personable, nobody deserved to leave this world lying on a cold concrete floor. Was her grief for Dorothy, a kind and gentle woman who'd just spent the last fifty years estranged from her favorite cousin over a teenage misunderstanding? *Such a waste.* Or was her sorrow for herself, a woman who couldn't help but alienate every man who tried to get close? Whatever the reason, Jill let the tears fall for several minutes before she showered, dressed, and put on her usual make-up. Yet her face still looked too pale and hollow-eyed. Jill considered more blusher and less eyeliner, but in the end she simply turned off the bathroom light and trudged down the steps to the kitchen.

Michael and Dot were both already at the table. In his navy-blue sport coat and dark slacks Michael looked like a kid dressed up for the junior prom. Aunt Dot, in her black dress, low-heeled pumps, and broad-brimmed hat, looked exactly like what she was: a widow about to face the worst day of her life.

'I'm so glad you're here in Kentucky.' Dot extended her hand to Jill. 'It's better to face tragedy with family.'

Jill hurried to clasp the woman's thin fingers. 'I'm glad we are too.' Although she felt like a poor excuse for family, she smiled and walked their innkeeper out to the car. Together they drove to Trehanny's Funeral Home where a select few had been allowed one last look at Roger before the casket was closed.

Surprisingly William, Michelle, Justin, Gordon and Billy Clark were already waiting for them, along with a scattering of relatives Jill didn't know. The Clarks rose to their feet and hugged Dorothy one by one. William, Michelle, and Justin hugged Jill as well, while Gordon offered a business-like handshake to her and Michael. Billy, dressed too casually for the occasion in black jeans and a white T-shirt, ignored Michael and looked at her like something stuck to his shoe. Unfortunately, the short sleeves didn't hide the panoply of skulls, crossbones, and bloody-fanged viper tats on Billy's arms.

Considering the fit of his suit, Will had weighed at least twenty-five pounds more when the suit had been purchased. Michelle was dressed in black knit pants and a cream-colored top that did nothing to hide her expectancy. Gordon's suit looked both expensive and well-tailored. His tie was silk and his shoes had been polished. Each of the Clarks approached the casket one at a time to pay their respects. When it was Jill's turn, she closed her eyes and uttered a simple prayer about forgiveness of sins.

Then like a shepherd, Joe Trehanny herded them outside to the waiting limo. 'Please, folks, make yourselves comfortable.' Trehanny swept open the door, while his employees loaded the casket into the hearse.

Dropping Jill's arm, Dot turned to her brother-in-law. 'Are your sons willing to serve as pall bearers?' she asked. 'I've already asked my houseguest, Michael Erickson. So along with Mr Trehanny we should have enough.' Dot peered at Will from beneath her hat's wide brim.

Will squinted at the stretch limo, the bright glare turning his face into a mass of creases. 'Of course, they're willing. But all this sure wasn't necessary.' He pointed a tobacco-stained finger at the vehicle. 'Our daddy would've called it worthless pretention.'

A blush brightened Dot's pale cheeks. 'Roger had paid for our funerals well in advance. It's part of the Trehanny *basic* package.'

'In that case, OK,' said Will with a shrug of his thin shoulders. He motioned his offspring into the third row of the limo and took his place next to Dot in the second row.

Michelle ducked in after her father. 'Jill, sit next to me. Michael can sit with the boys.' She patted the leather upholstery.

When Michael nodded agreement, Jill squeezed into the second row.

'I'd like to hang out with you today, if you don't mind,' Michelle whispered in her ear.

'It would be my pleasure.' She patted the woman's knee. Ridiculously, Jill hoped Amanda Posey would attend the funeral too, so the three could present a unified front to Jamie Shelby.

But once they entered the cool interior of Roseville Episcopal, a church filled to the gills with mourners, Jill dismissed her silly thoughts. As the family followed the casket up the center aisle, the widow grew weak-kneed and began to falter. Supported by William on one side and Jill on the other, Dot settled in the front row and began to weep, which continued throughout the one-hour service.

Parishioners offered readings from First and Second Corinthians, then Father Carl delivered a heartfelt homily about a man who seldom graced the inside of a church. But it was Gordon Clark's eulogy about his uncle and mentor that brought everyone to tears. Gordy spoke of fishing trips and building treehouses and white water rafting down West Virginia's New River, an adventure which had changed his life forever. Then Gordy described his training by one of the best bourbon masters in the business and how Roger taught him the ins and outs of a successful operation. There wasn't a dry eye in the house.

During the final hymn, Jill gazed over her shoulder at the congregation. Some people she recognized like Lindy at the front desk of Black Creek Distillery and Amanda, the county librarian. Jill spotted the clerk who sold her the black dress, along with the florist who provided a gorgeous arrangement of lilies and camellias at a reasonable price. Many of the friends and neighbors who had cleaned Sweet Dreams B&B and cooked the enormous amount of food were there. And toward the back of the church sat Jamie Shelby with an older, well-dressed couple who were undoubtedly his parents. His father sported the blotchy complexion and purplish nose which usually meant high blood pressure or alcohol over-indulgence or both. Jamie bobbed his head in recognition when their eyes met but looked away just as quickly. The rest of the congregation, though strangers to Jill and perhaps even to Aunt Dot, had known Roger as current or past employees, tradesmen, or fellow bourbon aficionados. Last but not least, Jill spotted the tall, gray-eyed cop from Lorraine, Kentucky and his shorter, bearded sidekick in the last row. The pair seemed to be watching everyone in attendance.

After the benediction, everyone filed out to their cars for the flagged processional to the cemetery. Roger would be laid to rest in the Clark family plot beside his mother and father. There was little chatter in the limo during the short ride to the outskirts of Roseville. Young Justin asked his father who was the lady in the navy polka dots who kept pinching his cheek, while Michelle complained about her need to find a ladies' room. With his focus out the window, William Clark ignored both of his children. Fortunately, the limo driver heard Michelle's plea and stopped in front of the cemetery office.

Jill found the custom of everyone trooping to the actual gravesite ridiculous. It was too tight an area for a crowd. People trampled over other graves and someone inevitably tripped on the green carpet and narrowly missed joining the deceased.

At last Father Carl asked people to bow their heads while he delivered a final prayer for the peaceful repose of Roger Clark's soul. 'On behalf of the Clark family,' he intoned, 'you are all invited back to the church hall for a luncheon. Additional parking is available at the elementary school and on both side streets. Now, please step forward and place your flower as a final tribute to Mr Clark.'

Trehanny's assistants ushered those standing in the back, presumed less closely connected to Roger, to place their flowers first. Jill noticed most mourners had been given white carnations, while the undertaker gave everyone in the limo a long-stemmed red rose. Jill wondered who had invented such customs, but when her heel caught in a carpet fold, she concentrated on remaining upright when her turn came.

Aunt Dot, her tears dried, delivered her rose on the sturdy arm of Joe Trehanny. William, his eyes red-rimmed and swollen, didn't look any steadier than Jill on her high heels. He leaned heavily on his son, Gordon.

At the church hall, Michael appointed himself parking attendant so that no one double-parked or ended up driving over the church's numerous flowerbeds. Jill manned the buffet of cold cuts and cheeses, fried chicken, and a variety of salads. She refilled bowls, washed serving utensils that fell on the floor, and kept an eye on the supply of soft drinks and bottled water. Thank goodness the luncheon was alcohol-free, something Uncle Roger would not have liked. Mourners talked, ate, and then talked some more. Apparently, those from small towns never ran out of things to say to each other. But by three o'clock most attendees had bid Aunt Dot goodbye and drifted to their cars or strolled in the direction of home.

'Anything I can do to help, Miss Curtis?' The husky voice of Nick Harris pierced her concentration as Jill refilled a coffee carafe from the urn.

'No, your offer is a tad late. The funeral seems to be wrapping up.' Her words sounded harsh. 'But thank you anyway.'

'It took me a while to work up my nerve,' Nick murmured. 'May I speak privately to you?'

Jill pulled off her apron with yellow flowers and carried a cup of coffee to an unoccupied table. 'Have you come to deliver another ultimatum?'

'Quite the contrary.' Nick sat down across from her. 'I'd like to apologize for yesterday. I had no business ordering around a private citizen, especially not one with a vested interest in justice.'

Jill took a sip of coffee and frowned. The coffee tasted like it had simmered all day. 'You should know I promised Aunt Dot I would stay to help for a while. And I intend to keep that promise.'

'I can't blame you. You have every right to be here, especially since Mrs Clark appreciates having family close by.' Harris laced his fingers together on the table. 'The truth is I've grown fond of you, so I don't want you getting hurt. That's why I wanted you out of Roseville until this is over.'

'*Fond?*' Jill gave an incredulous inflection to his term. 'Granny Emma is fond of me, while I'm fond of sweetcorn and sliced tomatoes in the summer. If you're hoping to make up, you'll have to do better than that.'

The dimple in his left cheek deepened. 'Very well. Jill Curtis, I think you are kind and pretty and funny and I am fascinated by you.'

She shook her index finger at him. 'You forgot that I am smart.'

'Plus, I think you're smart.' The detective tapped his forehead.

'I could be very helpful if you would let me.' Jill cocked her head to one side.

'The state police of the Commonwealth of Kentucky are here to serve and protect you. We have a hard time accepting help from citizens. But I'm willing to try as long as you don't put yourself in harm's way.'

'Fair enough,' Jill agreed. 'Now, I happen to be starving and I bet you haven't eaten yet either. Why don't you get us two plates of food before the church ladies pack it up for the homeless?'

Nick shrugged off his sport coat and rolled up his sleeves. 'Are there homeless in Roseville? I saw no evidence of that.'

'One of the church ladies found a family living in their car at the Family Dollar. They have since been taken under the Episcopal wing. The ladies also take meals to shut-ins and the elderly.'

'I knew I liked this town,' he said with a wink.

As Nick headed toward the buffet, Jill's fickle heart swelled beneath her ribs. She really should stay away from him, or at least stay angry. Whenever she gave in to her emotions, or wore them on her sleeve like a banner, her life careened out of control. But at least when Nick returned with two plates, loaded with fried chicken and potato salad, he wasn't alone.

Michael, his duties in the parking lot finished, plopped into the chair next to Jill. The videographer had created a sandwich that would have made Dagwood proud. 'Wow, as funerals go, that was quite a turnout. Some people had to park as far away as the fire station.' Michael squeezed his sandwich with both hands and took a bite.

'I'm surprised there was any food left.' Jill speared a sweet gherkin on her fork. 'Funerals in Chicago don't draw these kinds of crowds.'

'Not usually in Louisville either,' Nick said. 'I spoke with Mrs Clark in the kitchen. She was very grateful to both of you for all you've done.' He looked from Jill to Michael. 'William and his family were taking her home to rest. They plan to spend the night at Sweet Dreams before heading up the mountain tomorrow. They said they would see you this evening.'

Jill nodded. 'In the meantime, Lieutenant Harris, let's talk some more about the case.' She decided not to let the former topic get away. 'What about that security guard at Black Creek, Elmer Maxwell? He was the one on duty the night Roger died. Has anybody managed to track that shirker down?'

Nick chewed his mouthful of chicken and swallowed. 'No. The sheriff and I only spoke with Elmer Maxwell the next day. He said he felt nauseated at work and came home. He said he'd left two unanswered messages for Roger. His wife corroborated he had thrown up all night and still felt sick the next day. So we don't have enough for an arrest warrant or even to hold him if he did come back.'

Michael finished a chicken leg and licked his fingertips. 'Sounds like you're letting Jill stick her nose into your investigation.'

'Jill had me up against the wall.' Nick reached for his lemonade. 'So she can help as along as her participation doesn't jeopardize her health and safety.'

For some reason Michael chuckled over Nick's reply. 'An amusing notion – a mortal male controlling the actions of Jill

Curtis, but I wish you luck. And in case you or the sheriff would like to narrow your pool of suspects based on sorrowful expressions or the lack thereof, I videotaped everyone who showed up at the cemetery.'

'Thanks. I might just take you up on that offer.' Nick wrapped the other half of his sandwich in a napkin. 'Can I drive you back to Sweet Dreams? I'm not sure where you left your car when you rode in the limo.'

Since Michael's mouth was full, Jill answered for them. 'We're fine. Our car is on the street next to the church.' She ate another forkful of pasta salad and pushed away her plate. 'Aren't you going to finish your lunch, Trooper?'

'Maybe later. I want to get to the station and compare notes with Sheriff Adkins.' Nick glanced around the nearly empty church hall, then let his gaze linger on Jill. 'Will I see you this evening, maybe in Mrs Clark's backyard? I bought another mini-box of white wine.'

Michael's hoot of laughter echoed off the walls. 'A smooth move if ever I heard one.'

Jill ignored her partner. 'That's the best offer I've had in a while, but I'll have to see how things go. If Aunt Dot's in-laws are staying over, I should help entertain them.'

Nick stood and put his wrapped sandwich in his pocket. 'You know where to find me.'

At least Michael waited until the cop left to deliver his observation. 'I think that guy is starting to like you. How amazing is that?'

'It was bound to happen sometime. Finish eating, Erickson. We need to get back to the B and B. By now, Billy Clark could be rifling through Aunt Dot's jewelry box.'

Unsure whether or not she was joking, Michael wrapped the rest of his sandwich too and cleaned up the table. They were out the door and on their way to Sweet Dreams within five minutes flat.

ELEVEN

Tuesday evening

Now that Roger's funeral was over with, it felt as though a great weight had lifted from her shoulders. She and Aunt Dot talked to Michelle and William Clark long into the night. Justin had fallen asleep on the library couch soon after supper. And Gordon and Billy Clark? Jill never saw either of them after the luncheon in the church hall. And she didn't ask their whereabouts. It was much nicer not having either the multi-pierced thug or the cold-as-ice zombie glaring at her from across the room.

Sipping a snifter of bourbon, William told them stories about growing up with Roger near the banks of Knob Creek, the same creek that had caused so much trouble for Isaiah Shelby and Tobias Cook. During the summer the boys had fished for trout and pickerel, netted crawdads in the weedy shallows, and swung from a rope out to the one deep pool that according to their father had been formed by a sharp cut in the glacial rock beds. They hunted for squirrels and rabbits in the fall, ice skated on a nearby pond in the winter, and often skipped school in the spring. Will's favorite memory involved hopping a freight train to a thoroughbred farm near Lexington, where the brothers had watched newborn colts kicking up their heels for the first time. They had slept in someone's hay barn that night and caught a westbound train the following morning. Their excursion cost the boys a trip to the woodshed where the rod had not been spared. Years later, Roger and William still joked that the Lexington adventure had been worth it.

Aunt Dot shared tales about her early years with Roger – how they met, where they had gone on dates, and their July wedding at the smallest Baptist church in Kentucky. She described their cramped first apartment in Louisville when Roger worked on the Jim Beam production line. Listening to Dot describe their life with such joy on her face lifted Jill's spirits. Roger and Dot had been happy once, and maybe still were when he died. One argument didn't mean much when a couple had been married so many years.

Encouraged by her aunt, Michelle shared memories of her mother, a woman Dot hadn't known very well. When Michelle described how Wilma Clark taught her to cook, can, and preserve food the old-fashioned way, William's eyes filled with tears for the second time that day.

For the most part, Jill and Michael simply listened and kept quiet. Jill had no stories to share with people she'd only recently met, and Michael wasn't much of a storyteller no matter who he was with. Finally well past midnight, everyone was ready for bed. Michael took William and Justin to the only room with twin beds on the third floor, while Aunt Dot showed Michelle to the last room on the left in her wing.

Jill took Jack out to the backyard one last time, hoping to find a gray-eyed man nursing a glass of drug store wine. But the picnic table was empty of occupants. If Nick had been waiting for her, he wasn't anymore. Jill turned off the kitchen lights and crept up the steps. Leaving her clothes in a heap on the floor, she crawled between the sheets and slept the deep, dreamless sleep of the very young and the very lucky.

Wednesday morning

When she woke, Jill pulled on her last clean pair of shorts and a T-shirt and took the back stairs to the kitchen. Jack the beagle wagged his tail, ready for his walk, but no one else appeared to be up yet. She snapped on his leash and headed out the door. But when she reached the street, she saw William's beat-up old truck was gone. The Clark family had departed Sweet Dreams B&B without a final goodbye, at least not to her. Nick Harris's sedan was also missing from its usual parking sport.

Unfortunately, Nick's was the last vehicle Jill checked the whereabouts of before she and her companion broke into a jog towards downtown. The two of them passed every shop, restaurant, bar and municipal building before they ducked into the coffee shop for a latte and a complimentary dog biscuit. In no particular hurry, the two took the long, roundabout way home.

Jack noticed the commotion on the street the moment they

turned the corner. Jill had been admiring a neighbor's garden when the red and blue rotating lights of a police vehicle caught her attention in Aunt Dot's driveway.

'*What now?*' she muttered. Jack merely strained against his collar and barked.

'Where have you been?' Michael demanded when they were still forty feet away. He stood next to his car, which was on the street in front of the neighbor's house.

'What does it look like?' Jill said, closing the distance between them. 'I took Jack for a walk.'

Michael's normally rugged face was completely drained of color. 'Look at my car!' He pointed an accusing finger at his SUV.

Jill had no idea what he was talking about. Then she noticed Sheriff Adkins talking to Aunt Dot in the driveway and Nick Harris standing by the trunk of the Ford, jotting notes in his little book. 'What's wrong?' she asked.

Once she reached Michael's side, his agitation was all too apparent. Someone had smashed both passenger side windows with most likely a baseball bat. Shattered glass was scattered across the front and back seats and across the dashboard.

'This is so not good,' he moaned.

'Is anything missing?' Jill tightened her grip on Jack's leash since the dog's agitation had also ratcheted up.

'Yes, Jill, *everything* is missing.' Spittle flew from his mouth as he spoke. 'Whoever broke into my car took the video camera and all my equipment, including my light stands. They even stole the blank tapes and supplies I had stored in the trunk.'

Jill shook her head, confused. 'But you never leave your video camera in the car. I thought you slept with it every night.'

'I know, I know.' Michael sounded close to tears. 'I was so tired yesterday after the funeral that I didn't carry in my gear. Then we stayed up late listening to Mrs Clark and William's family. I meant to grab the camera before going to bed. But I forgot once everyone headed upstairs.'

Nick left his post at the trunk. 'I don't think this was a coincidence,' he said.

'What does that mean?' Jill asked.

Michael locked eyes with Nick. 'He means someone saw me videoing everyone who came to the funeral,' he stated flatly.

'Someone who didn't want law enforcement seeing the video and knew where you were staying.' Nick filled in the obvious details.

Jill pulled the beagle away from the vehicle. 'Most likely that person is the murderer. Have you dusted for fingerprints, Nick? Gathered any trace evidence they might have left behind?'

'Yes, Nancy Drew, those things occurred to me too. A deputy is on the way with the kit. I'm making sure no one gets close to the car and compromises any evidence left behind.' Nick bent down to scratch Jack behind the ears, then peered up at Jill. 'Looks like your exercise partner could use a drink of water. Why don't you and Michael wait for me inside the house? I'll join you in the kitchen once I'm no longer needed to secure the scene.'

Michael grabbed Jill's arm. 'He's right. We can't do anything out here. Let's get some coffee.'

As Jill and Michael walked up the driveway, Sheriff Adkins stopped talking to Aunt Dot as they passed. 'Morning, Miss Curtis.' Adkins tipped his hat.

'Good morning,' Jill gritted the words through clenched teeth.

When they reached the house, Michael held open the door for her. 'Did you happen to notice William, Michelle and Justin were gone before anyone else was up this morning? I believe they left while it was still dark, when nobody else was on the street.'

Jill shot him a glare on her way to the coffee maker. 'I think we would've heard if Justin took a baseball bat to your windows.'

'Not necessarily.' Michael slumped into a kitchen chair. 'We were sleeping in the back of the house with the windows closed and the air-conditioning on.'

She delivered two steaming cups of coffee to the table, along with the pitcher of milk. 'Why on earth would Justin or any of his family do that? You heard the detective – most likely it was someone who didn't want his face recognized at the funeral. Everyone saw William and Michelle at the funeral. Gordy got up in front of the congregation and gave the eulogy, for crying out loud.'

Michael blew on the surface of his mug. 'I'm not ruling out anyone. William and Michelle had no reason to leave so early.'

'It wasn't a member of the Clark family.' Jill kept her voice low but imbued her declaration with so much conviction Michael said nothing for several minutes. Instead, they sipped coffee and listened to the wall clock tick off the seconds and minutes.

'You're probably right,' he said at long last. 'Motive is important and the Clarks don't seem to have any.'

Jill didn't move a muscle, knowing more was coming.

'Nevertheless, as soon as the police release my car, I'm heading back to Chicago. Hopefully, tomorrow. I already called our boss while you were out with the dog.'

Jill's head snapped up. 'You already told Mr Fleming about the vandalism and theft?'

'Yeah, why not? That stolen equipment belonged to the news service. It wasn't mine.'

'What did he say?'

'Let's see . . .' Michael focused on the ceiling. 'He said it was a good thing I'd already sent in the first two segments, or our time here would have been a total waste. And he said to get back to Chicago as soon as possible with a copy of the police report, so he can file a claim with the company's insurance carrier.' He scraped his hands down his face.

'You're going home?' Jill studied the contents of her mug.

'Ah, yeah. Considering Fleming signs my paycheck and I can't finish the assignment with my iPhone. I think it's time for us both to head back to Chicago.'

'No way,' she snapped. 'I'm staying until Roger's killer is caught. Besides, there's a bigger story here in Spencer County.'

'Are we still talking about the same story – the popularity of bourbon tours?'

She squared her shoulders. 'Yes, that's one of the stories.'

'Jill, you're a travel writer, not an investigative reporter. And if you stop taking orders from headquarters, you might find yourself out of a job.'

'I realize that.' Jill released an exasperated sigh but refused to meet his eye. 'I'm hoping you can buy me some extra time.'

'I'll do what I can,' he said after a few uncomfortable moments. 'At least Mr Fleming liked what we've sent him so far. I'll tell him you're here working a fresh angle. And that I need to return with new equipment.'

'So you'll come back?' she asked.

'I will try, but I'm not losing my job.'

'Thanks, Michael.' Jill took hold of his arm.

With a snort, he shrugged off her grip. 'You realize that if we were boyfriend and girlfriend, I would have broken up with you long ago.'

Jill smiled. 'Yeah, I know. Partners are so much harder to get rid of.'

As he finished his coffee, his expression sobered. 'Just make sure no one takes a bat to your head, Curtis. I think you're under-estimating what's going on here.'

'I found Roger's body, remember? I'm not underestimating anyone or anything.'

Jill carried her second cup of coffee to the living room where she could watch the street in comfort . . . and watch the man in charge in secret.

Unfortunately, the action at Michael's car was soon over. Lieutenant Harris barked orders to the deputies with an evidence kit and pointed out the radius he wanted searched. Then he marched back to his car and drove away. No stopping in for a cup of coffee. No updating his new off-the-books assistant on the case. And no invitation for a romantic dinner that evening.

Jill had nothing to do but strip the beds used by the Clarks and start the laundry. Then she would figure out what to do with four cakes left over from the funeral.

Nick knew better than to connect potentially unrelated events into one grand conspiracy. Especially since acts of vandalism happened all the time in small towns – mailboxes smashed along a certain road or in a particular development, mustaches painted on posters of political candidates, and everyone's favorite, the town square decorated with streamers in a rival football team's colors. But the timing of Michael's vandalized car didn't fit within Nick's param-eters for random.

Most likely the deputies would find no fingerprints, no swatches of cloth ripped from a unique shirt, and no discarded cigarette butts beside the vehicle. Breaks like that only happened on TV shows with a sixty-minute window to bring the culprit to justice. Unfortunately, Erickson hadn't had time to download the video to his computer or upload it to the news agency's server before his car was ransacked. Nick's opportunity to view the faces of those at the funeral had been destroyed along with the windows.

On his way back to the station, Nick considered the recent vandalism at Founder's Reserve. Were overturned plants the handiwork of an inebriated wedding guest or someone with a darker agenda for the Shelbys? And which Shelby were they referring to in the epithet, *you ain't getting away with murder this time*?

All part of a grand conspiracy or random, unconnected events?

As Nick entered his temporary office, one of the officers who'd answered the malicious mischief complaint at Founder's Reserve was on his way out.

'Hey, Lieutenant Harris, I just put that report about the graffiti on your desk.' The deputy produced a cordial smile.

If they'd been back in Louisville, that officer wouldn't have been smiling. The deputy had answered the call at Founder's Reserve on Monday and now this was Wednesday. But Roseville wasn't Louisville and Nick wasn't his boss.

'Thanks, I'll take a look at it right now.' Nick was already seated with report in hand when he noticed Morris still lingering in the doorway.

'Was there something else, Deputy?' Nick peered over his reading glasses. 'Something that's not in the report?'

Morris slinked into the office and closed the door. 'Yes, actually. I grew up in this county and went to school with some of the guys who work for the Shelbys. The spray-painted graffiti wasn't the only trouble out at the distillery.'

'Have a seat.' Nick pointed at one of the padded chairs in front of his desk. 'I heard somebody tipped over the giant potted plants and made a mess on the patio. Is that what you're referring to?'

Morris checked over his shoulder before sitting down. 'Yeah, that's one of them. But there's been a string of incidents over a period of weeks. Usually when an employee discovers trouble they're told to clean up the mess or fix the problem but *not* call the police. Sometimes Mr Shelby calls his insurance agent, who takes pictures and files a claim. But sometimes the agent refuses to file a claim without a police report. Then the Shelbys have to eat the cost of the repair on their own.' Morris kept his voice barely above a whisper.

'Which Mr Shelby are you referring to?' Nick asked.

'Owen Shelby, the father. He's still the master distiller and in charge at Founder's Reserve.'

'Who told you this?' He pulled out his notepad.

Morris shook his head. 'One of the production employees spoke under the condition of anonymity.'

Nick rolled his eyes. 'So if I talk to Owen or Jamie Shelby, they'll deny all knowledge of these acts of vandalism?'

'That's just it, sir. My friend thinks that if you question Owen Shelby directly, he won't deny anything. Owen attends the same church as my friend and considers honesty his sacred duty.'

Nick considered the moral implication of omission of the truth versus commission of a falsehood but decided against questioning the man. 'Thank you, Deputy Morris. I think I'll drive out there right after I read your report. I appreciate your insight.'

Morris grinned and fled the office like a scared rabbit, his courage lasting only so long.

The incident report contained little information that could connect this to a larger crime, so Nick filled his travel mug and took the thirty-minute drive to Founder's Reserve. As he drove up the pristine tree-lined driveway, he contemplated a generational business: Owen had assumed responsibility from his father and grandfather before him, in hopes of one day passing the reins onto his son. But so much could happen to a corporate bottom line in the twenty-first century. The public's collective taste could change, while factors in a world economy could exert undue influence. Nick was glad he'd decided to pursue law enforcement and that his decision had been supported by his father, a mechanic, and his grandfather, a tobacco farmer.

Nick avoided the turn-off to the public parking and distillery tours, opting instead for the entrance marked Corporate Headquarters and Employees Only. 'Lieutenant Harris of the Kentucky State Police. I'm here to see Owen Shelby.' He passed his ID through the window of the security booth.

The guard studied his badge for a long moment. 'Is Mr Shelby expecting you, sir?'

'No, he is not, but I'm quite sure he'll make time for me.'

Actually, Nick wasn't sure of anything, but assumptions usually opened more doors than indecisiveness.

Picking up the phone, the guard turned his back on Nick. A

few minutes later, he handed Nick back his ID with a friendly smile. 'Follow this driveway to the end and park in any of the reserved spots. Enter the stone building through the double oak doors where Mr Shelby's assistant will be waiting for you.' Tipping his cap, the guard pushed a button to open the gate.

Nick followed the directions and was soon met by a well-dressed, middle-aged woman with a warm smile.

'Lieutenant Harris? I'm Deanne Orton. Will you follow me, please?' She led him down a long corridor of offices, all with their doors open, to the last office, this one with its door closed. With a well-manicured hand, she opened the door and gestured him in. 'Mr Shelby, this is Lieutenant Harris of the Kentucky State Police.'

Since Nick hadn't identified himself to her, Ms Orton must have paid good attention to the guard.

'Come in, Lieutenant. I'm Owen Shelby. Please, have a seat.'

In the few moments it took Shelby to reach his upholstered chair from his position at the windows, Nick not only assessed his surroundings but the man's appearance as well. Shelby looked to be in his late sixties, well-fed but not overweight, of medium height, with a thick shock of silver hair many men would kill for. 'What can I do for you today?'

'This morning I reviewed an incident report for vandalism in which a threat had been made,' Nick said, watching for a reaction.

'A threat? You must be mistaken, sir.' Shelby's face remained expressionless. 'Some kids decided to spray paint one of my rickhouses, but that was about it. My son never should have bothered the sheriff's department with this. I'm sure law enforcement has more important crime to worry about.' His smile revealed abnormally white teeth. At his age, they had to be veneers or dentures.

'The sheriff's department takes all complaints seriously, Mr Shelby, especially since that particular incident was by no means isolated.'

Owen grinned. 'You must be referring to those potted plants. Shoot, when a facility hosts a wedding with unlimited drinks, you learn how to handle a few drunks. It's hard enough to make sure nobody gets behind a wheel after they've been drinking. We sent two dozen people home in an Uber that night at our expense.

Potting soil spilled on the terrace is the least of our worries.' He held his stomach as he chuckled.

'Law enforcement appreciates your diligence in keeping our roadways safe.' Nick leaned forward in his chair. 'But there's been a lot of vandalism here at Founder's Reserve – incidents that you've chosen not to report.'

'Who told you that?' Shelby demanded.

'How I came by this information isn't important, especially since you're not denying it's true.'

The man's smile faded. 'You're not from the sheriff's department. I know most of the deputies that work for Jeff Adkins.'

Nick pulled a card from his wallet and placed it on the desk. 'No, sir, I'm not. I'm an investigator from the Kentucky State Police, the Louisville office.'

'Adkins requested reinforcement to track down hooligans with cans of spray paint? That's one big waste of taxpayer money!' A flush crept up Shelby's neck into his face.

'If that was the case, I would agree with you. But I was called in to investigate the murder of Roger Clark, the master distiller at Black Creek.'

'I know who Roger was,' he snapped. 'What I don't know is why you're wasting my time. My reasons for not reporting mischief by kids are my business.'

Nick picked a piece of lint from his pant leg. 'In a murder investigation anything out of the ordinary, anyone's behavior that's off the mark, becomes suspect. If a gang of punks has targeted Founder's Reserve, yet you refuse to report the crime at the expense of an insurance claim, then I want to know why.'

The two men glared at each other across the desk. Then Owen swiveled around in his chair. After he pressed a few buttons, several panels in the wall slid back, revealing a dozen security cameras with live feeds. Owen could watch everything happening at his distillery from the comfort of his office. Mashing, mixing, distilling, barreling, aging, bottling – every step in the process played out before their eyes. Other cameras mounted on the terrace and at various spots on the grounds kept track of what happened outdoors. There was even a camera recording who walked through the front door of corporate headquarters.

'Very impressive, sir,' Nick murmured.

'I run a multi-million-dollar business, not a moonshiner's still up in the hills. Keep watching this monitor.' Owen pointed at one scene as he pressed a series of buttons on a remote control. At first the screen went dark. Then a grainy video played out before their eyes of two young men weed-whacking the daffodils and tulips that surrounded the entrance and lined the driveway.

'This happened right before Easter this year.'

Nick walked around the desk and leaned in closer. 'That's Billy and Justin Clark, nephews of Roger Clark,' he said, after Shelby played the video a second time.

'I know who they are. Those boys are also Michelle Clark's brothers. That's why I'm not pressing charges.' Shelby switched the monitor back to the live feed of the bottling room.

'I don't understand.' Nick returned to the guest chair.

'Her brothers are angry because of the way my son treated Michelle. And I want my son to do the right thing.'

'And by the right thing, you mean . . .?' Nick let the question hang in the air.

'Jamie should marry that girl,' Shelby said. 'If he liked her well enough to sleep with her, then he should like her enough to walk down the aisle.'

'That's not really how things are anymore, sir.' Nick couldn't believe the words from his mouth. 'What I mean is your attorney can draw up papers to assure proper support until the child is an adult. Even visitation can be negotiated with a contract.'

Shelby flew into a rage. 'Well, that's how things are done in my family!' he shouted. 'Don't you think there are enough father-less children in the world? I won't have my first grandson or granddaughter growing up without a name!'

'I agree that a baby deserves a mother and a father, but you can't force Jamie to marry Michelle. What if she doesn't want to marry him?'

'She does. At least she did, before he publicly humiliated her.' Owen closed the wall of monitors behind his desk.

'And you think letting Billy and Justin get away with acts of vandalism will force your son's hand.' Nick tried to make sense of Shelby's logic.

'I told Jamie last night that the cost of every clean-up and repair is coming out of his cash flow. He's well aware that his bad behavior hurts business. This is still a God-fearing county we live in. So, Lieutenant Harris, have I clarified my off-the-mark behavior enough for you?' Shelby focused the scorn formerly directed at his son on Nick.

'I'd say you have. I appreciate your time today, sir.' Nick rose and stepped away from the desk. 'If there's anything the sheriff's department can do—'

'If I change my mind,' Shelby interrupted, 'I'll call Sheriff Adkins. Jeff can handle things in Spencer County just fine. We don't need any big guns sticking their nose in our business.' With that the master distiller stomped out of his office, summarily dismissing the trooper from Louisville.

But not before Nick plucked an empty Styrofoam cup from Owen's desktop. He headed back to the station to write his report, have the cup analyzed for DNA, and relay his conversation with Owen Shelby to the sheriff.

Adkins listened patiently until Nick finished. 'Can't say I'm surprised by the way Owen feels. Don't take this personally, Nick, but Roseville ain't like Louisville. People are used to handling matters on their own, especially a powerful man like Shelby.' The sheriff leaned back in his chair. 'His son's behavior might not raise eyebrows in Louisville, but it would in the circles Shelby runs in. Owen considers this a family matter. That's why he prefers to take care of it without police intervention.'

Nick swept a hand through this hair. 'For how long, Sheriff? What if the next time Billy and Justin start a fire and innocent people lose their lives? How will it look if the public finds out your office knew what was going on and did nothing?'

'The acts of vandalism took place on private property. Our hands are tied if Shelby refuses to press charges. If you have any suggestions, Lieutenant, I'm all ears.'

Nick thought for a moment. 'I think I'll drive up and pay a social call on the Clarks. Maybe Will doesn't know what his sons are up to. And even if he does, the boys might listen to some gentle persuasion.'

Adkins blew out his breath. 'You'd better take your friend along, Miss Curtis. Otherwise you won't make it halfway up their driveway. If they don't shoot you, they'll shoot out your tires. And that's a long walk back to town.'

Nick rolled his eyes. 'So much for law and order if I have to take a private citizen just to ask a few questions.'

'I'd be happy to send a few deputies, but I think you'd have more success with their newfound kinfolk.'

'I'll see if Miss Curtis is staying in town. Her partner plans to head back to Chicago as soon as we've finished processing his car.' Nick shoved his report back into the file.

'Let me know in the morning if you want those deputies,' Adkins said with a smile. 'The Clark land might be in the same county, but when you're atop that mountain you might as well be on the moon.'

Nick parked on the street and entered Sweet Dreams B&B through the kitchen door. He spotted just the person he wanted to see with her head in the refrigerator. 'Good evening, Jill. Looking for something to eat?'

'Hey, Nick.' Jill withdrew several containers as she straightened up. 'Tomorrow is trash pickup. Aunt Dot asked me to clean out the fridge of leftovers that got pushed to the back. If you're hungry, we've got chicken from yesterday that's still good.' She dumped the remnants of the party tray and the sweet potato casserole into a trash bag.

'Sounds good. When you're done, we can take that chicken and box of wine out to the picnic table. I've got a favor to ask you.'

Jill tugged down her T-shirt which had been showing a remarkable expanse of skin. 'I've got some news for you too. Why don't you take everything out now, along with Jack? I'll finish the fridge and wash up. I don't want to smell like pickled artichokes.'

Nick pulled the table in the shade and set out cups, plates, napkins and the container of chicken, along with extra plates in case Michael or Mrs Clark joined them.

When Jill arrived ten minutes later, her plaid shorts were gone, replaced by an ankle-length sundress and flip flops. 'I tossed a spinach salad so dinner will be at least halfway healthy.' She placed the bowl on the table.

'Anyone joining us?' Nick poured two glasses of white wine.

'Nope. Aunt Dot ate a sandwich and went to bed early. She's still tired from yesterday. And Michael is busy packing. He said he'll eat later. You have me to yourself.' Jill's grin could best be described as playful.

'When is Michael going back to Chicago?' he asked.

'He called a glass replacement company today. As long as you're done with his car, they may be able to replace the windows as early as tomorrow afternoon. Michael feels helpless down here without his video camera. And the boss wants a copy of the police report to submit to insurance.'

'You're not going with him?' Nick watched her over his wine glass.

'I am not.'

'Will Michael come back with new equipment?'

'He says he will, but the boss has the last word.' Jill took a swallow of wine.

'But he doesn't about you staying in Roseville without your videographer and with your story finished?' Nick tried to phrase his question benignly.

'You are correct. An excellent deduction, Trooper Harris. The boss has no say-so about that.' Jill's grin stretched from one corner of her mouth to the other.

'In that case, I'll ask my favor. I need directions to the Clark farm up in the hills. I want to talk to William about two of his sons.'

'Even with directions, you might not find the place.' Jill scooped spinach onto both plates and added sweet-and-sour dressing.

'That's what Sheriff Adkins thought too. So if you have no previous commitment for tomorrow, I'd like you to join me. Leg, thigh or white meat?' he asked.

'I'll take the small breast.' Jill pointed with her fork. 'Since I have no plans, and since I'd hate for my cousins twice-removed-through-marriage to shoot someone I'm *fond* of, I'll tag along.'

Nick divided up the chicken, then lifted his glass in salute. 'To a successful field trip tomorrow.' He clinked glasses with her. 'Now I'll fill you in on the case so far and also what I learned from Owen Shelby at Founder's Reserve.'

'I see you're taking our partnership seriously.' Jill took a bite of chicken and grinned.

By the time Nick had explained the recent exploits of Billy and Justin Clark, Jill's smile was long gone.

TWELVE

After her eventful day, followed by an insightful dinner with Nick Harris, Jill had not slept well. First, Michael's car had been broken into and his expensive equipment stolen while the car had been parked on a major thoroughfare. Then Lieutenant Harris had seen video of her cousins committing felony-level vandalism at Founder's Reserve Distillery, one of several instances according to Owen Shelby. Roseville no longer was the sleepy little town she and Michael had thought it to be.

Justin Clark might still be a minor, but Billy certainly wasn't. And Jill was willing to bet this wasn't Billy's first brush with the law. Fortunately Owen had chosen not to press charges against Michelle's brothers. And since Nick invited her along to ask questions, she might be able to keep one angry young man out of jail and another from having a black mark on his juvenile record.

Owen's decision to make his son bear the cost of clean-up and repairs had touched her heart. But knowing Jamie as well as she did, Jill put little stock in Owen's method of motivation. Men like Jamie weren't easily pressured by an inconvenient pregnancy.

Jill had just poured herself a second cup of coffee when Michael padded into the kitchen. Dressed in his Cubs T-shirt and baggy shorts, with his damp hair hanging in his eyes, her partner looked much younger than his twenty-seven years old.

'Are we the only ones up?' Michael reached for a mug from the cupboard.

Jill filled his mug to the rim. 'Nope, everyone's up. Mrs Clark left early for an appointment with her attorney. And Nick took Jack for a walk to get some exercise.'

'Has Nick made any progress on the case?' Michael added lots of sugar to his mug.

'Still no word on the security guard. Don't you think it strange the way the Maxwells just left their house like that?'

Michael's mouth dropped open. 'Just like that? They left without selling their house?'

'Not everyone can afford the American dream, Mikey. The Maxwells had been renters. The sheriff's department is trying to track them down through mutual friends, but I doubt Nick has enough evidence to arrest the guy. Looks like either Elmer Maxwell turned off the cameras for Black Creek on the night of the murder or someone else erased the tapes after Maxwell went home.'

'I thought Black Creek warehouse had no cameras.'

'True, but there were cameras at every exit and entrance. Seeing who came and went might be helpful.'

Michael thumped the package of bagels down on the counter. 'They should arrest the guy for obstruction of justice.'

Jill laughed. 'That's exactly what I said. But proving obstruction is no walk in the park. I gather by your outfit you'll be traveling today?'

'Nick emailed me a copy of the police report for insurance purposes and said me and my Volvo are free to leave town. As soon as I have the windows fixed, I'm getting on the road. The glass guy is coming at eleven. Weird, no? Nick's staying in the next room, yet we usually communicate with text messages.'

'Did I hear my name mentioned?' Nick and the beagle walked through the back door. One of them was panting, while the other had an attractive sheen on his tanned face.

Why did sweat look a lot better on men than it did on women? 'You did,' Jill said. 'Michael is leaving as soon as his windows are replaced.'

'It's not too late to change your mind and come with me.' Michael slathered both halves of his bagel with butter.

'Sorry, old boy,' said Nick. 'Jill agreed to come with me today. We're heading up the mountain to bust some moonshiners. Right now, Jack and I are going to take a shower.' Nick and the beagle headed up the stairs.

'You'd better be kidding, Harris,' Jill called after him. 'Otherwise you and I aren't going anywhere near the Clark homestead!' Her voice rose to reach the second floor.

'What's the matter with you?' Michael demanded, aghast. 'Why would you take a state cop to visit your family? You know either William or Billy has a still somewhere on the farm.'

'Nick was joking. He wants to question my cousins about vandalism at Founder's Reserve. I'll make sure his focus stays front and center and he doesn't meander into the woods. He's not an AFT agent.'

'He's still law enforcement. You're putting Nick in a precarious position if he spots something illegal.'

'I'll make sure he doesn't.' Jill made a brave statement, yet had no idea how she could ensure anything.

'This is a bad idea.' Michael swallowed the rest of his coffee.

'It was Nick's idea. He asked for my help. He's not interested in illegal bourbon production.'

'One of these days you'll learn, Curtis. You can't play both sides against the middle.' Michael picked up his breakfast and carried it to the front porch.

'I want Roger Clark's killer caught,' she called after him, something she'd been doing a lot lately. 'That's whose side I'm on!'

When the screen door slammed, Jill wasn't sure whether Michael had heard her or not. That was the thing about her partner: he had the uncanny ability to see through every one of her less-than-brilliant plans.

Jill packed sandwiches, several bottles of water, and a few pieces of fruit into a soft-sided cooler. Then she decided to clean Aunt Dot's kitchen while she waited. She had just finished mopping the floor when Nick and the dog reappeared at the bottom of the stairs. With his tail wagging, Jack skidded across the wet tiles.

'A woman's work . . .' Jill muttered as she turned to assess Nick's appearance. 'Jeans and sneakers – a good choice. Your usual suit, tie, and shoulder holster won't do for a visit to the Clarks. May I assume you'll be unarmed during our trip?'

'You may not.' Nick's gray eyes locked with hers. 'No professional lawman would venture into unknown territory without his weapon.'

Jill set the bucket and mop in the pantry. 'In that case, we're ready to go. I've got Mace in my purse in case Justin tries to get the drop on me.'

'Just make sure you aim it in the right direction.' Nick delivered his warning without a hint of a smile.

On the drive up the mountain, Nick talked about growing up with three sisters in a one-bathroom house. Jill opened up about being a lonely only child. Both would have readily switched places with the other. When they finally reached the hard-to-find driveway for the Clarks, Jill hopped out and tied a handkerchief to the sedan's antennae.

'Why are we running up the white flag of surrender?' he asked, rolling down the window.

'I don't know how they do it, but the Clarks know when someone's coming up their driveway. I want them to know we come in peace.' Jill climbed back in and buckled her seatbelt.

'They probably buried a trip-wire under the leaves and dirt that sets off an alarm.' Nick's expression remained unreadable behind his dark glasses, but a muscle tightened in his neck.

When the cabin came into view, he parked a fair distance away and reached for a handgun in the glovebox. 'Don't worry. I won't shoot unless I'm shot at.' He tucked the weapon into an ankle holster under his jeans.

'Clever,' she said. 'You only *look* unarmed.' Together they walked the remaining distance to the cabin.

Before they reached the front steps, Billy Clark stepped onto the porch with a shotgun. He leaned the gun against the railing. 'Now why would you bring a lawman on a social call, *cousin*?' Billy added a negative inflection to the word.

'Hi, Billy. This is Lieutenant Harris of the Kentucky State Police and he's a *friend* of mine.' Jill added her own inflection.

William Clark joined his older son on the porch. 'Stay in the house, Justin,' he barked over his shoulder. 'What's the meaning of this, Jill?'

Nick answered for her. 'Good morning, Mr Clark. I have a few *unofficial* questions for your sons.' He placed one foot on the bottom step. 'May we join you on the porch?'

William spat a blob of something into the bushes. 'Gordy ain't here. He's at work, trying to get Black Creek into full production.'

Jill stepped in front of Nick. 'His questions are for Billy and Justin. Could we sit with you a spell?'

William's glare softened when he focused on Jill. ''Spose we ain't got much choice. You sit there, Billy.' He pointed at one of the rockers. 'But leave the shotgun where it is. Justin, you bring out two kitchen chairs for Jill and her friend.' The patriarch lowered himself into the other rocker.

'That cop's got a gun at his ankle,' Billy sneered.

'Then don't give him a reason to use it. Do as I say, boy!' William shouted.

Surprisingly, both sons complied with their father's request. However, Billy grabbed one of the kitchen chairs from Justin and placed it ten feet away. 'I like the breeze better over here. You sit by Pa, cousin.' He pointed at the rocking chair.

Nick took one of the chairs and placed it across from Billy's. 'Now that we're all comfortable . . .' He jumped in without preamble. 'There's been a lot of vandalism around Roseville. On the night of your brother's funeral, someone smashed the windows of the videographer's car and stole his camera. They also broke into the trunk and stole his lighting equipment.'

William turned to face Jill. 'We were with you all night until we went home the next day.'

'Billy wasn't,' she corrected. 'He didn't come to Dot's house after the funeral.'

'I didn't steal no fancy camera,' Billy shouted at Nick. 'Wouldn't know how to use it and I don't wanna learn.'

Nick glared back with an equal amount of contempt. 'Maybe you wanted to sell the stuff. Or maybe you just smashed the windows and let someone else help themselves.'

Billy shook his head. 'I didn't smash any windows. And I ain't got nothing against Jill's partner.'

'That's good to hear.' Nick shifted on the ladderback chair. 'Because while Michael was shooting video in Black Creek a few days ago, someone switched off the power at his end of the building. Michael got stuck inside an elevator for hours, which could have proved deadly if Jill hadn't found him in time.'

'That sure wasn't me. Like I said, I ain't got nothing against you or your partner.' Billy directed this at Jill. 'And I ain't got a key to Black Creek Distillery.'

'Maybe the security guard left the door open for you,' Jill suggested.

William pulled a flask from his pocket and took a swallow. 'You two got this all wrong. My sons loved their uncle and would never cause mischief inside his distillery!'

'That could very well be the case, Mr Clark.' Nick's tone softened. 'But Spencer County deputies were recently called to Founder's Reserve on a vandalism complaint. Someone spray-painted the message *you ain't getting away with murder this time* across the back of one of Shelby's rickhouses.'

Jill kept her eyes on Billy while Nick described the graffiti. His brown eyes had darkened to black holes in his face.

'What's that got to do with us?' William squawked. 'My boys were home with me.'

'Hold on, Will,' Jill said. 'Lieutenant Harris hasn't told you which night the vandalism was. How can you be so sure of your sons' whereabouts?'

'Please hear me out, sir.' Nick took over the questioning. 'I'd heard damage had been done at Founder's Reserve that the owner refused to report to authorities. That didn't sound right, so I drove out to question Owen Shelby myself.'

Justin sprang to his feet. 'Michelle's been gone a long time. I'll go see if she needs help rounding up those goats.'

'Sit down, boy.' William's snarl lifted the tiny hairs on Jill's neck.

'Turns out,' Nick continued, 'the rumors of vandalism were true – trash cans had been dumped and contents scattered; potted plants overturned on the terrace with dirt spread everywhere, spring flowers weed-whacked into oblivion by the front entrance and up the driveway. Owen Shelby showed me a videotape of the weed-whacking right before Easter. There were your sons, Billy and Justin, front and centered.'

William gripped the arms of his chair so hard his fingers turned white.

'We didn't know about the cameras, Pa,' Justin whined, his complexion as pale as his dad's knuckles.

'Shut up, boy. This is what you were doing those nights you went to town? You said you were at the library learning on the computer.' William aimed his question at his older son.

'I needed to right the wrong done to Michelle by Shelby.' Billy rose to his full height.

'What are you talking about?' William's face contorted into a mass of wrinkles.

'Owen Shelby agrees that a wrong has been done to Michelle.' Not to be at a height disadvantage, Nick also scrambled to his feet. 'That's why he didn't press charges even though he recognized you two in the video. He hopes to motivate Jamie into doing the right thing.'

'What exactly would the *right thing* be?' A soft voice drifted from the interior of the cabin. A moment later, Michelle stepped onto the porch.

Nick spoke without considering the consequences. 'Owen wants Jamie to marry you, Miss Clark. He wants his first grandson or granddaughter to have the Shelby name.'

Michelle had little opportunity to react before William pushed to his feet and slapped her across the face. 'Jamie Shelby, that worthless scum? You told me that baby belonged to Carl from the Sunoco station.'

For several moments, it was pure chaos on the porch.

'Don't you dare raise a hand to your daughter!' Nick shouted, trying to squeeze between the two.

'Leave her alone,' demanded Billy, while he and Justin grabbed their father's arms.

And Jill? She was probably least effective when she jumped up and screamed, 'Stop it, Will. Think about the baby!'

It was truly a miracle that nobody got shot.

'Would everyone *please* sit down?' The bellowing voice of reason belonged to Michelle.

Three of the five did as she requested, while Nick and Billy took a few steps but remained standing, glaring at each other.

'I didn't tell you the truth, Pa, because I knew you hated the Shelbys. All because some long-dead Shelby stole a few acres from one of our long-dead ancestors.'

Will, back in his rocking chair, remained defiant. 'It was no small piece of land, girl. It was sixty of the best acres in the valley. Just look at what the Shelbys have today and look at how we live.'

Michelle perched on the footstool. 'The way I heard it, our ancestors preferred cattle-rustling and general thievery to farming anyway.'

Will leaned toward his daughter. 'Who told you that, Jamie Shelby?'

'Yeah, he did. And at first I didn't believe him. But I looked up the story in Spencer County history books. The Cook farm sat fallow for years. And three different books said the Cooks started the fight that got one of them killed. So when the Cooks set the Shelby house on fire, it was out of jealousy, not revenge.' Michelle reached for her father's hand. 'That feud was a long time ago and should be forgotten.'

'This was how you wanted to heal the rift between families?' Billy pointed at Michelle's rounded belly.

'Nope.' Michelle got back on her feet. 'I used to like Jamie and found him attractive. But I don't anymore and I sure don't want to marry him.' She grabbed hold of Billy's shirt. 'You never should have done that at Founder's Reserve. I won't have my brothers going to jail.' Michelle placed both hands on her belly. 'This is my baby. His or her last name will be Clark, same as mine. Now you tell Cousin Jill the truth about her partner's car.'

The porch grew very quiet. Then Billy turned on one boot heel towards Jill. 'I had nothing to do with Michael's broken windows or him being trapped in an elevator,' he muttered. 'And I sure didn't have anything to do with Uncle Roger's death.' Billy directed this at Nick.

'You can tell Owen Shelby there'll be no more vandalism at his distillery, Lieutenant Harris,' Michelle added. 'But he needn't worry about me. I would like him and all of you to stay out of my business.' Michelle glared at each of them in turn. Then she walked back into the house, letting the screen door slam.

THIRTEEN

Thursday afternoon

After Michelle stomped into the house, all the air on the porch seemed to have gone with her. For a few uncomfortable moments, Jill just sat there, wondering what to do next.

Nick broke the silence first. 'Thank you, Mr Clark, for allowing me to question your sons. As long as Owen Shelby refuses to press charges, and assuming there's no more vandalism at the distillery, Billy and Justin are in the clear.' His gaze moved from one to the other.

Justin lifted his right hand as though giving testimony. 'I'll never set foot on Founder's Reserve property again. You have my word, Mr Harris.' Then the boy ran inside the house as though chased by a swarm of hornets.

'What about you, Billy?' Jill moved next to her scruffy cousin.

'Trying to protect someone's honor and this is the thanks I get?' Billy shrugged with consummate ambivalence. 'Since Michelle don't want to get married either, I got no reason to drive all that way. Besides, I've got plenty around here to keep me busy.' He, too, pulled a flask from his pocket and took a hearty gulp as though baiting the state trooper.

Jill took it as their signal to leave. 'Bye, Michelle,' she hollered through the screen door. 'Let Aunt Dot and me know when your baby arrives.' Then spontaneously, Jill leaned over and kissed William's cheek. 'I promise less drama the next time I come over,' she whispered.

'Don't bring no lawmen and there won't be any drama,' Will said wryly, and started to rock.

Jill took hold of Nick's arm and strolled down the steps as though they were a couple going to the prom. She waited until they were away from the log cabin to express her opinion. 'Well, that wasn't the best use of taxpayers' money for gasoline or your time on the job.'

Nick lifted an eyebrow as he climbed behind the wheel. 'What do you mean?'

'We solved crimes that weren't actual crimes since Owen never filed any police reports. And we still don't know who locked Michael in the elevator or broke his windows.'

'Oh, I wouldn't say our time was wasted. At least we know Billy's vandalism had nothing to do with Roger's murder.'

'What we need is a lead.' Jill pulled a bottle of water from the cooler.

'What I need is food.' Nick turned the vehicle around and began the long trek down the mountain. 'I'm starving. If you share your lunch with me, I'll share what I found out from Mrs Clark.'

Jill pulled the cooler from the back seat and handed him a sandwich. 'Ham and cheese. Tell me what you know.'

'I can't eat and talk, especially not on this minefield of a driveway. Wait until I reach the county road.' Nick took a bite of sandwich.

Jill patiently waited until he accelerated to forty miles per hour on the paved highway, which was a breakneck speed considering the twists and turns. Then she handed him a fresh Georgia peach. 'Here's your dessert, but first it's time to talk, Detective Harris.'

Nick bit into the piece of fruit. 'No offense, but I'm really glad you threw out the fried chicken. I don't want to see another piece for a long while.'

'No offense taken.' Jill nibbled on her sandwich. 'Now, what do you know that I don't?'

'I saw Mrs Clark when I came downstairs this morning. She found Roger's will in their bank safety deposit box so she was on her way to see her lawyer. This was a *new,* updated version of the one they kept in their home safe.' Nick dabbed his lips with a napkin.

Jill stopped eating. 'She showed you a copy and not me?'

'Only because you were still sleeping. The new one will soon be filed and made public record, but she wanted us to know before we headed up Clark mountain.'

'Does the new will impact Roger's murder investigation?'

'It might.' Nick finished the peach and threw the pit out the window. 'In the old will, Roger left an eighty percent share of Black Creek Distillery to Gordon, his nephew and operations manager. The other twenty percent was to be divided between William, Michelle, Billy, and Justin. Each was to receive a five percent share, with the stipulation of no voting rights. Gordon would have assumed full control of the distillery and would make all decisions, including the decision if and when to sell or take the private company public.'

'And in the new will?'

'In the new one, the eighty percent share goes to Mrs Clark, but the other twenty percent distribution remains the same.'

'I guess crabby old Roger loved his wife after all,' she murmured.

'Was there any doubt of that?' Nick sounded confused.

'No. Don't pay any attention to me.' Jill threw out the rest of her sandwich. 'So Roger cut out Gordon, who'd been his right-hand man. I wonder why?'

'According to Mrs Clark, Roger and Gordon had a nasty argument the night before he died. He suspected Gordy of feeding information to Owen Shelby, among other things. Roger drew up the handwritten will the next morning. Since he had a bank teller and the manager witness and notarize the document, I'm betting it's legal.'

'What about Sweet Dreams Bed and Breakfast?' Jill's stomach flip-flopped with anxiety.

'That didn't change between the first and second documents. The B and B, along with their bank and investment accounts, goes to Dorothy Clark.'

'I hope this doesn't make Aunt Dot a suspect,' Jill said, only half joking.

Appropriately, Nick produced only half a smile. 'Not necessarily, since that's common among married couples.'

'Hmm. I hope I'm not back to being a suspect.' Jill studied the passing scenery. 'Where exactly are we going?'

Nick didn't answer right away. 'Have you noticed we never cross paths with Gordon Clark? I was hoping we'd run into him at the family farm.'

Jill peered at him over her sunglasses. 'Forgive me for stating the obvious, but Gordy had lots of responsibility before Roger died, and now he's running the show at Black Creek. He has no time to help pick peas in the garden.'

'I agree, but don't you find it odd Gordon hasn't visited his aunt since Roger died? And he went out of his way to avoid us at Trehanny's and at the funeral.'

'I noticed that too. At least we assume the guy in mirrored sunglasses and double-breasted suit giving the eulogy was Gordon. He looked more like a hitman than part of the Clarks. Instead of hanging with his family at the cemetery, Gordy stayed in the last row. Despite his rather heartfelt eulogy, when it was time to put flowers on the casket, old Gordy threw his rose on the ground and walked back to his car.' Jill tuned to a soft rock station on the radio.

'Why didn't you mention this before?' Nick pulled off the road and switched off the radio.

'Because my granny taught me to ignore rude behavior, since those people are just looking for attention.'

'Interesting. Care to report any other rude behavior by your quasi cousin?'

Jill checked to see if he was mocking her. 'There was the night of the wake. Gordy didn't come up to the casket to pay his respects like everyone else. And when he wasn't giving me the evil-eye, he seemed to be watching you, Lieutenant Harris. I guess the new boss at Black Creek Distillery doesn't appreciate Dick Tracy and his sidekick, Nancy Drew.'

Nick arched an eyebrow. 'I think of myself more as the Sherlock Holmes type.'

'No way, not with your southern accent.'

Nick laughed but his smile quickly faded. 'You told me Roger Clark rushed back to work Tuesday evening.'

'Yep, that was the day Nick and I arrived. He told Aunt Dot there was a problem at the plant.'

'Maybe that problem involved Gordon, since Roger changed his will the next day.'

'But would Roger have told his former heir about the change? Wouldn't it be more fun to save that juicy news for a big surprise?'

'Hard to say what a man like Roger considered fun, but it's time to have a chat with Gordon Clark.' Nick punched the address of Black Creek into the GPS, checked his rear-view mirror and pulled onto the pavement.

'And we won't take *no* for an answer.' Jill crunched up her empty water bottle.

Too bad workers at the distillery made sure *no* was the only answer they heard. From the security guard at the front desk: 'I'm sorry, Miss Curtis, Lieutenant Harris. Mr Clark is somewhere on the floor and cannot be reached.'

From the second-in-command in production: 'Mr Clark left specific instructions that he's not to be disturbed.'

And finally from his office assistant: 'If you'll leave your names and number and I'll see that Mr Clark calls you this evening.'

Nick flashed his badge a second time. 'I'm sure you don't mean to hinder a police investigation, Miss Keyes, but that's exactly what you're doing. Either get Mr Clark on the phone, or tell us his location, or I will arrest you. Those are your choices.'

The young secretary didn't know whether to cry or stomp her foot in sheer exasperation. 'One moment, please,' she sniffed. Then she turned her back while she typed in a text to the boss.

A ding soon signaled an answer. 'Mr Clark said if you'll wait in the conference room, he'll be with you as soon as possible.' Miss Keyes swept open the door.

'If Mr Clark's definition of *soon* is more than fifteen minutes,' Nick muttered, 'I'm calling the sheriff for backup.'

Pursing her plump pink lips, Miss Keyes nodded and tottered away on her stilettos. But she must have conveyed the message because Gordon Clark stomped into his office ten minutes later. Dressed in a pin-striped suit and starched white shirt, today the oldest of William's offspring looked more like a Wall Street stockbroker than a bourbon maker from a long line of moonshiners. Gordon shot his cuffs, straightened his silk tie and stretched out a hand to Nick.

'Excuse me for keeping you waiting, lieutenant. Please have a seat. With my uncle's passing, I'm trying to put out one fire after another on the production line. Figuratively speaking, of course.'

After shaking hands with Nick, Gordon turned to Jill. 'We haven't been properly introduced yet, Miss Curtis. I believe you're a distant cousin of my Aunt Dot's?' He offered his hand to her as well. 'It's funny Dot never mentioned you before.'

Jill formed two immediate impressions: one, Gordon's skin felt damp and clammy like the frog she'd rescued from Jack's jaw yesterday. And two, Gordy's eyes had only slightly softened their severe glint.

Jill withdrew her hand. 'Dot had a falling out with my grand-mother years ago. Granny never told me about her cousin until recently, when she heard about my upcoming Kentucky trip.' She sat down in one of the chairs. 'But I didn't come here to discuss my connection to your aunt. Lieutenant Harris and I have a few questions.'

'We?' Perching on the corner of his desk, Gordon directed his query to Nick. 'Why would a Kentucky State Trooper team up with a travel writer to investigate my uncle's murder?'

Nick flinched. 'Some of the backroads in Spencer County don't pop up on GPS. Jill was kind enough to show me the way to your father's farm. We're on our way back from there. The questions I have are informal, but if you prefer to have your attorney present . . .'

Gordon considered this. 'Ask me what you want. I have nothing to hide, but I do need to get back to work.'

'Sheriff Adkins's notes were unclear about several things. Why didn't you pick up when the security guard called you last Wednesday? Elmer Maxwell was sick and needed to leave.'

'I told the sheriff I was on my way home for a minor family emergency. Just like GPS is unreliable in the hills, cell phones don't always work either.'

'What kind of emergency?'

'My sister thought she might be in labor. But it turned out to be a false alarm.' Gordon crossed his legs at the ankles.

'Are you a trained medical professional, Mr Clark?' Nick asked.

'No, but I can follow step-by-step instructions in the birthing manual better than Billy or my dad, at least until the midwife gets there.'

'Michelle isn't planning to go to a hospital?' Jill almost fell out of her chair.

Gordy's evil glare returned. 'That is none of your business. Even if you are related to Dot, you're certainly not related to us.'

Jill swallowed the snide retort which sprang to mind. 'Whether or not I'm related has no bearing on the safe delivery of a child.'

'I'll pass that along, Miss Curtis. Now, do you have eight grand to go with your unsolicited opinion? Because I don't, and that's what the hospital requires upfront since Michelle has no health insurance.'

'I'll check my bank balance,' Jill mumbled, fuming.

'Getting back to Roger,' Nick interjected. 'Do you remember what you two argued about last Tuesday, the night before he died?'

Gordon huffed out his breath. 'You're joking, right? Not a day went by that we didn't argue. Uncle Roger might have put me in charge of production, but he never stopped micro-managing the distillery. I didn't take it personally.' He slipped off the desk. 'Now if that's all you need . . .'

Nick responded with another question. 'Were you aware that you were Roger's major heir in his will?'

As the color drained from his face, Gordon stopped picking imaginary fuzz from his sleeve. 'Roger left Black Creek to *me*?'

'He did. At least he did in his original will.'

'What do you mean by original?'

'Exactly that. Last Wednesday Roger stopped at the bank with a new will, this one handwritten which he had witnessed and notarized and locked in his safety deposit box. Mrs Clark emptied the box out yesterday and discovered the new document. She gave it to their attorney to file in probate court.'

'Can this new will be legal?' Gordon thundered. Oddly, he aimed his rage at Jill.

Nick shrugged. 'I'm not a lawyer, but I'm guessing it is.'

'And suddenly this little gold-digger is Roger's heir?' He hooked a thumb at Jill so there would be no misunderstanding.

'Why would he include me?' Jill choked back a laugh. 'Roger met me for the first time for five minutes last Tuesday.'

Gordon shook his head as though trying to dispel a nightmare. 'Look, we'll let the courts decide whether or not I inherit this white elephant. In the meantime, I still have a job to do. If you have any more questions, Lieutenant Harris, contact my lawyer. My secretary will supply you with the number. As for you,' he said to Jill, 'I'd appreciate you staying away from me and my family. The last thing we need is more cousins.' Gordy marched from his office without as much as a backward glance.

'Well, that was enlightening.' Jill stretched her arms over her head. 'I think we should celebrate by you buying me dinner.'

'It would be my pleasure, but I'm not sure what we're cele-brating.' Nick guided her out of Gordon's office and down the hall.

Jill checked to make sure no one was within earshot. 'If facial expressions can be trusted, Gordy already knew he was Roger's heir. Their argument on Tuesday must have been a real doosie. Other than that snide remark about me, Gordy didn't ask about the new will. If Roger threatened to disinherit him after the fight, Gordon plotted to kill him on Wednesday, not realizing Roger had already changed his will.'

'You have a vivid imagination, but we need proof to back up your theories.' Nick pushed open the front door, the warm air hitting their faces like a slap after the over-conditioned interior of Black Creek. 'Besides, Gordon Clark has an alibi for the evening of the murder.'

'You bought that baloney about rushing home to deliver Michelle's baby?' Jill grabbed his arm in the middle of the parking lot.

'Of course not. But by the time we get ahold of Michelle to verify his alibi, Gordon will have reached her first. Blood is thicker than first-cousins-twice-removed-by-marriage.' Nick patted her hand affectionately.

'You got that right.' Jill waited while Nick fumbled with his keys. 'Where do we go from here?'

'Pick a restaurant, Jill. The sky's the limit.'

'Let's go to that barbeque place by the fairground. But actually, I was referring to the case.' She ducked her head into his car.

'I intend to find out everything I can about Gordon Clark, and then take a hard look at Black Creek's financials.'

'What should I do?' Jill practically levitated with excitement.

'Like Gordon pointed out, a state investigator shouldn't need help from a travel writer. It's not . . . how things are done. But you could direct me to this barbeque place. I haven't found the fairground during my forays around town.' Nick punctuated with an amazing smile.

Jill sucked in a deep breath, crossed her arms and pouted. 'Google it, Harris. There's only one barbeque joint in Roseville. And just for the record, this isn't a date. Since I can't help, we're just two fellow travelers who happened to book rooms at the same bed and breakfast.'

Nick pulled out his phone. 'I seem to have shot myself in the foot.'

'You sure have. Just remember, Nick, this dinner is on you and I'm starving.'

In spite of herself, Jill couldn't remember so enjoyable a meal. She ate a vast quantity of pulled pork, three baby back ribs, five barbeque chicken wings, and enough coleslaw to keep America's cabbage growers happy, along with a mug of Bud Light.

Nick consumed even more, along with two mugs of Coors.

Once the karaoke started up, it became impossible to stay mad at Nick. Not that she'd planned to stay mad at him. He was right. She was just a travel writer, but she knew in her heart she had helped with the case. And he knew it too.

When they got back to Sweet Dreams B&B, both with leftovers in doggy bags Jack would never see, Nick paused on the front porch. 'Now if this had been a date, Miss Curtis, I'd try to kiss you goodnight. But since you drew a line in the sand, I'll simply tip my hat and say goodnight.' He opened the door with his key and followed through with his intentions.

'You are one exasperating man, Harris,' she called up the steps.

'Someday you'll let me change your mind.' And just like that he disappeared down the hall into his room.

Jill was left alone to take Jack out, get the coffee ready for the morning, and pace the floor of her room. When she couldn't remain upright another moment, she washed her face, pulled on jammies and crawled into bed. She had just started to doze when her phone dinged from its position on the charger.

Michael. With everything that had gone on today, she'd forgotten about her partner making the six-hour journey from Roseville to the Windy City. Bolting upright in bed, Jill read his short and sweet text: *Where the heck are you? I've called several times and you haven't picked up. If you're home, Jilly, and if it's not too much trouble, call me.*

She knew Michael was annoyed since he'd called her *Jilly*, her least favorite nickname. She glanced at the clock on her nightstand and then punched in his number. It might already be midnight, but he probably just got home. He picked up on the second ring.

'Hello, Mikey,' she crooned. 'You must have really missed me if you texted three times and called twice.'

'Of course I missed you, and I would've appreciated a little concern. What if I'd gotten a flat tire?'

'Calling Triple-A would make more sense than calling me. I've never changed a tire in my life.'

'What if I'd been worried about you heading up the mountain? Maybe your kinfolk wouldn't be as pleased to see you a second time.'

'I went with a cop who never goes anywhere without his firearm. And for the record, I never got your calls or texts because we were out-of-range for most of the day. Then my battery died because my phone roamed for a signal the entire time.'

'Your new nickname should be Queen of Excuses.'

'It's all true, Erickson. Now give me an abbreviated version of your news. I don't need to hear the number of potty-breaks you took or what you ate for supper. It's the middle of the night.'

'Mr Fleming . . . remember him? He's still our boss. This morning, while they were replacing the windows, I scanned the police report and sent it to him. Fleming said there shouldn't be a problem regarding my car repairs or replacing the stolen equipment—'

'Great!' she interrupted. 'See? You worry too much.'

'And you don't worry enough. Fleming isn't happy about you not coming back with me. His exact words were: "The Roseville segments are finished. Why should the news service pay her expenses while she visits with her Kentucky relatives?".'

Jill bolted upright. 'What did you tell him?'

'I convinced the boss that you were following a new angle down there, one that would take the cake on distillery tours.'

'Thanks, Mikey.'

'Don't thank me yet. Fleming said I should get my new equipment within a couple of days. Then I can head back down to Kentucky, but not to Roseville. He wants us both to head to Lexington.'

'Lexington? That's all the way on the other side of the state. There are plenty of other distilleries closer to Roseville.'

'Tourists have heard of Lexington and everyone who has driven south on I-75 has seen those huge thoroughbred farms. Even Mr Fleming has seen those horse farms. He thinks it would be a good angle to tie the bourbon tours to Kentucky horseracing. After all, bourbon is the key ingredient in a Mint Julep, served for over one hundred years at the Kentucky Derby.'

'Then the logical place we should be going is Louisville, the home of the Kentucky Derby. From what I understand, it has tons of distilleries. You need to talk to the boss again.' Truth was she didn't want to leave Aunt Dot so soon after the funeral, especially since her husband's killer was still out there. And she wasn't ready to leave Nick Harris. Roseville was less than an hour from the big city. 'How much time do I have left here?' Jill asked in a tiny voice.

'I can stall for a few days in Chicago, especially since we're almost to the weekend, and I'll try to get our location changed. But if I don't pack the car and head south on Monday, Fleming will be firing two people instead of just one.'

Jill swallowed hard. 'Is he really that mad at me?'

'Let's just say if you're not planning to join me *somewhere* on Monday, I suggest you call him yourself to explain.'

'OK, fair enough. I appreciate you going to bat for me.'

'Who will if not me?' Michael teased. 'The way I see it is you've got three days in which to decide if you're going to marry the eighth master distiller of Founder's Reserve.'

'No way, Jamie was just a passing flirtation. He still might be the murderer for all we know.'

'Or you could marry that Kentucky lawman. Given enough time he would turn you into a southern belle.'

'Nick and I are just friends.'

'No, Jilly, you and I are *just friends*. There are sparks between you and Nick. Nevertheless, I offer you a third option: remain in Roseville with Aunt Dot and help her run Sweet Dreams B and B. If you bring your granny down from Chicago and patch up their rift, it could be happily-ever-after for the three of you.'

Jill liked the mental picture. 'If I didn't know you better, I'd say you're trying to get rid of me.'

'Hey, if you're still serious about working your way up to the news desk, I suggest you show up for work on Monday. I should be there by six or seven in the evening. Good night, partner.'

Jill hung up with a smile on her face. She had three days . . . to find a killer and make up her mind about what she wanted in life.

It should be plenty of time.

That night she dreamed of being an innkeeper. But it wasn't a sweet Victorian mansion like Sweet Dreams and her partner wasn't the elegant Dorothy Clark. This place resembled a lunatic asylum from the nineteenth century and her partner was a cross between Nurse Ratchet and the hunchback from that famous cathedral. Jill awoke in a tangle of bedsheets with her hair plastered to her head. Usually she needed a cup of coffee before she could face the shower. But after one look in the mirror, Jill turned on the taps and jumped in, letting the warm water soothe every tight muscle in her body. By the time she padded downstairs, Jack sprang to his feet and attacked with his tail wagging.

'Good morning, Jill,' Aunt Dot greeted. She was kneading a ball of dough, preparing to bake a delicious treat. 'Would you mind walking Jack? I'm afraid you've spoiled him.'

'I'd love to.' Jill filled a travel mug with coffee, added a bit of milk and sugar, and clipped on Jack's leash. 'Have you seen Nick yet?'

'As a matter of fact, I have. He came downstairs for breakfast and took his toast back to his room. Shall I mention you inquired about his whereabouts?' Dot's expression was close to a smirk.

'No, just ask him not to leave before I get back with Jack.'

'It would be my pleasure.' Dot winked as she rolled the ball of dough out on waxed paper.

'First Michael, now Aunt Dot?' she asked Jack. 'Has everyone gone crazy or am I sending out the wrong signals?'

Jack cocked his head left and right, yet the beagle had no answers.

Jill headed downtown, rounded the square, and paused briefly at the dog park so he could greet a few pals. When they headed back to the house, Jack looked disappointed, especially when they turned up the driveway.

But Nick, refilling his mug at the kitchen counter, did not. 'Good morning. Rumor has it you wanted to see me before I left for work.' He aimed a grin at Mrs Clark, who was spreading a thick layer of chopped nuts across her rolled dough.

Jill bent down to unsnap Jack's leash. 'Just curious if you have any updates since last night.'

'Actually I do. I was looking into Elmer Maxwell's financials, courtesy of the state police database, when I got a call from the sheriff. Apparently, the Maxwell family seems to have returned to Roseville. One of the deputies saw his kids playing in the yard and the lights on in the house.'

'Why would Elmer take off and then come back?' Jill took an apple from the bowl.

Nick shrugged. 'I don't try to figure out why people do what they do, not anymore. But it couldn't be easy to go on the run with two little kids and a wife. That same deputy talked to the bartender at the Brew Pub. Elmer liked to bet on sports, any sports – football, basketball, horseracing – but the guy wasn't very lucky. He owed some bookie from Frankfort a lot of money and that bookie didn't like waiting to get paid. The bartender had been expecting Elmer to pack up and skip town.'

'Which he did,' Jill interjected.

'Nope,' Nick corrected. 'Five days ago Elmer came into the Brew Pub and paid the guy in full, over ten thousand dollars. Then he left town. Since the Maxwells had been up to their eyeballs in debt, the pay-off was enough to have a warrant issued for Elmer's arrest. I'm on my way there now to bring him in for questioning.' Nick poured his coffee into Jill's travel mug and snapped on the lid.

'Great. I'm going with you. Let me just grab—'

'Sorry, Jill, this is police business. No ride-alongs for journalists today.'

'I thought we were partners.'

'No, you and Michael Erickson are partners. Sheriff Adkins will help me bring in a potential bad guy. But if there's any breaking news, I promise you the inside scoop.' Nick patted her head like a small child or worse . . . a dog.

Jill fumed until he disappeared out the door. Then she turned to her cousin, who pretended not to be listening.

'May I please borrow your truck, Aunt Dot?'

'Keys are on the hook.' Dot pointed with her spatula. 'But don't follow Nick too closely. By the way, the Maxwells live on Greenbriar Drive in case you lose him.'

'Thanks, you're the best innkeeper in the world.'

'Just make sure you give me four stars if and when you ever check out.'

FOURTEEN

Friday morning

For all of ten minutes, Nick felt bad about hurting Jill's feelings. Then he spotted Roger Clark's beat-up old truck in his rear-view mirror. He thought about calling her and ordering her to back off, but he just couldn't bring himself to do it. He liked Jill. And that wasn't very smart, because after they caught Roger's killer, he would return to Louisville and she'd go home to Chicago. He should call the sheriff so he wouldn't be surprised when Jill bounded up the front walkway, notepad in hand. But in the end, Nick pretended not to notice her following him and let the chips fall where they may.

At the home of Elmer Maxwell, Nick parked next to the sheriff's cruiser and headed towards the front door, which stood open to every fly and mosquito in Roseville. Unfortunately, Jill pulled right behind his sedan, effectively blocking him in with her truck. With a few long strides, he reached the driver's side window. 'This is private property, Miss Curtis,' Nick warned. 'If you get out of that truck, I will arrest you.'

'I wouldn't dream of it, Trooper. I'll stay right here in case you need me.' Jill smiled innocently.

'No, you won't. Move your vehicle into a legal parking spot on the street.'

'Fine,' she agreed, rolling up her window.

With Jill dealt with, Nick looked around the yard. Why wasn't Elmer's van parked in the driveway or his children playing outside on such a warm summer day? Suddenly a shrill voice came from inside the house, and Nick bolted to the doorway.

'Why is your deputy tramping all over my house?' Janice Maxwell screeched. 'I told you Elmer's not here.'

'Just doing our job, Miz Maxwell.' Adkins maintained his soft, unhurried drawl despite her agitation. 'Don't worry. Deputy Frank won't mess anything up.'

'May I come in, ma'am?' Nick asked, stepping across the threshold. It took a minute for his eyes to adjust to the dark interior of the one-story house.

Janice's head snapped around. 'Why not? Everybody else seems to do whatever they please. And close that door!'

'Let's go over again what happened for the benefit of Lieutenant Harris.' Adkins rested his hands on his knees.

'Fine, but you are wasting time.' Janice released a weary sigh. 'One night, Elmer came home from the bar and told me to pack the car 'cause we were leaving. I asked him where to and he said I'd know when we got there.' She shook her head and took a gulp of Coke. 'Then he drove us to my sister's house in Washington County. Just like that, we show up without calling first or bringing any food with us. My sister is worse off than we are!' Janice looked from one to the other to make sure they understood the significance.

'That had to make you uncomfortable,' Nick murmured.

'You got that right. My sister started fussing about where we were going to sleep and my brother-in-law demanded the money Elmer owed him. I didn't even know he'd borrowed money from Al.' She breathed in and out as though to calm herself. 'Well, Elmer pulled a couple of hundreds from his wallet and handed them over saying he won a few races at Keeneland. I never saw my husband with so much cash.'

Nick and the sheriff exchanged a glance. 'Go on, Miz Maxwell,' Adkins prodded.

'That money shut Al up for a few nights. Then one fine morning, he was back to badgering Elmer that he still owed him more. The two of them starting yelling and carrying on and before I knew it, Al kicked us out. Just like that. My kids didn't even finish their bowl of cereal.'

This time when Janice met the eyes of her audience, Nick felt a welling of sympathy deep in his gut. Was this what people meant by hand-to-mouth? He pitied any mother forced to raise children under such circumstances. 'Where did your family go next?'

Janice expelled a hollow laugh. 'All his big plans . . . Elmer didn't know what to do. He took us to breakfast at Hardee's and then just drove around, wasting gas. I knew we weren't going anywhere. Then he brought us back here.' She waved dismissively at the sparsely furnished room. 'There ain't a bit of food in this house and what does my husband do?' The frustrated woman didn't wait for an answer. 'He just took off and went to the bar last night.' She reached for a cigarette from a pack on the coffee table, adding smoke to the stale smell.

'How do you know that's where he went?' The sheriff's brow furrowed.

Another listless shrug. 'That's the only place Elmer ever goes. Everybody knows him at the Brew Pub on Fifth Street. It's like his second home when he leaves the distillery.' Janice laced her words with plenty of scorn.

Adkins pulled out his phone, then strolled into the kitchen to make his call.

'But Elmer has never stayed out all night before,' she said, turning to face Nick. 'He knows we only have one car so I got no way to get food.'

Nick peered out the window overlooking the driveway. 'I noticed a Chevelle Super Sport in the carport. Couldn't you drive that to the grocery store?'

'That car hasn't run in years.' She snorted with contempt. 'It is just a hole in the ground where Elmer throws our extra money. Not that we've had much lately.'

'Before the sheriff and I leave today, we'll make sure you have groceries in the house. I know the Episcopal Church has a community outreach program,' Nick said, half-expecting a stinging rebuff.

Instead Janice nodded and murmured, 'Thank you.'

'Where are your children, Mrs Maxwell?'

'I told them to stay in their room. I don't want them listening while we're talking about Elmer. Every kid should respect their daddy.'

Nick's opinion of the woman lifted a notch.

Sheriff Adkins strolled into the room and slipped his phone back into his pocket. 'The manager of the Brew Pub said Elmer stopped in last night, but he only drank two beers and left. He didn't talk to anyone and he ignored the ballgame on TV which for Elmer was very strange.' Adkins delivered this news to Nick, not Mrs Maxwell. 'I put out an APB on his vehicle, a late model Chevy van.'

Janice's eyes filled with tears. 'Why are you doing this, Sheriff?

Can't you wait until he comes home? This nice cop said he would help us get some food in the house, so let's just be patient.' She gestured in Nick's direction.

'I'm afraid we can't, ma'am.' Adkins hiked his belt over his belly. 'Your husband is wanted for questioning in the murder of Roger Clark. So if you have any knowledge of his whereabouts and refuse to tell us, you could be charged with obstruction of justice.'

'If I knew where he was, I would tell you.' As Janice's tears turned into downright hysterics, she buried her face in her hands.

The sheriff perched on the arm of the sofa. 'It's just some questions. If Elmer had nothing to do with the murder, he's got nothing to worry about.'

'My . . . husband . . . wouldn't . . . hurt . . . a . . . fly.' Her words were a staccato between sobs.

As the sheriff waited for Janice to compose herself, Nick wandered down the hallway off the living room. Behind door number one was the master bedroom in a condition best described as post-tornado. There were so many clothes strewn across the floor none could be left in the closet. Behind door number two Nick found a little girl around four years old and a little boy around six. They were building a fort with interlocking plastic sticks. The room was so overwhelmingly pink it had to belong to the Maxwell daughter. Both children glanced up when Nick opened the door.

'Hi, there,' he said, momentarily at a loss for words. 'Your mother sent me to check on you. You continue to play nice and she'll join you in a few minutes.'

The last two rooms were the boy's bedroom, tidy but very blue, and a long narrow bathroom. Nick gazed out the bathroom window at a backyard filled with toys and half a dozen fruit trees. Apples in various states of decomposition lay scattered on the ground.

One of Adkins's deputies cleared his throat from the doorway. 'I went through the whole house as soon as we arrived, Lieutenant Harris, including the attic and the crawl space. Elmer Maxwell isn't here.'

Nick glanced back at the familiar face. 'I'm sure you did, but did you check that building out back?' He pointed at the barn beyond the mini orchard.

Deputy Morris squeezed in beside him. 'You think that barn's on the Maxwell's property? I figured it belonged to the people on the next street.'

'Let's go find out.' Nick couldn't get out of the airless bathroom fast enough.

In the living room, Janice had regained some of her composure. 'Does that barn out back belong to you, Mrs Maxwell?' Nick asked.

'You mean that old shed? Yeah, it's ours. Elmer used to work on his racecar in there, before the landlord put up the carport. Some racecar . . . can't even get down the driveway.' She wiped her face with a sodden tissue.

'What's it used for now?'

'Nothing. I don't think anyone's been inside in years.'

From the bathroom Nick had seen tracks where the grass had been bent down. 'Mind if we take a look inside?'

'Knock yourself out,' she said after a moment's hesitation.

Sheriff Adkins locked eyes with him. 'Take Deputy Morris with you, Nick. I'm going to stay with Mrs Maxwell in case her husband calls.'

Unsure why Adkins didn't want the wife left alone, Nick headed out through the kitchen with Morris on his heels. The backyard was even more cluttered with discarded toys than it had looked from the window. Every step through the knee-high grass offered a trip hazard.

'Look at this, Lieutenant.' Morris bent down to inspect the tire tracks. 'Somebody drove back to the shed recently.'

'Yeah, I saw those indentations in the grass from the bathroom.' Nick withdrew his gun from the shoulder holster. 'Best to be prepared,' he added in response to Morris's expression. 'I'll go around to the left. You go around to the right but watch your step. Snakes love to hide in tall weeds.'

Slightly paler, the deputy withdrew his service weapon and made his way along the property line.

Nick followed the tire tracks around to the opposite side where double doors and a wide ramp led into the barn, easing the entry and exit of vehicles and garden tractors. Unfortunately, all of the barn's windows had been covered over with cardboard.

'We'll be going in blind,' Nick whispered as Morris reached

his position. 'Be ready, but don't start shooting. Follow my lead.'

Morris saluted with his gun barrel.

'Elmer Maxwell,' Nick shouted. 'This is the Kentucky State Police and Spencer County Sheriff's Department. Come outside with your hands raised. We need to ask you some questions.'

Neither of the law men moved as they listened for movement inside the barn. When they didn't hear a sound, Nick repeated his demand. 'Come on out, Maxwell. There's no place for you to go.'

'Cover me,' Nick whispered after another minute. 'I'm going in.'

As Morris gripped his weapon with both hands and raised it to shoulder height, Nick slid back the door and entered, ready for anything. But there was little to be ready for. Nothing moved inside the dim interior. The first thing Nick noticed was a rag stuffed in the exhaust pipe of a vehicle. Then he saw a man behind the wheel, his head slumped to one side. With his weapon still trained on the van's occupant, Nick approached the driver's side.

'He must've really tied one on last night,' Morris muttered from the doorway. 'Wake up, Elmer. We need to ask some questions.'

From the sag of the shoulders and the tilt of his head, Nick suspected the former security guard wasn't sleeping. 'Open up the barn,' he shouted to Morris. 'Get some oxygen in here.' When he yanked open the van's door, Maxwell almost fell out. Nick checked for a pulse at Maxwell's carotid artery and his wrist but felt only cool, damp skin.

'Is he dead?' Morris asked hesitantly.

'I believe so. Don't come in here. Radio for an ambulance. Then ask Sheriff Adkins to join us but say nothing to Mrs Maxwell. We'll let EMTs make the call.' Nick reached over the body to turn off the ignition, but the van had run out of gas long ago. Glancing around, a whitish layer of dust covered the cement floor of a building which appeared not to have been used in years. As carefully as possible, Nick backed out of the barn, trying to re-step in his same footprints. Once outdoors he filled his lungs deeply with fresh air.

Sheriff Adkins met him halfway back to the house. 'What do we have, Nick, a suicide?'

'That's how someone wanted it to appear. There's a rag stuffed in the tailpipe, a blueish tint to Maxwell's skin, and the van's out of gas. But other than mine, I saw only one set of footprints to the tailpipe and back to the driver's door. So who closed the barn doors after Maxwell backed the van inside?'

Adkins stroked his chin. 'Good point. Looks like someone else coerced him into making that decision. Did you see any other tire tracks in the grass?'

'No, only one set. Nevertheless, let's make sure the footprints match Maxwell's shoes and the tracks match the van's.'

'You got it. I'll get our forensic guy out here. I'll make sure no one obliterates those footprints before they're measured and photographed.' Adkins tipped up his hat brim. 'In the meantime, why don't you break the news to Janice? You seem to have developed a rapport with her.'

On his way to the house Nick remembered Jill Curtis and detoured around to the front. Was she still sitting in Roger's truck in the hot sun? Or sneaking through the bushes trying to scoop the local news station? He would prefer she not take photographs as they brought Elmer out on a gurney.

Jill exited the pickup as Nick approached. 'What's up?' she asked. 'Have you taken Elmer Maxwell into custody?'

'We found him in an outbuilding. It appears he might have taken his own life.'

Her eyes grew very round. 'That's just awful. Is his wife home?'

'She's inside the house, along with two little kids. I need to tell her the bad news and you might be able to help.'

Jill blinked several times. 'What could I do?'

'The family had packed up and left town, but then returned unexpectedly. There's no food in the house and her kids are probably getting hungry. Do you think you could rally the Episcopal ladies to help out?'

'I've only attended that church twice and once it was for a funeral.'

'I know, but I promised Mrs Maxwell. Maybe Mrs Clark will help you.'

Jill smiled. 'Lead the way, Trooper, but I sure never took you for a softie.'

'Only with women, children, and small animals.' Just as Nick and Jill entered the house, the sound of sirens could be heard in the distance.

Janice jumped to her feet. 'What's going on, Lieutenant Harris? Did you find Elmer?'

'Yes, ma'am. Your husband had parked his van in the barn in the backyard.'

'What was he doing in there?' Her face mottled with confusion.

'We're not sure, but whatever it was he might have been overcome by carbon monoxide. EMTs and an ambulance are on the way.'

It took a few moments for the significance to sink in. 'Is Elmer dead?'

Nick chose his words carefully. 'I wasn't able to find a pulse, but medical professionals will soon be here with oxygen. Let's hope for the best.'

Janice wobbled on her feet. She dropped onto the sofa as her knees gave out.

Nick squatted in front of her. 'If it's OK with you, one of the deputies will take your fingerprints, just so we know which prints belong in the van.'

Mutely, she bobbed her head.

'And in the meantime, this is Miss Curtis,' Nick continued. 'She attends the Roseville Episcopal Church. She will see to it that your home is restocked with groceries.'

Jill stepped forward and offered a sympathetic smile. 'My first name is Jill. Why don't I call for a pizza, then we can say a healing prayer for your husband. You are not alone, Mrs Maxwell. I'll see that you get the help you need.' Sitting down next to the widow, Jill wrapped one arm around her shoulder, while she Google-searched pizza shops with her other hand.

Nick stared with utter amazement. It was just like his mother used to say, 'If you want something done fast and done right, ask a woman to do it.'

FIFTEEN

J ill didn't have much experience dealing with children. But she thoroughly enjoyed playing with Janice Maxwell's kids while they waited for the pizzas to be delivered. After an initial bit of shyness, daughter Amy talked Jill's ear off about each member of her stuffed animal family. Then her older brother, Brandon, carefully explained how they'd built the two-room fort. Without shedding a single tear in front of her kids, Janice supplied a bed sheet to convert the open-air fort into a secret cave. Then Jill, Janice, and the well-mannered children each ate two slices of pizza inside the new private domain.

Jill remained with the Maxwells until Aunt Dot arrived to replace her. Once Jill had explained the family's dire circumstances on the phone, Dot had insisted on coming to the house. On her way out, Jill received a heartfelt hug from Janice and from Aunt Dot she received the assurance the Episcopal Ladies Guild would take good care of them.

'Thanks for the pizza,' Janice said in the doorway. 'I don't know how we would've managed. We should never have come back here. We had enough money to make a fresh start. But Elmer thought he could get a little more.'

More from whom? Gordy? Did Gordy pay Elmer to kill Roger Clark? Or did Gordy kill both of them? Jill wanted to ask Janice but she had dissolved into another round of tears.

'Don't worry,' Dot said. 'I'll take Janice to see Elmer at the hospital as soon as she's ready.' She wrapped her arms around the woman and led her back to the sofa.

Jill was free to wander around the backyard, looking for Nick. But neither he nor Sheriff Adkins were still at the crime scene and none of the deputies bagging forensic evidence knew where they had gone. Deputy Morris reported that the EMTs had been unable to revive Elmer Maxwell before transporting him to the hospital.

Jill considered calling Nick, but in the end she let him do his job and she headed back to Sweet Dreams B&B.

After twenty minutes of playing with Jack in the backyard, Jill poured a glass of iced tea and carried it to the front porch. She'd had little time to herself since arriving in Kentucky. But with Michael in Chicago, Dot helping a family in need, and the man-of-her-dreams – or a reasonable facsimile – trying to determine if someone had helped Maxwell to an early grave, Jill settled down in the glider.

However, her amount of relaxation measured exactly eleven minutes. Before she could finish one glass of tea, Gordon Clark parked in front of the house and strolled up the walkway. Lost in his thoughts, Gordy didn't notice her until he stepped onto the porch.

'Oh, Miss Curtis. Is my aunt home? I'd like to talk to her.' He bent down to scratch the beagle behind the ears.

'Hi, Gordy. No, I'm afraid she's not.'

When Clark looked skeptical, Jill grudgingly offered more information. 'Elmer Maxwell, one of your security guards at Black Creek, died of carbon monoxide poisoning last night. Your aunt is with Elmer's widow, probably at the hospital by now. Before Dot comes home she'll arrange for groceries and meals to be brought in by her friends at church.' Jill kicked with her heels to get the glider moving.

Arching his neck, Gordon gazed at the sky, as though answers could be found in the skittering white clouds. 'That sounds like Aunt Dot – always thinking of other people, unlike myself who thinks of no one but me.' His deeply shadowed, haunted eyes left Jill unnerved.

'I don't know you well enough to agree or disagree, but you could wait for your aunt in the parlor.' Jill sounded like a talking robot, even to her own ears.

Gordy forced a smile. 'I would rather wait with you, Jill. I owe you an apology,' he added after a pause.

'Apologize for what?' Her uneasiness grew by leaps and bounds.

'I went out of my way to snub you, because I was sure you were a gold-digger, out to get my uncle's distillery.'

Jill planted her feet to stop the glider's movement. 'You don't think that anymore?'

'I'm the one obsessed with power and money. Uncle Roger had

taken the time to teach me everything he knew about bourbon. And how did I repay him? I gave him a hard time about working me so hard at the distillery.' Gordon dropped down on the top step. 'Roger had busted his butt his whole life. Why would he expect anything less from me?'

'You should know hard work since you grew up in a family of moonshiners.'

Gordy shook his head. 'Not by a longshot. What my father and brother do up in the hills is nothing compared to running a full-scale, legal operation. As it turned out, my uncle had left me the majority of Black Creek in his will. All I had to do was my job and wait.'

'Sounds simple enough. Why couldn't you be patient?'

'Because my family refused to let the old ways die.'

Jill struggled to keep her voice level. 'What did William and Billy have to do with Roger's death?'

Gordy's face contorted. 'With his death? Nothing. I'm talking about making a few extra bucks at Black Creek's expense. That's why Uncle Roger changed his will. Every month I took home a few cases of empty bottles and a pack of labels. My father would put his moonshine into Black Creek bottles. Then Billy sold them to the mom-and-pop stores as the real stuff. Dad made enough cash to pay the real estate taxes and buy groceries.'

'And did this little scam make a difference to your family?' Jill glanced at her watch, hoping someone would come home soon.

'It did, but that five or six hundred a month cost me my job, my inheritance, and my future.' Gordy's voice cracked with emotion. 'Uncle Roger discovered the missing cases during inventory and figured out what I'd been doing. That's what we argued about Tuesday night.'

'So on Wednesday you waited until the production crew left and then killed him. Too bad Roger had already changed his will earlier that day.'

'Killed him?' Gordon swiveled around to face her. 'I didn't kill anyone. When I went to work on Wednesday, I begged Roger not to fire me. I didn't know anything about his will – new or original – until you and that cop came to my office yesterday.'

'Have you heard what's in Roger's new will?' Jill felt her shirt stick to her back with sweat.

He nodded. 'Aunt Dot asked me to meet her at the attorney's office this morning so her lawyer could read the new will. Then she told the lawyer she wanted to give me her share, because Roger usually regretted decisions made in haste. Those were Aunt Dot's exact words.'

'Well, it sounds like things are coming up roses for you.'

Gordy frowned. 'That's why I'm here. I plan to tell my aunt about stealing the bottles and labels and passing off moonshine as Black Creek bourbon. I won't let her give the distillery to a thief and a fraud.'

'Not to mention her husband's killer.' Jill rose to her feet and took a step backwards.

He looked like someone had kicked him in the stomach. 'I didn't kill Uncle Roger. When I left work on Wednesday, he was still alive. Like I told you and that cop, I drove up the mountain to check on my sister. Ask Michelle, she'll confirm my story.'

'Michelle would probably say just about anything to protect a family member.'

Gordy stood and locked eyes with her. 'Yeah, she probably would, but Michelle loved Uncle Roger. So she would never cover up his murder. Plus I'm not the only one with a key to Black Creek.'

'That's right. Michelle has one too.'

His face flushed with anger. 'So do several security guards, including Elmer Maxwell. Maybe he killed Roger and couldn't live with himself.'

'Sure, blame it on a dead man. What motive do you think Elmer had?'

'I have no idea. I only know I'm not lying. I wasn't anywhere around when my uncle died. And I had no idea Roger planned to leave me the distillery.'

'We'll let the cops sort this out. Right now, I want you to leave.' Jill backed up until she felt the door handle in the middle of her spine.

Pointing at the glider, Gordon walked towards her. 'Why can't I wait here until my aunt comes home?'

In an instant, Jill bolted inside the house and pulled out her cell phone. 'I'm punching in 9-1-1,' she said through the screen door. 'I suggest you leave before the cops arrive. You'll have to chat with Aunt Dot some other time.'

'I don't blame you for not trusting me. Tell my aunt or the cops or anybody interested I'll be on the farm with my family.' Gordon trudged down the steps with none of the swagger displayed in his office at Black Creek. He climbed in his Jeep, cast a final glance at Sweet Dreams B&B and headed in the direction of home.

Once his car disappeared around the corner, Jill locked the door and returned to her 9-1-1 call. She identified herself, claimed she'd dialed the number by mistake, and breathed a sigh of relief when the dispatcher hung up. Jill couldn't wait for Dot to get home, or for Nick to finish work, or even for some strangers with reservations for tonight to arrive. Unfortunately, her phone rang just as she stepped out of the shower. And the caller was none of the above.

'Hello, beautiful. How was your drive back to Chicago?'

It took Jill a moment to recognize the vaguely familiar slow drawl. 'Jamie Shelby, is that you?' Swallowing her disappointment, she toweled off with one hand.

'Right as rain. I can't wait to see the Founder's Reserve segment on TV. Now that you're back to work in the Windy City, I thought maybe you could email me a copy of the article you wrote.'

'I would be happy to, but I'm not in Chicago. I'm still at Sweet Dreams B and B.'

'Didn't I hear through the grapevine that someone broke into your car and stole your equipment?' Jamie's question followed a brief pause.

'News travels fast in Roseville, but I should be used to that by now.' She chuckled. 'Only my partner drove to Chicago to pick up new equipment. Remember, Michael Erickson?'

'Of course, I do. That guy sneezed if he got within twenty feet of grain. Michael really should stay in the city.'

'Not just grain,' she said. 'Michael is allergic to cat dander, tree pollen, ragweed in the fall, and a ton of other allergens. I hope our next assignment will be in a bigger city than Roseville. Of course, distillers need corn, barley and well water, so that's unlikely. I'm supposed to meet him on Monday after I tie up a few loose ends with Roger's murder. Michael got our next destination changed to Louisville.'

'Roger's murder? You're a travel writer, not a homicide detective. I thought Sheriff Adkins brought some hot-shot state investigator in to help out.'

'Yes, he did.' Jill let the mental image of the *hot-shot investigator* float through her mind. 'But since I finished my article on the first two distilleries, I don't have much else to do.'

'Have you narrowed down your pool of suspects, Miss Marple?' Jamie teased.

'I prefer Nancy Drew, and yes, I think I know whodunit. Time will tell if I'm right.'

'Bravo, Nancy. Hey, since you're still in Roseville, why don't we have dinner tonight? I can read your article on Founder's Reserve and double check for minor inaccuracies. Plus, I would love to hear your theory on who killed Roger.'

Jill pulled back the curtain, hoping to see Nick's car in the driveway. She couldn't wait to tell him about Gordon's recent visit, not spend time with a Shelby. 'I'll email you the article,' she said, 'but I really should stick around Sweet Dreams tonight. I'm not sure when Mrs Clark will be home and new people are supposed to check in.'

'That's just plain silly,' Jamie stated flatly. 'Your innkeeper knows exactly what time her guests plan to arrive. Maybe you're still a little afraid of me, even though the police ruled me out as a suspect. After all, Miss Curtis, you were my alibi.'

Suddenly Jill remembered the snide remark made by Gordon Clark in his office: *Do you have eight grand to go with your unsolicited opinion? Because I don't, and that's what the hospital wants upfront since Michelle has no health insurance.*

Jill had a sudden thought. Most likely Jamie has eight thousand dollars and he's also the father of her child. Michelle might be too proud to ask for money, but a first-cousin-twice-removed-by-marriage wasn't. If there was even a chance of getting Michelle the upfront money, she needed to try. Besides, Nick should be back to Sweet Dreams soon. He could let in any guests who arrived before Dot got home. 'On second thoughts, Jamie, I'd love to have dinner with you. Where should we meet?'

'*Meet?* You city slickers sure have odd habits. Since this will be my last chance to wine-and-dine you, I insist on picking you up. Can you be ready in half an hour?'

Jill smiled even though he couldn't see her face. 'Southern men are such gentlemen, no? All right, I'll be on the porch. Don't be late, Shelby.'

Not only was he not late, he turned out to be five minutes early. Jamie screeched his sports car to a stop in front of the house. The low-slung vehicle would make entering and exiting discreetly in her short dress almost impossible. But her choice of outfits was the least of her worries. From the moment Jamie showed up at the front door with a huge bunch of flowers, Jill regretted her decision to go out with him one last time.

'These must have cost you a fortune,' Jill murmured, accepting the bouquet from his outstretched hand. 'And they can't be a bribe for glowing media coverage, since I already turned my article in.'

'Does a man need a reason to buy flowers for a beautiful woman?' He stood so close Jill could smell his aftershave and maybe even his shampoo.

'I'll put these in water and leave a note for Dot.' Letting the screen door slam, she backed down the hallway.

'Tell her not to wait up,' he called after her. 'I've got an evening of seduction planned – first the flowers, then a gourmet dinner with champagne and candlelight at a romantic seaside cottage.'

Frowning, Jill stuck the flowers in a vase, turned on the tap, and penned a succinct note: *Having dinner with Jamie Shelby. Driving Roger's truck so I can come home early.* Setting the flowers on the breakfront, she marched back to the porch.

'Let's get one thing straight, Shelby.' Jill crossed her arms. 'This will be a casual dinner between business acquaintances. No attempts at seduction will be tolerated.'

Jamie hid his laughter behind a cough. 'Relax, Jill. I was joking. Consider just how far we are from the ocean.' He slicked a hand through his thick hair. 'We're having dinner at a country inn popular with the after-church crowd and couples celebrating their anniversary.'

'I see, but why can't we stay in Roseville?' She forced her arms down to her side.

Jamie sighed with dramatic exaggeration. 'Because I don't want fast food, or pizza, or a cheeseburger and a beer. I thought we could have a *nice* dinner tonight.'

He looked so earnest, so sincere, she relented. Besides, a *nice* place would make it harder to refuse her request for Michelle's eight grand. 'The country inn sounds lovely, but we'll drive separately.' Jill pointed at Roger's truck in the driveway.

'What on earth for? The restaurant is forty minutes away.'

'Because I want to run an errand on my way home,' she lied, bracing herself for more argument.

But Jamie merely shrugged. 'Fine, I'll lead and you follow. Flash your lights if I go too fast.' At the bottom of the steps he pulled out his phone and tapped the screen. 'This is where we're going in case we get separated.' He showed her the inn's website with a rambling white house surrounded by flowers and a picket fence.

Jill tapped the address into her GPS, climbed into the pickup, and backed it down the driveway. They would be dining in a public place with her vehicle in the parking lot – it was time to relax and look forward to some good food.

SIXTEEN

Nick returned to the Spencer County Sheriff's Department feeling more frustrated than he had in a long time. It had been one dead end or time-wasting detour after another since his arrival in Roseville. His gut told him that Elmer Maxwell's death wasn't a suicide, yet the deputies had found no fingerprints inside the car that didn't belong to Elmer or a member of his family. Unfortunately, the footprints next to the car had been too obliterated by himself or one of the deputies to prove he hadn't driven home alone and closed the barn door himself. Upon inspection, the fence that separated the Maxwell property from the one behind them had a missing section, making travel between the two yards easy and relatively unseen. None of the adjacent homes had windows overlooking the two backyards. Someone could have ridden home with Elmer, rendered him unconscious, and escaped in a car parked around the block.

Nick tossed his notebook on the desk and leaned precariously back in his chair. Had someone paid the security guard to erase the videotape for the Wednesday before last? So it would appear, yet Maxwell had taken that person's identity with him to the grave.

'Excuse me, Lieutenant.' Deputy Morris interrupted Nick's woolgathering. 'Remember the partial blood sample we gathered at Roger Clark's crime scene, but found no match in the databanks?'

Nick waited, assuming more was forthcoming. 'Yes,' he finally prodded.

'And remember the coffee cup you took off old man Shelby's desk?' Morris's grin stretched from ear to ear.

Nick smiled too. 'The DNA matched?'

'Right on the money – a perfect match. Owen Shelby was with Roger Clark the night he died.'

'Have you told Sheriff Adkins?'

'I did, because he was only six feet away when the results came in.'

Nick righted his chair and walked into the main office. Adkins stood at the counter with a stack of parking tickets in front of him. 'Did you contact the DA about an arrest warrant for Owen Shelby?'

Adkins shook his head and stared out the window into the parking lot.

'On its way, but I don't think we're going to need it.'

'Why not?' Nick asked. 'Blood evidence found at the crime scene matched the elder Mr Shelby's DNA. He was with Roger the night he died.'

'I agree, but Owen Shelby is heading toward the front door. He appears to want to talk to us.'

A moment later Owen shuffled through the doorway, looking nowhere near as dignified as he had a few days ago. His complexion was mottled, his shirt rumpled, and the lapel of his suit had a greasy stain. As he crossed the linoleum floor, Owen looked left and right as though confused what to do.

'Mr Shelby,' called Nick. 'Why don't you come back to Sheriff Adkins's office? We can talk privately in there.'

Shelby met Nick's gaze with bloodshot eyes, nodded, then shuffled wordlessly around the counter. As he followed the sheriff down the hall, Nick stayed close behind him, breathing in the strong smell of alcohol and nervous perspiration.

'Have a seat, Mr Shelby.' Adkins pointed at a chair. 'Have you changed your mind about pressing charges against Billy and Justin Clark?'

Shelby's face went blank as he lowered himself into the chair.

'For vandalism, sir,' Nick interjected. 'We spoke to you in your office the other day.'

Shelby waved his hand through the air. 'No, I'm not here about that. I want to confess to killing Roger Clark. But on my ancestors' graves, I swear it was an accident. Roger threw the first punch and from there, things turned ugly.'

Nick glanced at the sheriff who looked just as surprised as he felt. 'In that case, sir, we advise you to say nothing more until you have legal counsel present.'

Shelby gripped the arms of the chair. 'I waive my right to legal counsel. Let's just get this over with.'

'I'll go set up the conference room,' Adkins said to Nick as he walked from the room.

'It's standard procedure to videotape all confessions, so Sheriff

Adkins will have that ready in a few minutes. In the meantime, you can start by explaining why you went to Black Creek on Wednesday night.'

Owen blinked several times. 'Business has been lousy this year. I thought we could generate bigger profits with flavored small batches. We would age the bourbon for the required minimum of two years, and then market the product to twenty- and thirty-year-olds. Those millennials have money to burn, but they prefer whiskey that tastes like apples or peaches or cinnamon. The small crafts must be hurting as much as us.' He shook his head sadly. 'I thought Founder's Reserve would cover the cost of raw materials, then Black Creek could mix and distill, since our facilities are geared for mass production. Then we would handle aging and bottling, along with the cost of promotion and distribution.' Owen blotted beads of perspiration which had formed on his brow. 'So I called Roger up and mentioned the idea of a partnership. He told me to come by after supper and we could discuss my idea. He said to drive up to the loading dock and his guard would let me in.'

'Why did Mr Clark want you to come in through the back door?' Nick asked.

'He wanted to give me a tour, and not what they normally show tourists. So we started in his warehouse, where his barrels of bourbon are aged.'

'Did Mr Clark like your business proposition?'

'Oh, Roger liked my idea all right. He fetched a couple glasses and a bottle of his best product. So I pulled out a flask of my thirty-year-old bourbon. We drank a toast, but I never should have used the word *partnership* on the phone. That crazy old coot thought we would share the profits fifty-fifty. Why would I split fifty-fifty if I'm fronting the cost of raw materials, tying up my rickhouse for two years, and bearing the full expense of promotion? When I suggested a seventy-thirty split, Roger called me every foul name in the book. Then he said I was a thief just like my ancestor.' Owen's face flushed to a dangerous shade of plum. 'I've never cheated anyone in my life. How dare that upstart from the hills—'

'We're ready for your statement in the conference room, Mr Shelby.' Sheriff Adkins interrupted Shelby's description of his arch nemesis.

Owen pushed to his feet and lumbered through the doorway. Once he was settled in an upholstered chair, the sheriff sat down on Shelby's right. 'Are you sure you don't want your attorney here during questioning?' he asked.

'I told you, we don't have time to get my overpriced lawyer off the golf course.' Shelby thumped the arms of his chair with his fists.

Nick switched on the video camera and leaned across the conference table. 'If Clark's death was an accident—'

'It was an accident, I tell you. Like I said, Roger went crazy when I refused a fifty-fifty split. He accused me of trying to cheat him, like when the Shelbys stole sixty acres of land from the Cooks. When he called me a thief like my grandfather, I told him it was better to be a thief than an arsonist who torched a house with a grandmother inside!'

'Is that when Roger threw the first punch?' Sheriff Adkins asked.

'Yes, he threw a hook and caught me on the chin.' Shelby fingered the spot as though it were still tender. 'Then I threw a punch and it was no holds barred after that.'

Nick couldn't imagine fisticuffs between these two men, yet his gut told him Shelby was telling the truth. 'We found drops of your blood on the floor near where we found Mr Clark's body. Is that how it got there, during this fistfight?'

'Yeah, I guess so. Roger connected with my nose pretty good, and you know how those things bleed. Tempers were on edge because business was bad all around, but neither of us wanted someone to die.' Shelby peered from one to the other, hoping they understood.

'Did you push Mr Clark into the metal rack?' Sheriff Adkins asked in a quiet voice.

'Roger had me up against the barrels. I pushed just to get him away from me. But he slipped in the spilled bourbon and fell. That's when he hit his head on the edge of the rack.' Owen touched the back of his head.

Nick locked gazes with the sheriff. 'The medical examiner in Frankfort said the fatal blow to Mr Clark was to the frontal portion of the skull. It wasn't the superficial laceration on his scalp.'

The elderly man blinked several times. 'I don't know anything about that. I'm just telling you his death was an accident.' Sweat ran down the side of Owen's face and dripped onto his already rumpled suit coat.

'What happened after Roger Clark slipped in the bourbon and hit his head?' Nick picked up the questioning.

'I didn't know if he was just out cold or dead, so I panicked. Business was already bad, and publicity like that could put us under.'

'What did you do?' Nick demanded.

Owen twitched, like a cornered animal without a way to escape. 'I got out of there the same way I came in. The guard was busy watching a ballgame and didn't even see me leave.' His lip curled with contempt.

'The guard was Elmer Maxwell, right?' asked Adkins.

'Yes, that's what I was told. I have a contact at Black Creek. He lets me know when good employees are unhappy in case we want to make them a better offer.'

'Who is your contact, Mr Shelby?'

'Gordon Clark.' Shelby's distress visibly increased.

'Why would Roger's second in command help Founder's Reserve?'

'For money, what else? If Roger had paid a decent wage, his employees would've been more loyal. Besides, Gordy never gave up proprietary secrets, only information on personnel.'

Nick circled the table until he stood next to Shelby. 'You mentioned twice that we didn't have time for your lawyer to get here. Before I lose my temper, why are you in so big a hurry?' He leaned until he was inches from the man's face.

Shelby's features contorted with hatred. 'I want you to charge me, Lieutenant, and notify the media I confessed to the accidental death of Roger Clark.'

'Just because you're rich you don't get to decide what happens,' Nick muttered under his breath.

'Then charge me with manslaughter, I don't care. I just don't want anything else bad to happen.'

'Something bad like Elmer Maxwell taking his own life?' asked Sheriff Adkins.

'Or someone coercing him by putting a gun to his head?' Nick added.

Shelby shook his finger. 'I asked my son to check on Clark and get my antique flask back. I dropped it during the scuffle, but I didn't ask him to pay that security guard to erase the tapes with me on them. That's it.' Shelby dropped his face into his hands. 'I know I should've called the police right away. If I had, maybe Roger would still be alive.'

'We asked around at the bar where Maxwell drank and placed bets on sports events. He had flashed a wad of money on the day Roger died, and also on the day before he allegedly took his own life.' Sheriff Adkins kept his voice low and controlled. 'If we subpoena your son's financial records, will we find large cash withdrawals to match those dates?'

'Maybe, but my son didn't kill him and I didn't either. Elmer Maxwell was a married man with two kids, for goodness' sake.'

Nick placed his hand on Shelby's shoulder. 'A man being black-mailed might do something stupid. What else do you know, Mr Shelby?'

A tear slipped down Owen's face. 'Jamie didn't like that travel writer and her sidekick asking so many questions – questions that had nothing to do with tourists or making bourbon. That woman writer – Jill something – had been sticking her nose into Jamie's relationship with Michelle Clark.'

Ice formed in Nick's veins. 'What did your son do to Jill Curtis?'

'Nothing to her,' Owen blubbered. 'Jamie thought she was really pretty, but he wanted them both to go back to Chicago. They had finished their stories on Founder's Reserve and Black Creek. Anything personal about Jamie and Michelle didn't belong in a travel article and certainly nothing about Roger's death inside the distillery. Publicity like that won't bring more folks to Kentucky for the tours. He said he was going to keep an eye on her – make sure she didn't cause too much trouble for us. He wanted to make sure she had only glowing praise for Founder's Reserve.' Owen lifted his chin and focused on the sheriff.

Nick switched off the video camera. 'I am out of patience and that doesn't bode well for you. What did your son do to the videographer?'

'Jamie got mad when he saw him taping everyone who came to Roger's funeral. So that night he went to the B and B where they were staying and smashed his car windows with a baseball bat. Then he stole the guy's equipment.'

'Did your son cut the power at Black Creek and trap Michael Erickson in the elevator?' Nick demanded.

Shelby's forehead furrowed. 'I don't know anything about that. Jamie just told me about trashing the car.'

'Does Jamie have a key to Black Creek?' When Owen didn't immediately answer, Nick grabbed his shoulders and shook him like a ragdoll.

'Michelle gave him a key the night of Roger's fundraiser and he never returned it to her. I don't want Jamie to do anything else stupid. This nightmare has gone on long enough.'

Nick sprang from his chair. 'If you could record the rest of Mr Shelby's confession, Sheriff, I want to check on Jill.'

'You got it, Lieutenant,' said Adkins.

But Nick was already out the door with his phone in hand. He punched in Jill's number and waited. When all three tries to reach her went to voicemail, he jumped in his car and drove straight to Sweet Dreams well above the speed limit. Let whoever was on duty chase after him. Maybe the backup would come in handy.

Jill flashed her lights several times trying to get her date's attention. A four-cylinder pickup was no match for Jamie's late model sports car, either in speed or maneuverability. And the route he picked out of Roseville had plenty of curves. At long last, Jamie got the message and slowed down enough so she could enjoy the scenery along the way.

Once they reached the restaurant, Jill began to feel a little foolish. The Pine Hollow Lodge was just as charming as Jamie had described. The rambling three-story building had plenty of porches and wrought-iron balconies attached to most second-story rooms. A flagstone path led to the front door, while a second path took guests beneath a grapevine-covered arbor into the flower garden. Old-fashioned larkspur and hollyhock grew along the picket fence enclosing the property.

Jill parked the battered truck next to his shiny car in the last row of the lot. 'This place is adorable,' she murmured, taking hold of his elbow.

'It doesn't look like a dangerous lair for psychopaths?' Jamie's smile deepened his dimples.

'Definitely not, at least not from the outside.'

As though to underscore the safety a group of elderly women in red hats and purple outfits trooped through the doorway. All seemed to be talking at once.

'Reservation for Shelby,' Jamie said to the hostess.

Without a moment's hesitation, they were shown to a table in a semi-private alcove. Candlelight reflected in the crystal stemware and illuminated a budvase of tiny roses. Despite the romantic setting, Jill didn't feel the least bit nervous. Dozens of other diners were only yards away. 'If the food is half as good as the ambience, we're in for a treat,' she said as he pulled out her chair.

Jamie sat across from her. 'And since we're miles from the ocean, your virtue is safe with me.'

It took a moment for his joke to sink in. 'So I won't have to feign a headache after all?' she teased.

Jamie straightened his tie and leaned across the table. 'Look, Jill, I get it. You're not physically attracted to me, but I thought we worked well together on your article. I read what you wrote about Founder's Reserve the moment it hit my inbox. You did a great job with Black Creek too, without mentioning the unfortunate circumstances with the master distiller.'

Jill shuddered at the memory of Roger lying in a pool of blood. 'The circumstances were beyond *unfortunate*, Jamie. My cousin's husband was murdered in cold blood. What I emailed you was the first draft. I might just include something about Roger if they arrest the killer before the article goes to press.' She reached for her water glass and took a sip.

His friendly smile vanished. 'What would be the point? Isn't there enough negative news already in the media? People want to read about interesting places to visit without tawdry tabloid rubbish.'

Tawdry tabloid rubbish? Jill swallowed as heat rushed to her cheeks. 'Why don't we pick out something to eat?' She hid her face behind the extensive menu.

'If you like seafood, I recommend the mountain trout,' he said after several minutes of silent study. 'The filet mignon is always good if you're a steak lover. And I understand the pasta Florentine is wonderful if you turned vegan since the last time we were together.' Jamie placed his menu on the edge of the table.

Jill lowered hers as well. The sooner they got this meal over with the sooner she could get back to Sweet Dreams. 'I'll have the trout with wild rice, along with a Caesar salad and iced tea to drink.'

She sat back as Jamie gave their orders to the waiter. Surprisingly, he requested a bottle of Roderer champagne instead of the iced tea she requested. 'I hope that's not an expensive bottle of wine,' she said after the waiter left their table. 'Since I don't drink much, I wouldn't know the difference between vintage champagne and the cheap stuff. Plus, I'm driving tonight.'

Something flashed in his dark eyes: anger? Disappointment? He stared at the flickering candle before speaking. 'I realize that, Jill. That's why I made the wine selection. And the fact we're in two different vehicles is a perfect example of your annoying stubbornness.'

Before she could respond, Jamie burst out laughing as though he meant his comment to be funny. Jill hadn't felt this uncomfortable on a *date* since the eleventh grade, when a boy had described his previous conquests in a misguided attempt to impress her.

'You're not the first man to say I'm stubborn.' She forced herself to meet his eye. 'My partner describes me that way all the time. So far the trait has served me well.'

'Lucky for me, women like you are a rarity in these parts.' Jamie hooked his thumb at the tree-covered hills in the distance.

Jill also focused on the view until the waiter delivered two glasses and the bottle of champagne. After Jamie pronounced the taste acceptable, the waiter began to fill both flutes. Jill covered her glass with her hand. 'Thank you, but I would prefer a glass of iced tea instead.'

Jamie pried loose her fingers. 'Since you'll be eating a full meal, you won't be impaired after just one glass. I want you to know what the good stuff tastes like.'

Feeling the waiter's and Jamie's gazes on her, Jill drew back her hand. 'Fine, one glass, but I would still like that glass of tea.'

'Absolutely, ma'am.' The waiter filled her flute, then fled their table.

'To just comeuppance to Roger's killer and great success for your travel series.' Jamie raised his glass in a toast.

How could she not drink to that? After they clinked glasses, Jill sipped her champagne and tried not to sneeze from the tiny bubbles. 'This tastes better than I thought it would,' she declared, scooting her chair to the table. 'When you referred to women from these parts, it reminded me of something . . . or rather someone. Michelle Clark.'

Jamie moved closer to the table too. 'For someone who says she's uninterested in me romantically, you seem obsessed with my ex-girlfriends. Why is that, Jill?' His mouth twisted in an unappealing fashion.

'Maybe because Michelle is a distant cousin through marriage.'

He leaned back as the waiter delivered Caesar salad to the table and divided it between bowls with great fanfare. 'Your kinship with the Clarks is a stretch, even in the South.'

Jill ignored his comment. 'As you know, Michelle is expecting a baby and plans to have that baby at home. In all likelihood, the baby is yours,' she added and waited for dispute.

'Lots of women still use midwives in the hills. It's her choice.' Jamie's tone revealed utter disinterest in the matter.

'You're probably right, but in Michelle's case, her decision stems from a lack of money, not due to some archaic tradition she wishes to maintain. The hospital in Roseville wants eight thousand dollars upfront before she can deliver there.'

Jamie chewed a mouthful of salad thoroughly. 'And you think I should come up with the cash?'

'Yes, I do. Whether or not this will be your son or daughter, you described Michelle as a longtime friend, besides an occasional lover. Her life, along with the baby's, could be in danger if she delivers far from professional medical care.' Jill stabbed some romaine with her fork.

Jamie studied his cuticles while considering. 'All right, Jill, but I don't have that kind of cash sitting around. I'll give Michelle my credit card number and authorize an eight-thousand-dollar charge at Roseville General.'

Jill almost choked on her lettuce. 'You have that kind of credit available?'

'Of course, I do.' He took a drink of champagne. 'Now, can we enjoy the rest of our meal without any more bones of contention?'

'Yes, Mr Shelby. I can't think of a single other contentious matter.' She picked up her fork and dug into the salad with gusto.

Soon his filet mignon arrived, along with her mountain trout on a bed of wild rice with tender asparagus spears. Jill couldn't remember a better tasting fish. And judging by the rate Jamie devoured his steak and baked potato, his meal must have been satisfactory as well.

Jamie set his knife and fork on the side of his plate and pushed it away. 'It just occurred to me how close we are to the Clark *farm*.' He added a derisive inflexion to the word. 'I should drive up the mountain and tell Michelle my decision, in case she goes into labor during the next day or two. You could tag along to make sure I follow through.'

Jill sipped her iced tea, which the waiter finally remembered. 'That would imply I don't trust you.'

'Eight grand is a lot of money, Miss Curtis, especially if the baby belongs to a local yokel and not me.'

'You really can be incorrigible.' Her appetite gone, Jill slapped her napkin down next to her plate. 'Fine, I'll come with you. But first I need to use the ladies' room.'

'You're not the first woman to describe me as such.' Jamie laughed merrily as she walked away.

The two glasses of water, plus a glass of iced tea, weren't the only reasons she needed the restroom before setting out for the Clarks. Jill also wanted to let Nick and Aunt Dot know exactly where she was and where she was going. But after several attempts to reach them, she couldn't even get their voicemails to answer.

When Jill arrived back at the table, a slice of cherry cheesecake was waiting for her, while some kind of pie-a-la-mode sat in front of Jamie. 'Ughhh,' she moaned. 'What have you done?'

'Would you rather we switch?' Jamie asked, lifting his plate of rapidly melting dessert.

'Enjoy whichever one you prefer, but I couldn't eat another bite.' She glanced at her watch. 'When you see the waiter, please ask for the check.'

'Of course, but in the meantime, you must try this pie. I swear the peaches were picked yesterday.' He waved a spoonful through the air, stopping inches from her lips, as though he were enticing a toddler.

'Fine, one bite.' Jill opened wide and swallowed.

'Good, no?'

'Delicious.' She peered around the room for their elusive waiter.

Jamie launched into a story about his grandmother's ability to pick fruit based on sight alone, while eating his pie at a snail's pace. 'Are you sure you don't want the last bite?' He held up his spoon.

'I do not, thank you. Check, please?' Jill called to their waiter at another table.

'What is your hurry?' Jamie whined, his voice ratcheting up a level. 'It's not that late. Plus you promised to drink a glass of champagne to know what the good stuff tastes like. For crying out loud, you've eaten a full meal.'

Jill scowled and lifted the long-stemmed crystal glass to her lips.

'And don't guzzle it down like Kool-Aid. I intend to eat your dessert too.' Mulishly, he reached for the cherry cheesecake.

Jamie ate the second dessert so slowly, she had plenty of time to savor the expensive bubbles and even drink more iced tea. Finally the waiter delivered the leather folder, Jamie finished stuffing his face and he handed the man his credit card.

Unfortunately, Jill tripped over something on their way out. If Jamie hadn't caught her arm, she might have sprawled across the flagstones in front of other diners exiting the restaurant.

'Stop playing around, Jill,' he hissed, holding her upright. 'You had *one* glass of wine.'

'I'm not playing, Jamie. I suddenly felt lightheaded.' Jill pulled away from him.

Jamie studied her face. 'If that's true, then you should leave that piece of junk here and ride with me.' He slipped a steadying arm around her waist.

Jill looked to the west where the sun was about to drop below the trees. 'It'll be dark soon. Since you said we're not far away, I think I'll follow you to the Clarks. Then if I don't feel like driving home, I'm sure William will let me spend the night.'

'Whatever . . . you . . . say . . .' Jamie dragged out each word, adding as much scorn as possible. 'I'll drive slow but try to keep up. We don't want you making the wrong turn and getting lost.' He jumped in his car, slammed the door and started the engine.

Jill struggled to climb into the truck. Then she tried Nick's number once more before putting the pickup in gear. No service. She considered heading back to town, but she didn't trust Jamie to make good on his promise to pay the hospital bill. And the dull pain which had begun behind her eyes blossomed into a major headache. So when Jamie turned left out of Pine Hollow Lodge, Jill followed him and for the next fifteen minutes, it took all her faculties to keep the vehicle on the road.

Then without warning, Jamie turned into a narrow lane, drove about a hundred feet and stopped the car. Jill pulled in behind him and looked around. Despite the overgrown mountain laurel and rhododendrons, the canopy of pines and the number of potholes, the driveway didn't look remotely familiar.

Jill set the emergency brake and waited for Jamie to walk to her. She spotted poison ivy climbing every tree trunk. 'Where are we? This doesn't look like the road to the Clark homestead.'

Jamie yanked open her door. 'It's not, but I saw you weaving across the road in my rear-view mirror. There aren't many guard-rails along this stretch, so I got worried.'

When she opened her mouth to disagree, a wave of nausea hit her stomach. Jill swiveled around so her feet rested on the running board, put her head between her knees, and waited to vomit.

After a full minute of nothing happening, Jill lifted her chin and locked eyes with Jamie. 'I don't know what's wrong. My head is swimming and it feels like every limb of my body has turned to lead.'

Jamie helped her to sit up and lean her head back. 'Don't worry, Jill. This will soon be over.' He tenderly planted a kiss on her forehead.

And that was the last thing she remembered before her world went dark.

SEVENTEEN

When Nick roared into the driveway of his temporary home he almost rear-ended a Jeep he'd seen parked at the Clark farm in the mountains. Taking the front steps two at a time, he burst through the front door and into the house with little consideration of what he'd find.

Dorothy Clark and her nephew, Gordon, were huddled over computer printouts that covered the dining room table. Both glanced up with startled expressions. 'Lieutenant Harris, what on earth is the matter?' Dot asked.

'Excuse my interruption, Mrs Clark, but it's urgent that I find Jill Curtis.'

The innkeeper's expression remained the same – bewildered, while Gordon's jaw tightened and his face turned ashen.

'I don't know where Jill is,' said Dot. 'I haven't seen her since she left the Maxwells. If I'm not mistaken, she had planned to look for you.'

Gordon ran his palms down his pant legs but focused his gaze on the printouts.

'If you know something, Mr Clark, I suggest you tell me now. Otherwise, I'll charge you as an accessory if anything happens to Jill.'

'What is going on here?' Dot's focus shifted from Nick to her nephew.

Gordon's lips drew together in a line. 'I have no idea where Jill went. All I know is Jamie Shelby came by while I was waiting to talk to my aunt. Jill kicked me off the porch, so I drove around and then sat in my car across the street until you got home,' he said to Dot.

'When was this?' Nick asked.

'An hour, maybe ninety minutes ago,' Gordon said to Nick. 'Jamie pulled up and laid on the horn until Jill came out. Then he strolled up to the porch and handed Jill a bouquet of roses. She made a big deal out of smelling them, like it was the first time she got flowers. After they talked for a while, Jamie walked to his car and opened the passenger door. Jill shook her head and they started to argue.'

'You heard their argument?' Nick flattened his palms on the table.

'No, but it doesn't take a genius to tell by their expressions. Jamie wanted Jill to go somewhere in his car and she didn't want to. I saw her point at Roger's truck next to the house.'

Dot wrung her hands, like most women her age did when they got upset. 'Did you hear where Jamie planned to go?'

'No, ma'am, I didn't, but pretty soon Jill crossed her arms like this.' Gordon mimicked the gesture. 'Jamie must have given in because his face became real friendly again. Then he took out his phone and showed her something on the screen.' Gordon directed this information to Nick. 'I'm guessing it was a restaurant, because Jill punched in something on her phone before she got in the truck. Then Shelby drove off and Jill followed him. That's all I know.'

'Which way did they go?' Nick demanded. 'Towards downtown?'

'Nope, they went the opposite way, to the south.'

'What restaurants are in that direction?' Nick asked Mrs Clark.

'Only a few fast food joints and a diner for truckers. Nowhere that Jamie would take a woman on a date.' Dot looked to her nephew for confirmation.

Gordon turned his focus skyward as though deep in thought. 'There is one place I pass on my way home, but it's quite a distance away. Pine Tree Inn or something like that.'

'Pine Hollow Lodge,' Dot interjected. 'Roger and I went there for our anniversary once or twice. Quaint and charming, good food, too. Jill would like it there.'

Nick typed the name into Google on his phone and waited. 'Is this the place, Mrs Clark?' He showed her the website's image.

'That's it.' Dot shifted her weight from foot to foot.

'If my aunt doesn't mind postponing our discussion for another day, I'd better ride along and show you the way,' Gordon suggested.

Dot began gathering the papers into a pile. 'We can pick this up tomorrow, but I do have a pie I wanted to send home with you, nephew.' She disappeared through the swinging door and returned a moment later. 'This note was on the kitchen counter,' she said, handing the note to Nick.

'"Having dinner with Jamie Shelby. Driving Roger's truck so I can come home early",' Nick read aloud. 'Not much here we don't already know, but I'll keep this if you don't mind.' He tucked the note in his pocket and headed out the door with Gordon at his heels.

'Stay in touch, Lieutenant,' Dot called.

'You don't have to come with me, Gordon. GPS can direct me to the restaurant. If it was that hard to find, they couldn't stay in business.'

'True, but you never know when a rockslide will close the main route.' Gordon strode to the passenger side of Nick's sedan. 'I know these mountains like the back of my hand.'

Nick hit the unlock button. 'Get in. And on the way you can explain what you still have to discuss with Mrs Clark. Roger cut you out of his will. *If you don't mind.*' He added a heavy dose of sarcasm.

Gordon climbed in and buckled his seatbelt. 'I don't mind at all. I already told Jill, so you would find out anyway.'

As Nick followed the main route south from Roseville, Gordon launched into a convoluted tale about stealing empty bottles and labels and letting his family sell unregulated moonshine under the Black Creek brand.

'My uncle was ready to bequeath his proudest accomplishment to me and my family. And we'd been stealing several hundred dollars' worth of profits for months.'

Nick uttered the first thing that came to mind. 'You're lucky no one got poisoned on your uninspected, unregulated moonshine.'

Gordon looked at him curiously. 'My dad uses pure water from a very deep artesian spring, Trooper. Besides, bacteria won't grow in one-hundred-twenty-proof bourbon. The point is I was ashamed of what I'd done and didn't blame Roger for changing his will.'

'So you found out he left everything to his wife.'

'Aunt Dot asked me to come to her attorney's office this morning. That's when I heard. All I wanted was to keep my job until she lined up my replacement. But she told the lawyer she wanted no part of the distillery and was giving it outright to me.'

'Isn't today your lucky day?' Nick sneered. 'Instead of pressing charges for theft and fraud against you, Mrs Clark wants to hand you a fortune.'

Gordon shrugged. 'Black Creek isn't worth a fortune, at least not right now. I just told Aunt Dot everything and that I didn't deserve her generosity. She said we would work out a deal so I can repay what I owe. After that we would split the profits for as long as she lives, and then I'd inherit. So I am lucky, after all.'

'I'll be keeping tabs on Dorothy Clark,' Nick said. 'She had better stay healthy.'

'You do that, Lieutenant. I love my aunt and plan to pay back every dime I owe.'

For a short time, neither spoke. Nick followed the GPS directions while Gordon watched scenery he'd probably seen his entire life.

Finally Nick broke the silence. 'You think Jamie would take Jill to a restaurant this far out in the county?'

Gordon straightened in the seat. 'Yeah, I do. My sister mentioned that Jamie took her there a lot – fancy dishes, lace tablecloths, candlelight, expensive wine. Michelle said she could order anything she wanted. Chicks just eat that stuff up.' He rolled his eyes. 'Oh, and they also have rooms upstairs and a few cabins out back for rent. So after Jamie got my sister drunk, they didn't have far to go.'

Nick gripped the steering wheel tighter. 'No offence to your sister, but not every woman will be as susceptible to Shelby's charm.'

'None taken. I just hope Shelby gives Jill a choice in the matter.'

Nick pressed down on the accelerator, taking the next curve faster than any sane man should.

'Slow down, Lieutenant. Dinner at Pine Hollow Lodge takes forever. We can still get there in time.'

Nick released his foot from the gas, letting the car slow down on the next uphill. 'Thanks. And Jill can take care of herself until then.'

'You really like her, don't you?'

He glanced over for half a second. 'Yeah, I do, but I won't know if those feelings are mutual until Roger's killer is behind bars.'

'Rest assured, I'm no killer.' Gordon released his death grip on the door handle.

Nick nodded, but he didn't plan to be *rest assured* of anything right now. Fifteen minutes later he turned into Pine Hollow Lodge, spinning gravel as he braked to a stop by the entrance. True to Dorothy Clark's description, the place was most definitely quaint – wraparound porch, wrought-iron balconies, picket fence, and a flagstone path leading to a gazebo. 'You're right,' he murmured as they headed toward the copper-clad front door. 'Most women would want to stay for a week, if not buy the place outright.'

'Let's see if my twice-removed-cousin-by-marriage and that sleazebag are still in the dining room.' Gordon tried to bypass the hostess stand until Nick grabbed his arm.

'I know you have an axe to grind, Clark, but I'm in charge here.'

Grudgingly Gordon stepped back while Nick approached the young hostess. 'I'm Lieutenant Harris from the Kentucky State Police. I need to speak to the manager immediately.'

The timid woman pressed a button on the side of the podium and stepped back. 'He'll be with you in a moment, sir.'

A few minutes later a middle-age man marched through the swinging doors, presumably from the kitchen. 'I'm Mr Prescott. What seems to be the matter?'

Nick repeated the introduction, flashed his badge, and showed a photo of Jill Curtis from his phone, taken during the evening of deluxe pizza and drug store boxed wine. Then he handed the manager a mugshot of Jamie Shelby, taken after his arrest for drunk driving.

Mr Prescott perused both photos carefully, then handed Nick back his phone and mugshot. 'Yes, they were dining here earlier. The gentleman called ahead for reservations and ordered a bottle of our best champagne.'

'Oh, not Founder's Reserve bourbon?' Gordon spat out his question.

The manager shook his head. 'No, sir. The gentleman specified vintage champagne, so we served a bottle of our best.'

Nick's lip curled with contempt. 'That was Jamie Shelby and Jill Curtis in the photos. Check to see if this couple checked into a room for the night. Let me remind you, this is a police matter. If I need a warrant, I can get one, but I'll shut down the restaurant in the meantime.'

Prescott tapped the computer monitor with a shaking hand. 'No need to make threats. I'm willing to cooperate.' He tapped the screen a few more times and looked up. 'They are not staying with us tonight. The gentleman paid the check with a credit card and they left.' His gaze moved from Nick to Gordon.

'You're absolutely sure? Shelby might have checked in under an alias.' Nick tried to read the screen over the manager's shoulder.

'Sir, I am positive.' Prescott straightened his tie for a second time. 'The three couples who are here are regular guests and much older than the people in the photos. No one has checked-in since. Now, if there's nothing else . . .'

'Which way did they go when they left?' Gordon asked.

Mild indignation replaced some of Prescott's discomfort. 'I'm sorry, but we don't keep tabs on our guests when they leave.'

'They turned left out of the parking lot,' said the hostess who had been hovering in the background. When the manager gaped at her, she continued, 'I wanted to make sure the woman didn't get behind the wheel. She seemed in no shape to drive since she tripped on her way out.'

'*And?*' Nick prodded.

'Unfortunately the man got into his car,' she said, 'and the woman followed him in a beat-up truck. I didn't know what to do.'

'Officer, if they had appeared impaired, the waiter would have cut them off.'

Nick ignored the manager and addressed the hostess. 'You're sure they turned left?'

'Yep, they headed up the mountain.'

'Let me talk to their waiter,' Nick demanded of Prescott.

'He's already left for the day,' he whined.

Nick turned to the hostess. 'How long ago did they leave?'

'Not that long ago . . . maybe fifteen minutes? The man seemed mad about something, like maybe he didn't want her to drive.'

'Thank you, miss. You've been very helpful. If by chance either of them comes back, call me immediately.' Nick laid his card on the podium, glanced around an almost empty restaurant and walked outside.

'What now?' Gordon asked.

'What else is up this road?' Nick pointed in the direction Jamie and Jill had headed. 'A roadhouse? Maybe an after-hour joint?'

'Heck, no. Nothing is up this way except a few abandoned farms. My dad's property is at the very top and that's where the road dead-ends. The state bought up most of the land and handed it over to a conservation organization.' Gordon stuffed his hands in his pockets. 'And Shelby sure wouldn't take Jill to our house. Either my father or brother would shoot him on sight. Jamie must have turned around somewhere and headed back to town.'

Nick muttered an uncustomary expletive and climbed back into the car.

'Should we start checking those farms?' Gordon jumped into the passenger seat.

Nick didn't answer. Instead he switched on his police radio and summoned the Spencer County Sheriff's Department. 'I need to speak to Sheriff Adkins,' he told the dispatcher. 'This is Lieutenant Harris of Kentucky State Police.'

In less than a minute, Sheriff Adkins's voice crackled across the radio. 'What's up, Nick?'

As succinctly as possible, Nick explained his location and the situation with Jill Curtis and Jamie Shelby. Then he asked, 'Where is Owen? I hope you haven't released him.'

'Nah, he's sitting in a cell, still waiting for his lawyer. I don't want him signing a statement without legal representation. Owen must've been right about the guy being on a golf course.'

'I need you to call Owen's wife and ask if she's seen her son. And if not, call the security office at Founder's Reserve to see if Jamie passed through the front gate recently. Then radio me back.'

'You got it.'

Like the consummate professional he was, Adkins didn't ask unnecessary questions. But it was a long time before he came back on the line, during which Gordon fiddled with his cell phone, and Nick pictured what he would do to Jamie if he hurt one hair on Jill's head.

Finally the radio crackled to life. 'Negative on both counts,' said Adkins. 'Mrs Shelby hasn't seen her son all day, and Jamie hasn't passed through either entrance since he left the office hours ago.'

Nick clenched down on his back teeth. 'Could you bring Owen Shelby to the radio? I want to ask him a few questions.'

'Hello?' asked a hoarse voice five minutes later.

'Mr Shelby, this is Lieutenant Harris. We're trying to track down your son's whereabouts. Does your family own any properties other than your house in Roseville and the distillery?'

'Let's see.' Owen paused to think. 'We used to own a winter home in Naples, Florida. It was my wife's pride and joy. But we sold it to buy new automated equipment for the distillery. So Norma now spends winter in Roseville, a fact she never ceases to complain about if we get even a few flakes of snow.'

'Think, Mr Shelby,' Nick commanded. 'Are you sure you have no other properties, maybe something that's usually rented out?'

Again, silence ensued while the elderly man pondered. 'We once owned a rustic cabin up in the hills. But when Jamie and I stopped hunting, we haven't been there in years.'

'Who did you sell it to?'

'No one. The place really wasn't worth much, so we just stopped paying the taxes and let the state of Kentucky take it. I guess it's part of the new conservancy now.'

'Do you remember the address?' Nick asked. 'Would your wife have it written down somewhere?'

'Goodness, no, Lieutenant. That cabin didn't have an address or a mailbox. It was on an old logging road without a name.' Owen chuckled as though Nick had asked something amusing. 'The cabin didn't even have indoor plumbing. It was for men who wanted to rough it, so you can understand why it grew distasteful as I grew older.'

Nick gritted his teeth, yearning to grab Shelby by the throat. 'What highway was it off? How did you get there?'

'Back then it was called Roseville Road. I think the route number was seventy-three.'

With his thumb, Gordon gestured to the road they were on.

Nick rolled his eyes. 'All right, I want you to explain to a local resident *everything* you can remember. There must've been a landmark to help you find the turnoff.'

'It must be twenty years ago. I would never be able to find it,' moaned Shelby, sounding close to tears. 'Besides, my son wouldn't go there. The roof has probably fallen in.'

'Do your best, Mr Shelby.' Nick played the only card he had. 'Then maybe the prosecutor will show some mercy towards you.'

'Let me think,' he said. 'I remember passing the restaurant with the all-you-can-eat buffet on Sunday.'

Gordon pointed at the lodge behind them.

'Then there were two farms on the right and then several logging roads. We turned down either the third or fourth one with an oak tree on the corner. That tree trunk branched so many times the loggers just left the tree behind. I can't remember any other landmarks.'

When Gordon rolled his eyes, Nick got a bad feeling in his gut.

'Thank you, Mr Shelby. If you remember anything else, tell the sheriff to radio me right away.' Nick started his engine. 'Let's look for those two farms.'

'The houses might have fallen in and some of those old roads could have grown over,' said Gordon. 'Let me ask my sister if she knows this cabin. She and Billy roamed all over these woods when they were young.'

Nick pulled up to the pavement and checked for traffic. 'Don't waste time. You'll never reach Michelle on your cell phone.'

'True, if Michelle is inside the house. But she loves to hang out at the goat barn with her favorite critters. And if she's up there, the call might go through. The barn sits high enough to get a signal from Roseville.' Gordon punched in his sister's number and waited, letting the phone ring for a long while.

To Nick's utter astonishment, they both heard a tentative, 'Hello?'

'Michelle, it's me, Gordy. I'm with Nick Harris, and we're trying to track down Jamie Shelby.'

'I have no idea where—'

'Just listen, Michelle,' Gordon interrupted. 'This could be urgent. Shelby could be with Jill Curtis and he may wish to harm her.'

'Why would Jamie want to hurt Jill? You're not making any sense.' Michelle's words were broken by static.

'Because Jamie thinks Jill figured out who killed Uncle Roger.'

'And who would that be?' Michelle asked.

'We'll explain later. Right now, do you know the whereabouts of an old hunting cabin the Shelbys used to own? It can't be very far from our house.'

'Yeah, that's where a bunch of us hung out during high school. We used to drink beer and roast hot dogs and crash on the floor in sleeping bags. But the Shelbys haven't owned that cabin in years. It's part of—'

'I know, Michelle,' Gordon snapped. 'Have you been there recently?'

Michelle remained quiet for so long, they thought they had lost the connection. 'Not recently, but I could still find it,' she finally said. 'Shelby once asked me to meet him at the cabin for a *romantic* picnic supper. That creep told me he'd fixed the place up, but all he'd done was patch the holes in the roof and put sheets on the rusty bed. And his idea of dinner was a bucket of chicken and a six-pack of beer.' She clucked her tongue. 'I told him the place was a dump and if that was the best he could do he shouldn't call me again.'

'So you started meeting him at the Pine Hollow Lodge?' Gordon sneered. 'You deserve so much better than Shelby!'

'I'm a grown woman, big brother. I'll make my own decisions.'

Nick pulled the phone from Gordon's hand. 'This is Nick Harris, Miss Clark. If Jill is still with Jamie, she might be in danger. Could you tell us how to find this cabin?'

'It's down one of those old logging roads. I don't remember which one. When I went I always took the path through the woods. It was quicker that way.'

Nick frowned at Gordon. 'We'll need to check down every logging road between here and your place.'

Gordon took his phone back. 'Don't get any ideas of going there, Michelle. Your baby is due any time. You stay right where you are and we'll find Jill if she's still with Jamie.'

'Fine, brother dear,' she said. 'But make it snappy. Jamie has a bad temper when things don't go his way.'

Gordon slipped his phone in his pocket, while Nick peeled onto the highway, heading north. He didn't want to think what a desperate man in a bad mood might do in the middle of nowhere.

EIGHTEEN

Jill regained her senses in a dimly lit, dusty log cabin that reeked of mildew. When she tried to breathe deeply, she ended up coughing and choking against the smelly rag over her mouth. Willing herself not to panic, she scanned the room from one end to the other. An old-fashioned metal bed sat against the wall with a flowered bedspread and two pillows with matching shams. Compared to everything else inside the hovel, the bedding looked fairly new. An antique trunk sat at the foot of the bed, perhaps containing whatever the owner wanted to keep safe from mice. In the center of the room was a kitchen table beneath an oil lamp hung from a rusty chain. What looked like dates had been carved into the oak surface, perhaps notating the cabin's most recent occupants. Two more chairs exactly like the one she sat on were at the table, while a fourth broken chair was sticking from the kindling box on the hearth. Streaks of black soot and several loose flagstones hinted at the unsafe condition of the chimney, and there was enough dirt on the floor to write your name. A breakfront cabinet with mismatched dishes that hadn't been washed in years and a sofa which might have been blue plaid in better days completed the furnishings. Sheets of plastic, yellowed from age and weather, covered the windows. The cabin had one trash can, overflowing with beer cans and takeout containers, but no stove, refrigerator, or sink where a person could wash their hands.

Why would Jamie buy me an expensive meal, a fancy bottle of champagne, and two desserts in a nice restaurant, and then bring me to a dump like this?

Jill remembered using the ladies' room, finishing the glass of champagne, and tripping over uneven carpeting on her way out. She remembered feeling lightheaded in the parking lot and Jamie helping her into Roger's truck. Then she had followed his red sports car down the road until he turned into a driveway. By that time her mild case of lightheadedness had become full-blown nausea. Once they had pulled off-road, Jill had swung her legs out of the truck, bowed her head, and waited to throw up.

Nothing after that rang a bell.

Now she was tied to a chair inside an abandoned shack with a gag in her mouth, making it impossible to call for help. *Talk about bad dates gone wrong.*

Jill tried to recall where they had been going after the restaurant, but a sharp pain pounded behind her eyes. For a while, she could do nothing but concentrate on not choking on her own bile. When the pain finally subsided, images of a very pregnant Michelle floated across her mind. She and Jamie had been headed to the Clark farm, to give Michelle money for a hospital delivery. Jill didn't need a second perusal to confirm she wasn't inside the Clark's mountain-top cabin. Although modest in décor, Michelle kept their home spotlessly clean.

After struggling for a few minutes against the restraints, she succeeded only in tipping over the chair and whacking her head on the floor. Once again, her world went dark until a harsh voice pierced her fog.

'For heaven's sake, Curtis.' As Jamie yanked her chair upright, his angry face loomed into view. 'Couldn't you just sit still until I got back?'

He was still wearing the same pants and white shirt from dinner, but his sleeves had been rolled up and his suitcoat was gone. He pulled the dirty rag from around her mouth.

'Jamie,' she muttered after a short coughing spasm.

'Very good,' he said. 'You haven't knocked yourself completely witless.'

'Where have you been? And where am I?' Her voice sounded weak, almost feeble.

Jamie dragged over one of the kitchen chairs, straddling it to face her. 'First things first. I had to run an errand, thanks to your unrelenting stubbornness. But while en route I thought of the perfect solution to my dilemma.' He held a water bottle to her lips.

'So what is this place?' she asked after several swallows of water. 'I thought we were on our way to see Michelle.'

'We'll get to that in a minute.' Jamie gazed around the room. 'I have such fond memories of this cabin. I used to come here hunting with my father and uncles a long time ago. That's when dear old Dad had time for such pursuits. Then more recently, Michelle and I hung out drinking beer and making love.'

'How charming. Judging by the dust those trysts must have been a while ago.'

'Suddenly, my Mountain Mama got picky about the accommodation and insisted I spend the big bucks on her.' His laugh was downright malevolent.

'Can't blame a gal for having standards, but why am *I* here? Surely you don't have visions of us cuddling on the pink peonies.' Jill angled her head towards the flowery bedspread and shams. 'That is so off the table.'

He snorted. 'I would've enjoyed that when we first met, but not anymore. Your virtue is safe, since romance by force isn't my style. I'm just not that kind of guy.'

The gleam in his eyes sent a shiver up Jill's spine. 'OK, then why are we here?'

'I want to know why your truck was parked outside the Maxwell house. You forget what a small town Roseville is. Why couldn't you just go back to Chicago when you finished your article?'

'Maybe I have ambitions of becoming an investigative reporter.'

'That ship sailed a long time ago. Newspapers are laying off reporters these days. People prefer the highly biased stories from the internet and TV talk shows. Your partner was smart enough to heed my message and leave town.'

The blood in Jill's veins turned to ice. 'What did you do to Michael?'

'Nothing lately. Michael is back in Chicago, where you should be now. Several claustrophobic hours in an elevator and a few smashed car windows sent that boy packing his bags.'

'*You* locked him inside the elevator at Black Creek? But you didn't have a key.'

'Michelle gave me hers the night of Roger's fundraiser. But we got so caught up in the excitement she forgot to get it back. That key came in handy more than once. After all, I had to wipe the security tape clean and lock up the room after I paid Maxwell to leave his post.' He grinned malevolently. 'Seeing the videographer snooping around was a bit of good fortune for me.'

'But why Michael? My videographer never did anything to you.' Jill wiggled her wrists against the ropes.

'Michael's allergy to grain was a little annoying,' he sneered. 'Then I saw him videotaping everyone who came to Roger's funeral, as though a guilty face might betray the killer.'

'Is that why you stole his camera? Would the tape have betrayed your guilty face?'

'Not mine, you little ninny. I was with you, remember? I just wanted you both to stop butting your noses in my family's business.'

Jill strained against her restraints. 'Well, Roger was my family and he's why I stayed.'

'You didn't even know the guy a few months ago. If you had, you wouldn't have liked him much.' Jamie jumped up and started pacing the room. 'Roger Clark wasn't very nice to his employees or to your precious Aunt Dot. He was a bully with delusions of grandeur with his little distillery.'

'What do you mean?' Jill noticed a flush had risen up Jamie's neck.

'Roger tried to recruit Founder's employees every chance he got, hoping to steal our secrets along the way. My father went to see him with an idea that could have benefited both companies. Instead of being grateful, Roger wanted to reap the majority of the profits.' Jamie's hands bunched into fists as he paused by her chair. 'My grandfather and great-grandfather built Founder's Reserve into what it is today after years of hard work. Then my father poured every dime of his and Mom's savings into improving operations. Roger thinks he can move into the same position with his insignificant upstart?'

'Not very realistic, huh?' Jill didn't like the sweat on Jamie's forehead or the spittle in the corner of his mouth.

'No, Jill, not very.' Jamie started pacing again.

'So when their discussion took a nasty turn your dad killed him?' Jill asked the question to gauge his reaction.

'Not on purpose. Roger threw the first punch. Then they started wailing on each other like a pair of barroom brawlers. Hard to picture, no?' Jamie shook his head. 'Roger, who was younger and stronger, had my father against the rack, so Dad pushed him away. Unfortunately, Roger slipped on some spilled bourbon from a toast-gone-wrong. When he fell, he hit his head on a sharp metal edge.'

'Sounds like self-defense to me or manslaughter at worst.' Jill squirmed to loosen the ropes.

'What difference does that make? My father's reputation, along with Founder's Reserve's, will be ruined. Our sales would tank. With so many bourbons on the shelf, people choose a brand that represents a true American legacy.'

'And Elmer Maxwell?'

'We'll get to him in just a minute.' After rummaging around in the trunk, Jamie pulled out a bottle of Founder's Reserve.

'Are you really gonna drink that? Who knows how long it's been in there.'

Jamie opened the bottle and tipped it up for a healthy swig. 'Bourbon doesn't go bad. You should know that considering all your research.' He pressed the bottle to her lips.

Jill shook her head. 'I can't swallow like this. Untie my hands so I can drink properly.'

He straightened his spine. 'I'll untie one hand. After all, you've got nowhere to go.'

With one arm free from the restraints, Jill reached for the bottle. 'Before I imbibe, I want to know if you drugged my champagne.'

'Not only your champagne but also your iced tea, while you were in the ladies' room. I couldn't take any chances. Then the stuff worked so fast, you almost passed out before we left the restaurant.' Jamie chuckled with amusement. 'But have no fear about the bourbon. Michelle never needed one iota of encouragement.'

Jill swallowed a sip. 'If you had no romantic intentions, why did you bring me here?' She flourished her hand through the air.

'To find out what Janice Maxwell told you and what you figured out on your own.' Jamie took the bottle for another drink.

'Janice said they should've stayed away when they had the chance and not gotten greedy. Had Elmer been blackmailing you?'

'What a stupid man,' Jamie said, a slight slur to his words. 'First I paid him five grand to erase the tape of my dad's visit to Black Creek. Then when Gordon fired him for not showing up to work, Maxwell came to me for money to start a new life. So I gave him another five grand and he left town. Unfortunately he came back for more because he needed to pay off his bookies. When I turned him down, he decided to take his own life.'

'I'm betting you helped him along.' Jill worked at the rope on her left wrist.

'Maybe I did, but neither you nor that hot-shot cop can ever prove it.'

The little hairs on Jill's neck stood on end. 'Why are you telling me this now?'

'Because it doesn't matter anymore.' He stopped pacing in front of her chair. 'You know too much.'

'I really don't know anything.'

'I can't take that chance.'

'What do you have in mind? At least do me the courtesy of knowing my fate.'

'Sure, why not?' he said with a smirk. 'When you insisted on taking two cars to the restaurant, you helped hatch a plan. So I made sure you were drunk when you left the restaurant, or at least that's how it looked.' Jamie's smile was colder than a glacier. 'You were unfamiliar with the roads and going too fast. Unfortunately, there's no guardrail where you missed a curve and lost control. Roger's piece-of-junk truck went over the edge and burst into a ball of flames.' He leaned close to her face. 'In other words, Jill Curtis, you are about to have a horrible accident on your way home.'

'I left a note at the B and B that you and I were dining together.'

'So what? Several employees saw you stagger from the restaurant, yet you still insisted on getting behind the wheel. You will suffer the same fate as most hapless drunks in these parts.' Jamie poured a goodly amount of bourbon down the front of her dress.

'Where is my piece-of-junk now?' Jill asked, trying to work her hand loose.

'Exactly where you left it. You came here in my car. But soon the sedative in the water bottle will start to work. Then I'll take you back to your truck under the cover of darkness and drive to a perfect spot past Pine Hollow Lodge.' Jamie glanced at his watch. 'By then, all the employees will have gone home and the overnight guests will be fast asleep. No one else lives up this highway other than *your kinfolk*, and they should be well into their cups by now. So nobody will witness one drunk travel writer careening to her death. It could be weeks before anyone spots the wreckage over the embankment.'

Jill remembered drinking his bottle of water when she first came to. She had very little time to think of something to save her life. Then, out of the corner of her eye, she saw movement outside. One of the pieces of plastic had come loose, exposing a corner of the window. If Jill wasn't mistaken, Michelle Clark had just peeked through the streaky glass.

Jill yanked her focus back to her host. 'Let's not be hasty. You need to make sure Pine Hollow employees have gone home. And I don't feel all that sleepy. Tell me, Jamie, were you ever planning to pay the hospital for Michelle's delivery?'

Jamie dragged the kitchen chair back in front of her. 'I would like to, considering the baby is probably mine. But if I pay Roseville General, I would lose any future paternity suit and get stuck supporting the kid till he or she turned eighteen.'

Jill reached for the bourbon and surprisingly Jamie relinquished it. 'Would that be so bad? You're a rich man.' She swigged a hearty amount but didn't swallow.

Jamie rolled his eyes. 'Everyone thinks the Shelbys are loaded, but the truth is we're far from it. I like Michelle. We've had a lot of good times in the past. But she'll have to support this little *mistake* all by herself.'

Infuriated by his term and total lack of responsibility, Jill sprayed her mouthful of bourbon into Jamie's face. Then she lifted the half-empty bottle high into the air and crashed it down on his head.

At the same time, a very pregnant woman stormed through the doorway with a hefty stick in her hand. Michelle delivered a resounding *craack* to the side of Jamie's head. 'My little mistake?' she wailed. 'My only mistake was hooking up with a loser like you. My baby will know the joy of a loving family.' Michelle stood over him, waiting for the unconscious man to make a move.

'Ah, Michelle?' Jill mumbled as the room spun before her eyes. 'Thanks for showing up, but I'm about to pass out again. Untie my other wrist and use the ropes to tie up Shelby. We don't want him coming around too soon.'

Michelle patted Jill's shoulder. 'Gotcha covered, cousin. My brother and your boyfriend should be here soon. Until then, I can keep Shelby in check. You sleep tight.'

'I know Gordon's your brother, but who's my boyfriend?' Jill asked as the room darkened around the edges.

'Nick Harris, the cop from Louisville. Everybody but you has been aware of the attraction.'

'Has it been that obvious?' Jill felt herself smile, but that was the last action she was aware of for a while.

NINETEEN

Nick swerved into the first logging road north of Pine Hollow Lodge. 'There's Jill's truck,' he shouted, stopping just behind it.

'Now all we have to do is find Jill.' Gordon bounded from the sedan and headed to the truck's passenger side.

Nick yanked open the driver's door. 'Here's her purse and her cell phone is still inside.' With a push of a button, the home screen lit up. 'Thank goodness, Jill hated passwords,' he said. 'Looks like she tried to call me, Sweet Dreams, and the sheriff's department several times, but none of the calls went through. So much for her cell phone provider.' Nick took off his sunglasses in the fading light and looked around.

Gordon was already searching the brush around the car. 'Let's see where this road goes.'

As Nick beat back the weeds on the left side with Gordon on the right, they hadn't gone a quarter mile when the road ended in a clearing. Two large piles of discarded branches indicated this had been a loading zone for logging trucks.

'Jill's not here,' Nick said after a quick perusal.

'On to the next road.' Both men broke into a run back to the sedan.

Within minutes, they reached the next logging road to the north. But Nick had barely pulled off the pavement when his wheel dropped into a deep rut. 'This road is impassable. If there's an old hunting cabin up ahead, nobody has visited in years.' Nick thumped the steering wheel with his fist.

Muttering an expletive, Gordon climbed from the car. 'I'll push while you back out in low gear.'

It took ten minutes of rocking the car back and forth before the wheel popped free. By this time Gordon was fairly well covered in mud.

'Sorry 'bout the mud, Clark,' Nick said once on Highway 73.

'Not to worry. I'll take it out on Shelby when we find him.'

'If we find them in time.' Grinding his teeth, Nick sped past the next logging road. He backed up and turned onto a gravel roadbed in much better shape than the last with fresh tire tracks along the edge. The two men exchanged a look.

'Let's keep our fingers crossed.' Gordon rolled down his window.

Nick crept along the narrow lane, watchful of potholes and any sign of Jill. Half a mile later, they rounded a bend and spotted a shiny red sports car.

'That car belongs to Shelby,' Gordon exclaimed.

'I know, just remember to stay behind me.' Nick withdrew his weapon as he climbed from the vehicle. 'I'm taking the lead.'

As quietly as possible, they made their way through dense undergrowth to a dilapidated cabin with a lopsided chimney and plastic covering the windows. After circling the shack, Nick got his first view of inside the cabin through one corner of a window. 'Looks like the situation is under control, Gordon. See for yourself.' Nick holstered his weapon and stepped to the side.

Jamie Shelby was on the floor with his wrists and ankles bound, while Jill and Michelle sat on kitchen chairs on either side. Above their heads burned a kerosene lamp on a rusty chain, the sole illumination in the room.

'I'm not so sure about that. Michelle might be going into labor.' Gordon bolted through the front door. 'Is the baby coming?' he asked his sister.

Michelle's grimace of pain changed to an honest-to-goodness smile. 'Either that or I've got the worst case of indigestion in the world.'

'I told you to stay home!' Gordy shook his finger, his face full of fear.

'Easy, Gordy, we've got this.' Nick snapped handcuffs on Shelby's wrists. Then he turned his attention to Jill, whose head had lolled to one side. 'What's wrong with Jill?' Nick checked Jill's breathing and listened to her heartbeat.

'She's just sleeping,' said Michelle in between painful gasps. 'Jamie slipped her a sedative so he could murder her in cold blood.' She kicked Shelby in the ribs just as he roused to consciousness. 'Worthless, murdering philander.' Michelle kicked him a second time.

'Stop, we need to get you to the hospital.' Gordon helped his sister to her feet. 'I'll sign for the bill and pay Roseville General each month.'

Halfway to the door, Michelle paused as a contraction took her breath away. 'Not to worry, big brother.' Once the contraction passed, she held up a slip of paper. 'Jill gave me Jamie's credit card number. She witnessed him pledging an eight-thousand-dollar charge for the safe delivery of his son or daughter.'

Nick, who hadn't left Jill's side, tossed Gordon his car keys. 'Take Michelle in my car, but first let me radio the dispatcher to have EMTs meet you along the way. Just in case this baby is in a big hurry. We'll also tell Sheriff Adkins to send a cruiser to pick up Shelby.'

'You're sure you two will be all right?' Gordon cast a sympathetic gaze towards Jill.

Nick nodded. 'Jill's vitals are strong and stable. I think she's just sleeping like Michelle said. Go, or you'll end up delivering your nephew or niece by yourself.'

The new master distiller needed no additional encouragement. Nick followed the Clarks out the door, radioed for medical assistance, and left a message with the dispatcher for the sheriff. He heard the subsequent start of his engine on his way back into the cabin, where he picked up Jill's limp hand to wait. At one point Shelby roused to consciousness, so Nick tied a discarded rag around his mouth. The last thing he wanted to hear was Jamie's arrogant mouth.

After what seemed like an interminably long amount of time, Jill's left shoulder twitched. Finally she opened one eye, then the other, and released a weary sigh.

'Have you had enough fun for one trip to the Blue Grass State?'

'Where is everybody? How long have I been asleep?'

'Hello to you, too, Miss Curtis. I have no idea how long, but Gordon Clark and I got here about twenty minutes ago.' Nick offered her a bottle of water. 'He and Michelle are on their way to the hospital in Roseville. Her baby is coming.'

Jill's face bloomed with a smile. 'I'm so glad I don't have to play midwife. I never read that manual.' She tried to stand but fell back down.

'Stay in that chair,' Nick insisted. 'Who knows what drug that creep gave you.' Nick scowled down at Jamie on the floor.

Jill focused on the bound-and-gagged man at her feet. 'Know what Shelby had planned? He wanted to stick me in Roger's truck, push the truck over a cliff and then drive home, business as usual. How do people get so nasty? Is it because of money?'

'I don't think so. It was his father who tipped us off that Jamie was up to no good.'

Jill's chin snapped up. 'Owen, really? I'm surprised.' Then she dropped her head into her hands. 'I have a major headache.'

Nick gently massaged her neck with his fingertips. 'Drink more water, Jill. You're probably dehydrated.'

'Where did this water come from?' She studied the plastic bottle in her hand.

'I brought it with me from the station.' Nick took the chair formerly occupied by Michelle.

'You didn't add anything, did you? I'm rather skeptical when a man gives me something to drink.'

'Go ahead,' he said with a wink. 'Trust me.'

Jill studied Shelby, bound and gagged on the floor, then gave him a long hard look. 'Fine.' She downed half the contents of the bottle and wiped her mouth.

'How did it taste?' Nick teased.

'Like water. Why?' She arched one eyebrow.

'Because I did add something – Love Potion Nine.' He struggled to keep a straight face.

'There's no such thing.'

'Yes, there is. And it was in that bottle.' Nick leaned forward so that their noses were inches apart. 'So what do you say, Curtis? I'm laying my cards on the table. Do you feel anything for me other than friendship?'

'Must we talk about this now?' Jill squirmed in her chair. 'I've just been drugged twice, kidnapped, and locked inside a tacky shack without a proper bathroom.'

Nick bit back his smile. 'I'm afraid so, because while you're at the outhouse, deputies will arrive to whisk Shelby to jail and us back to civilization. Then we'll rush to the hospital to see Michelle and her new baby. And before we know it, you'll be headed to Chicago and my one big chance will be lost.'

'Wow, Nick. That was a lot of words.'

'It was, but I need an answer.'

'First of all, I'm not going back to Chicago. On Monday I'm supposed to meet my partner in Louisville for our new assignment. Michael asked the boss to change the destination from Lexington partly because it has four major distilleries, tons of small crafts, and mainly because it's your current hometown. Is that enough answer for you, Lieutenant Harris?'

Nick pointed at the bottle. 'Do you suppose potion number nine worked?'

'It might have. My casual interest seems to have morphed into affection with a dash of physical attraction. I'm willing to date you a few times.' Jill pushed up from the chair, rose on tiptoes, and planted a kiss on his lips. 'Is that good enough?'

'It'll have to be, because I hear sirens in the distance.' He wrapped an arm around her waist. 'I need to get you to the outdoor facilities and then to a hospital. I want to know exactly what Shelby put in your drink.' He nudged the man on the floor with his toe.

Jill gingerly moved toward the door. 'Are you planning to drive my truck? Gordon took Michelle to Roseville in your car.'

'Nope, after the sheriff takes Shelby into custody, we'll let a deputy drive Roger's truck back to town.' Nick pulled the key fob from Jamie's pocket and smiled at her. 'I've always wanted to drive a hot car like his. And now I'll have a pretty girl by my side.'

CPSIA information can be obtained
at www.ICGtesting.com
Printed in the USA
LVHW051308211021
701072LV00001B/2

9 781780 297279